THE CORPSE
IS INDIGNANT

THE CORPSE IS INDIGNANT

Douglas Stapleton
and
Helen A Carey

COACHWHIP PUBLICATIONS
Greenville, Ohio

To Harry Link, who believed in the Judge as a person—who contributed many anecdotes about him—and who had faith in him as a character between the pages of a book.

—D. S. and H.A.C.

The Corpse is Indignant, by Douglas Stapleton and Helen A. Carey
© 2018 Coachwhip Publications

Published 1946
No claims made on public domain material.

CoachwhipBooks.com

ISBN 1-61646-436-4
ISBN-13 978-1-61646-436-3

1

MURDER CUM LAUDE

Judge James Massie made one concession to gallantry. He removed his feet from the second drawer of his desk and planted them firmly but not happily on the floor. Then he peered at Willie over the steel rims of his spectacles. "Git Miz Jensen a cheer—a comfortable cheer," and then watched his sixteen-year-old and self-adopted son and assistant swing a chair awkwardly under the knees of the woman who swayed uncertainly in front of the Judge's massive desk.

"You'll hafta sorta excuse Willie. He ain't as used to having murders dropped in his lap as I am." The Judge glanced down at the mound of his waistcoat with its sagging meridian of a gold chain and sighed. "But come to think of it, I ain't got much of a lap to drop murders into. I occupy most of it m'self." He nodded to Willie, "And git Miz Jensen a glass o' water . . . mebbe a mite of ammonia."

The woman sank into the chair and laid her hands flat on the desk top, as if she were too weary to move them.

"I'm not . . . joking, Judge. I . . . I just killed my husband."

Judge Massie nodded, and the pink accordion of his several chins folded over the melting dignity of his collar. His blue eyes, bright behind the rims of his spectacles, regarded her carefully. "You used to be a right perty woman, Sylvia."

One hand jerked convulsively, and the woman raised it to her sallow, gaunt cheek, where the remnants of a ghost-ridden beauty still remained. One finger traced the high cheekbones, touched the tired, sagging corner of her mouth—and very slowly

5

the woman smiled. "Thank you, Judge. I needed that. To remind
me of . . . of . . . saner times." She bit her almost bloodless lips
and shook her head, as if to clear it of nightmares.

Willie handed her a glass of water cloudy with ammonia and
she drank it almost greedily, and then sat back, color flushing her
thin cheeks. "I needed that, too. Now I can tell you about it."

"Don't know's I rightly want to hear it, Miz Jensen. Me an'
Willie, we're sorta tired. Been in court all day, defending young
Westmoreland, an' we jess come up to the office to git away from
a mite o' celebratin'. Nine o'clock at night's perty late for us to
be here."

"I know." Her voice took on a new eagerness. "I read about
it in tonight's paper. You defended him so brilliantly." Her voice
dropped huskily. "And I want you to defend me."

"Agin' what?" Judge Massie tented his plump fingers over his
paunch and regarded his thumbs curiously, as if he had just discovered them. "Anybody accused you of anything?"

Sylvia Jensen shook her head dazedly. "Not yet . . . but they
will . . . when they find . . ."

Judge Massie held up a broad pink palm. "Ain't interested in
what's gonna happen. Never was much at fortune-tellin', an' lawyers cain't afford to be too much beforehand. Known as connivin'
. . ." the Judge twinkled gravely at Mrs. Jensen, "an' I never was
much at connivin'."

Only the Judge's swift glance kept Willie from making a startled denial. Judge James Massie loved conniving—and Willie
knew it.

"Also, was I to hear anything about murder, le's say, an' didn't
immediately report it to the police, then mebbe they'd think I
was accessory after the fack."

Sylvia Jensen frowned perplexedly. "But surely a client's com-
munication to her attorney is sacred . . . and if you take my case . . ."

"What case?" Judge Massie looked bland and surprised. "Ain't
heared of any case—yet."

The woman sat up straighter in her chair, baffled, puzzled
and angry. "You're being obstinate. I'd expect that of Edgar Willebrandt—he clucks and putters—but I expected more of you."

Judge Massie nodded slowly. "An' I'm a complete disappointment. An' there's so much of me to be disappointin'. Now Edgar Willebrandt clucks, but he's handled your estate fer a good many years—and done a perty shrewd job of it. But, o'course, he does cluck. Howsomever, there's young Charlie Detweiler, his assistant." The Judge regarded her from under shaggy brows.

"He makes me sick . . ."

Judge Massie coughed. "Warn't aware you used slang. But come to think of it, that warn't slang. You really mean it. He sorta makes my stomach churn, too."

Sylvia smiled gently. "He does, doesn't he? That's why I couldn't go to him."

"Been waitin' for that smile . . ." The Judge sat up. "Now, mebbe we can talk business."

Sylvia Jensen relaxed in her chair. "Oh, I knew you'd take my case. You see I killed . . ."

"Jess a minute . . . Jess a minute!" The Judge held up an imperious hand. "I said business. Got a kid sister, ain't you? Jess back from college?" Sylvia nodded. "Name o' Cordelia, most generally called Deedie?"

"But what's she got to do with . . ."

"Now, effen you was to tell me you wanted to mebbe deed her some property an' wanted me to handle it . . . why, then I'd be your attorney. And effen you was to tell me, as your attorney, jess why you thought mebbe this here kid sister would be needin' some property—like you was scared you'd be arrested—then mebbe, as your attorney, I could ask you why you thought you was gonna be arrested . . . an' you'd tell me . . . in the confidence of a client to her attorney."

Willie, who had listened with growing disappointment to the earlier conversation, sat up, beaming. Such deviousness belonged to the Judge and he approved of it.

Sylvia followed the reasoning carefully, with dawning appreciation—and then she smiled, a little wistfully, but a smile. "Of course! And as it happens, that's exactly what I want to do." She reached in her bag and then shook her head. "I didn't bring them. They're at the bank. It's my Chelsea Motors stock. I want

to transfer that to my sister, Cordelia Storme." Sylvia Jensen was
being very precise.

"Willie, got that down?"

Willie nodded. His shorthand was not spectacular, but adequate. "You kin fill in the stock certificate numbers later. How
much does this here stock amount to?"

"About two hundred and fifty thousand dollars." She went on
hastily, "It's my own, left me by my uncle—and isn't tied up in
the estate."

Judge Massie nodded ponderously, his several chins quivering. "An' why would you be wantin' to give sech a large sum to
your sister, when she's well provided for under the terms o' yore
father's estate?"

"Because . . ."

Judge Massie again held up his hand. "Jess a minute. To sorta
make this, legal an' bindin', rightly I should have a retainer. Now
effen you was to make it in cash, I wouldn't have to fool around
with checks and mebbe explain to a bank how-come I didn't
deposit a check on the right date an' sech, effen sech a question
ever was to come up."

Sylvia Jensen looked startled for a moment and once more
dived into her bag. "I have some cash. I got it to pay off the servants tomorrow. I always pay them on Friday . . ."

"Tomorrow's Thursday," murmured the Judge—and pocketed
a wad of bills without counting them. "Now, don't nobody know
when I got cash, an' you kin tell me why you think your sister
might need this money."

Sylvia Jensen's hand clenched on the desk and then relaxed.
"Thank you, Judge. You've helped a lot . . . and now I can tell
you. You see, I'm anxious for Deedie to have this money because
I may be arrested for murder and the estate will be tied up."

Judge Massie pursed babyish lips and nodded thoughtfully, as
if this were the first time he had heard of a murder and classified
it among less desirable but more or less expected crimes. "Got
any reason to believe you'll be arrested for murder?"

Sylvia drew a deep breath and let it out. "Yes. You see, I
just killed my husband, Dr. Frederic Jensen. I shot him in my

bedroom because I was afraid . . ." She shivered and hid her face in her hands, "I was afraid for my . . . my . . . sanity . . . even my life."

"Aside from bein' a mite upsot, Sylvia—an' I figger if I'd jess shot somebody, I'd be upsot, too—I cain't see but what you're sane as anybody I know. An' I've known you mighty nigh thirty years—since three-cornered pants was yore exclusive style o' dress."

Sylvia began again, her voice stronger. "You don't know. For some time I thought I was going crazy. Little things happened . . . well, it has even been difficult to understand or realize even when they are happening. I mean, I'd tell the maid something quite ordinary—just a household order—and he'd come in and say, 'Now, my dear, I'm sure you didn't quite mean that. The girl hasn't been insolent.' Well, she hadn't, it was quite true, and there was no answer. At first I thought he'd misunderstood what I'd said to the girl and then, well, what began to frighten me was that I wasn't sure myself of what I'd said. I'd go over it, trying to find something wrong, until I began to wonder if I even knew what I'd been saying at any time . . . whether what I imagined was what I'd really said."

"Cain't nothin' bother a body like tryin' to recommember what's been said. Do it m'self sometimes. Catch m'self thinkin' out a long conversation, an' then wonderin' mebbe effen I'd said any of it. Happens sorta reg'lar-like when I git on parties that's jess a mite dull." Judge Massie shook his head at his own shortcomings. "Downright embarrassin' sometimes."

"Yes . . ." She breathed easier, as if she had just been waiting for that confirmation, and the Judge lifted a kindly, shaggy eyebrow at her. "Yes . . . and then once he asked me what I meant by telling old Mrs. Parsons that she smelled like a goat wearing patchouli, and he seemed quite honestly upset about it. Now old Mrs. Parsons weighs two hundred and sixty, and can't manage a bath too frequently, and *does* wear patchouli—that sickening perfume—and I've often thought she *did* smell like a goat with patchouli," and Mrs. Jensen answered the Judge's twinkle with a brief, timid smile, "but I'm sure I wouldn't say it, for she's the dearest old thing. But it made me begin to doubt, you know . . . wonder if I might have said it, and not remembered—to wonder, perhaps, if I were going crazy."

Mrs. Jensen plucked at her bag with nervous fingers and was quiet for a moment. When she looked up the horror was again in her eyes. "That's why I killed him. He was *trying* to drive me crazy. He was making me think I was crazy . . . and then I would go mad, completely, wildly mad . . . so I shot him. I had gone up to lie down. He stood there, grinning at me from the doorway at the foot of my bed. He looked curiously flat and unreal for a moment, and then he grinned . . . so sneeringly, so triumphantly . . . and I shot him . . . I shot . . ." Suddenly she broke off, flinging her hands across her mouth.

Judge Massie creaked his chair forward. "Wouldn't be wonderin' where you got the gun, would you? Don't strike me as a body that would keep a gun handy-like."

"Yes . . ." Her voice was the smallest bit of a whisper. "Yes . . ." It almost whistled through her tight lips. "I never had a gun before . . . I never shot a gun before . . . I . . ." Terrified, her eyes sought the Judge's kindly, calm face, and then she bent over her bag, scrabbling among its miscellany with shaking fingers before she drew out a little Spanish automatic. As if the gun were a reassurance, she settled back. "I don't remember buying it. Could I have done it and not . . ."

Judge Massie extended a plump hand. "Mebbe I'd better take care of it. Them popguns ain't very good, but they kin do a sight o' damage at close range." Sylvia Jensen passed it over docilely enough. The Judge slipped out the clip and emptied the cartridge from the chamber. He held the gun under his bulbous nose and sniffed. "Been fired recent-like." He counted the shells in the clip, and added the unfired one from the chamber. "One missin'. Reckon that checks. Now let's get this here thing straight, jess for the record. Dr. Jensen stood in the doorway at the foot of yore bed. I take it you got them new-fangled notions 'bout married folks sleepin' in different rooms. Tain't natchel. But did he say anything?"

"He didn't need to . . . I knew what he was thinking. I just grabbed the gun and said, 'you won't touch Deedie', and . . ."

"Jess a minute, Miz Jensen." Judge Massie tweaked the bulb of his nose thoughtfully, and cleared his throat with a loud "errumph." He shifted a paper on his desk. "Miz Jensen, I've knowed you sence the day you was borned an' I knowed yore paw an' yore maw, an' I ain't one to see jealousy where it ain't, but moughtn't there be a mite o' jealousy in this?"

Sylvia Jensen was plainly bewildered. "Jealousy? Jealousy of what?"

"This here little sister of yourn that jess come back from college."

"Ohhhh . . ." She stopped to consider that. "Jealousy? Oh, no. You see . . . just a minute. I've got to stop and be very reasonable about this, Judge Massie, or I'd . . . I'd go crazy, really crazy. It isn't like that at all. The doctor and I haven't, well, haven't been man and wife for months, a year, I guess. I haven't cared particularly about the other women—and there've been many of them, and I've known it. Dr. Frederic didn't even try to hide it from me. He even boasted slyly of them, offered to show his motion pictures of them. But Deedie . . . Deedie's different . . . and I've seen him looking at her. She's so terribly young, just eighteen. But he wanted her—I could see that—and I had to stop him . . . to save her . . . to save me . . . to save my sanity."

"Yassum, an' that sorta settles that. Now, 'bout this here shootin', it ain't jess clear to me how come it happens. You're lyin' down, an' you see him come in. Were you lyin' down with the light on?"

"Light on?" Sylvia Jensen frowned. "I suppose it was . . . I think so . . . it must have been. I saw him quite clearly, except that I had awakened suddenly and he looked—well, I suppose it was my eyes, but he looked—well, a little different . . . out of focus. I've been having a little trouble with my eyes lately, and headaches. I had gone upstairs to lie down after dinner. We had intended to go to the theatre but something, well, something came up. It was early, the servants' night off, and Deedie had gone to a dinner dance with that nice Coleman boy . . ."

Judge Massie pursed his lips and shook his head. "Don't know's I'd call him anything short of a rascal, or mebbe scamp. Drinks too much, drives too fast, hits p'licemen—though I've seen p'licemen as I'd like to hit, m'self—gits into jail an' 'spects his money to git him out . . . an' it generally does. Makes a feller feel a mite Bolshevistic seein' a wuthless, no 'count scamp with too much money ridin' roughshod over the right of others. How-somever, scamps and rascals is generally reformable, when rascal-lin' an' scampin' come o' high spirits an' not real, low meanness, an' I don't figger Pete is mean. But git 'long with yore story."

"It was deadly quiet after the shot. I walked over and looked down at him, touched his hand, and he was cold . . . and then I screamed . . . but no one heard me, because it was the servants' night off. We dismiss all the servants on Thursday . . ."

"Thursday?" Judge Massie ruffled the fringe of his hair and consulted a preposterously gay calendar on the sedate wall, a calendar that advertised hardware through the dubious medium of a girl in a sunbonnet. "This here is Wednesday, Miz Jensen." Willie nodded solemn confirmation.

"Thursday," corrected Mrs. Jensen. "I had dismissed the ser-vants and there was no one else in the house unless . . ." She paused and considered. "No, Mrs. Hardecker—she's our house-keeper—went to visit her cousin." After she had passed the ac-tual shooting, she talked normally, even brightly, perhaps a little feverishly. "I slipped on my coat—I hadn't undressed—and came down here to see you."

"How come you didn't phone? Jess a mite o' luck you caught us here. Willie an' me, we been up to the court all day, and jess come in fer a bit o' reee-laxin'."

Sylvia nodded slowly. "The Westmoreland case . . . and you won. I read the late edition."

"This?" Judge Massie shoved an afternoon paper across the desk. "Says we done right well. An' lookee there, it mentions Willie." A plump forefinger pointed

She glanced at it and nodded. "Yes, that's it."

"Effen you'll jess read the date, Miz Jensen." The Judge urged it on her gently. "Go ahead . . . read it out loud."

"Wednesday, August third . . ." She crumpled the paper on the desk and buried her face in it. She wasn't crying. The rigidity of her shoulders and her silence denied it. Suddenly she sat up. "You think I *am* crazy." It was an accusation.

"Well, Ma'am," Judge Massie ventured cautiously, "it's a defense that's got a heap of 'em off."

"No . . . no . . . no! You can't . . ." She stood up, facing him, glaring. "No! Deedie . . . you can't . . . it would kill her. She'd always wonder . . . I mean . . . she's my sister, and Father was always considered eccentric, and if I . . . Oh, no! You mustn't! I forbid you to use that . . . absolutely. I'm *not* crazy." Willie, who had leapt to her side, eased her into her chair, and she smiled at him.

"Shucks, Miz Jensen," Judge Massie's voice was gentle, his hands quiet on the broad, battered expanse of his old desk, "ain't a soul sayin' you're crazy. An' come to think of it, I ain't preparin' a defense yet. I ain't even yore counsel for defense. I'm only hired to transfer a deed o' gift, recommember?" Gently he did it, as if he were soothing an excited child.

"Oh, yes," she nodded dully. "Oh, yes. I remember. But even . . . even when they arrest me you must promise not to use *that*."

"Miz Jensen, I ain't heared all the evidence in the case. Fact is, th' ain't any case as yit, so I cain't say's I see a defense right handy." Judge Massie fondled the second of his several chins and frowned. "Howsomever, effen you say so, I'll give you my promise—come time they try you fer murder, I promise I won't use insanity nor nothin' borderin' on it, 'cause, from what I hear so far, this here is one case of murder cum laude, or in less legal-soundin' language, he got ev'ything he deserved. An' now 'bout this deed of transfer, or deed o' gift . . ."

"Oh, thank you . . ." It was almost a prayer.

"Willie, here, is right handy at poundin' things out on a type-writer, an' he kin write it up an' salt it down with *wherefores* an' pepper it with *parties o' the first an' second parts*, an' even third parts, effen it's necessary. You kin sign it, an' Willie, who is right ambidextrous at times, kin seal it as notary."

Willie whipped the cover off his very new typewriter, sat at his very new desk and wrote rapidly. He handed over the brief paper with a flourish and Mrs. Jensen signed it.

"And not a bat of an eyelid," as Willie said afterward, "when she gave away a quarter of a million bucks."

She waved the paper until the signature was dry and then handed it to Judge Massie. "That money is my own, from an uncle. It's all I have, really . . ."

Judge Massie folded the paper and tucked it into his waist-coat—he called it *weskit*—pocket along with the cash she had given him. "All 'ceptin' 'bout fifteen millions yore paw left you."

"Oh, but that's all in the trust. Father tied it all up so that I get only the interest, and I'm to take care of Deedie. If I should die, a share for her stays in trust, and my share is distributed among some charities Father has listed. Unless, of course, I have children—and I haven't any. But this is mine. I can do with it whatever I wish, and I want to be sure Deedie is taken care of. A case like this might tie up the estate for some time."

"Dad-gum if that ain't the ca'mest way to be ree-guardin' yore own possible trial fer murder! But Sylvia Jensen, I sorta like you fer it, an' fer thinkin' o' that little sister." The Judge heaved himself laboriously out of his deep leather chair. "Reckon we got the details sorta hung up to dry. Better git goin' an' notify the p'lice. It's gonna look perty awkward effen you delay too long—not that the whole thing ain't a mite on the awkward side."

Mrs. Jensen reluctantly reached for the new streamlined phone, incongruous on the Judge's old-fashioned desk, but Judge Massie shook his head. "Don't work. We ain't got our own pus-sonal phone in. That there thing is jess on this here buildin' exchange, and Susie Wilford goes home at six o'clock. Susie's the telephone operator."

"Then I'll phone from the house. You'll go with me?" She rose, gathering her gloves and purse, ignoring the blunt, ugly little automatic on the desk.

"Land o' Goshen, yes. Ain't aimin' to turn you loose in that there house with nobody but *him*—and the p'lice acomin'." He escorted her gallantly to the door. She went on through and the Judge waited for Willie.

Willie swaggered out, attempting an unsuccessful compro-mise between the toughness popular among sixteen-year-olds and the dignity emulated from Judge Massie. As he passed the Judge he lowered one eyelid: "Looks to me like one old gal has fixed herself a swell set of evidence that she's crazy as a coot . . . and that's a honey of a defense, Jedge, in any man's court. But jess the same, I'm all for her, same as you."

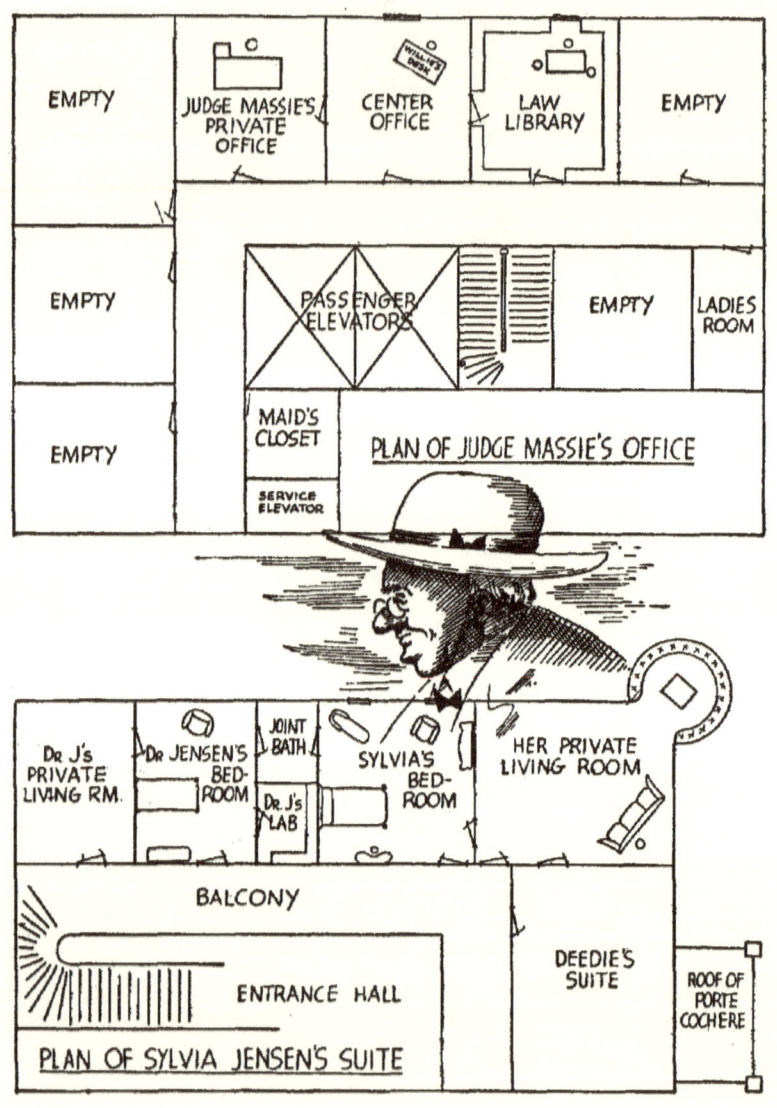

PLAN OF JUDGE MASSIE'S OFFICE

EMPTY

JUDGE MASSIE'S PRIVATE OFFICE

CENTER OFFICE

WILLIS'S DESK

LAW LIBRARY

EMPTY

EMPTY

PASSENGER ELEVATORS

EMPTY

LADIES ROOM

EMPTY

MAID'S CLOSET

SERVICE ELEVATOR

PLAN OF SYLVIA JENSEN'S SUITE

DR J'S PRIVATE LIVING RM.

DR JENSEN'S BEDROOM

JOINT BATH

DR. J'S LAB

SYLVIA'S BEDROOM

HER PRIVATE LIVING ROOM

BALCONY

ENTRANCE HALL

DEEDIE'S SUITE

ROOF OF PORTE COCHERE

2

A CORPSE WALKS

Judge Massie, his panama in full sail, waddled with astonishing rapidity down the corridor, whipped around the corner and came to a rumbling halt before the door of the automatic elevator. He complained to Sylvia Jensen, who had kept pace with the Judge's sally only with an effort. "Doo-dads . . . that's what they is, doo-dads." He included the concealed lighting, the soft-glowing aluminum ceiling and the mirror-like elevator button in one sweeping gesture. "An' that there Pete Coleman put Ambler Truxton up to this. New fangled ideas! Don't like 'em. Howsomever," he added with a twinkle, "they's a heap o' comfort in 'em—sometimes."

Willie was eager to show off the automatic elevater. "You jess push that button an' the elevator comes right to you, an' opens the door, an' everything." He gave the button a staccato series of rings.

"Sometimes," grumbled the Judge amiably, "sometimes. Allus afeared I'm gonna git caught in the dad-gummed thing, an' fer a man o' my weight an' general circumference it'd be plumb disconcertin'. It ain't agonna work, son," he added with gloomy satisfaction.

As if to disprove the Judge's words the door slid noiselessly back, disclosing a small cubicle of severe simplicity. The Judge shook his head. "Effen they'd made it a shade smaller, they'd 'a had to take me down in sections." He ushered Mrs. Jensen in, moved his own bulk testingly on to the elevator, and sighed as it gave no sign of breaking loose. "An' push the right button, Willie. I'd plumb hate to go to my reward in sech a fancy coffin."

Willie hastily covered the Judge's reference to coffins with an explanation. "This ain't the real elevator." He pushed a button. "It's only the service elevator to the basement, where they got a garage. You can keep your car practically in your office . . . kinda . . ." He finished lamely when it was obvious that Sylvia Jensen had heard not one word of the conversation.

The Judge rambled amiably along, filling the pause adequately with the genial rumble of his voice, covering the suffering silence of the weman who had murdered her husband. At the basement level he helped her out and led her to the only car in the gaunt, bare room—a Ford of ancient vintage and many idiosyncrasies. "Ain't nobody understands *Jessie Mae* 'ceptin' me—or would want to. Mind that there step, it's a mite rickety."

But Sylvia Jensen was scarcely aware of the car or of the Judge's guiding hand. She had sunk into an apathy that even *Jessie Mae's* thunderous awakening to life did not shatter. A young man in immaculate overalls opened the great door, and Jessie Mae sailed out into the night, drowning the young man's cheery farewell.

"Young spriggins," the Judge complained genially, "haulin' himself 'round in dungarees that don't git dirty. How kin a man really work 'thout he gits himself dirtied up? Good night, Joe," he bellowed over the roar of *Jessie Mae's* motor, and swung into traffic.

On the level street the ancient car settled down to a less thunderous roar but somewhat erratic pace and course, for the Judge's driving was strictly utilitarian. It got him places, but without grace or charm. He liked to talk as he drove, and occasionally swiveled his fat neck to watch the reaction to his words. And he sometimes emphasized a strong line with a satisfying but dangerous gesture.

Suddenly Sylvia Jensen sat forward and touched his shoulder. "Judge, Judge, what shall I say? I'm . . . I'm beginning to be frightened. What shall I do?"

"Cain't do nothin' rattlin' 'long in *Jessie Mae*. One comfortin' thing 'bout travelin'—cain't do a thing till you git where you're goin'." Judge Massie sighed at the dubious comfort of traveling. "Been doin' some figgerin' on my own. Ain't easy figgerin' fer somebody else, 'cause most likely they won't be wantin' you to do it anyhow. Howsomever, I done my figgerin', an' here 'tis. You jess up an' tell 'em the truth. Truth's got a way o' comin' out anyway, mebbe with its shirt-tail a mite ragged an' tore in spots, but it most ginerally always comes out. An' effen you're standin' 'round introducin' it pussonal like, same as if it was a friend you been long acquainted with, it sorts remains yore friend. But come a time you deny the truth, like it was a redheaded stepchild with sore eyes, then you cain't expect it to up an' defend you when you need it. Truth is a powerful friend but a mighty mean enemy."

"Truth!" Mrs. Jensen was scornful. "Truth! And have it hurt Deedie, leaving her wondering and miserable . . . doubting herself . . . believing perhaps that I was crazy. Oh, I know whatever I say to her about him would make her wonder about me. He's got her hypnotized. She thinks he's wonderful and kind and thoughtful. She hasn't seen underneath. She's too blinded with his glamour—and he was glamorous, and handsome. I've tried to tell her, but he counteracted it all before I even got a chance. He has told her about my 'nerves,' about my day-dreaming, about my 'imagining' things . . . and he's been *so considerate* and *so clever* at dissembling that she believes him. She hasn't connected it with Father . . . yet. But after *this*, she will. She'll begin to wonder about me, about Father—and then about herself. She'll always be afraid, then, because she's so sensitive."

"Mebbe you ain't givin' her full credit fer sensitiveness. Mebbe, effen we went to her with the truth right away, fust thing, that there sensitiveness would be all sympathy for you. An' her sympathy would be all the sweeter fer havin' been on the wrong side. Folks is sometimes like that. Show 'em they been misjudgin' and they're downright pathetic tryin' to make up fer it."

"I can't . . . I can't take the chance. I won't. I'll lie. I'll say I just came in and found him. They'll believe me . . . they'll believe you," she ended triumphantly.

Judge Massie shook his head. "Sylvia Jensen, me an' truth is somewhat alike. We're good friends, but we're powerful mean when we're agin' you . . . an' you'd be turnin' me agin' you effen

you do that. I don't know's I done right in listenin' to you, and
mebbe I ain't done right in givin' you some o' the advice I already
turned loose. But this here thing you're a'plannin' an' a'schemin',
that there is downright suppressin' of evidence."

"Evidence? Evidence? What evidence? You can't call the word
of an hysterical woman 'evidence,' and that's all you have to go
on. I don't quite see you, Judge James Massie, coming forward
with the story of an hysterical woman. No, I'll do this my way."

"Sylvia Jensen," the Judge's voice was kindly, soothing, "I
recommember a time, long ago, when you warn't much more'n
knee high to a hop-toad, an' you come to me 'bout somethin'
you'd done. I disremember what 'twas—mebbe breakin' a winder—you were right much of a tomboy in them days. An' you ast
me what to do, an' I tole you then, same as now, that truth is always a good friend. Mebbe you don't recommember that, mebbe
it don't seem important now. But it was sure an all-fire matter o'
life an' death then. An' you took my advice, an' you lived long
enough to fergit it. Mebbe this here is a mite more important
than breakin' a winder, but the winder-breakin' then seemed jess
as big an' troublesome an' unyieldin'. 'Pears to me you gotta go
through a period o' trial an' tribulation now, same as you went
through 'bout that winder, but you foller that same advice now.
An' it's wise to take advice of a lawyer in matters concernin' the
law, same as you'd take bitter medicine from a doctor effen you
was ill."

"I see." Suddenly she sat forward, gripping the tattered back
of the front seat. "But Judge, you don't know how it has been
tormenting me. You couldn't know. I, well, sometimes I almost
believe I'm mentally ill. Yes, Judge, he's done that to me. Like
recently, I saw two of Dr. Frederic . . . or seemed to. I left him in
the library in his brown suit and came upstairs, and I could have
sworn I saw him up there, too—but he was wearing a blue suit.
Probably there's some simple explanation, some trick of light.
Perhaps it took me longer to walk upstairs than I thought, and
he had hurried up the back stairs. And yet I was sure he had
changed his clothes. Don't you see, if he deliberately did that
to me, then, well, those things could happen to Deedie, and if I

were—if it were even suggested I were insane—you can see what it would do to Deedie." She touched his shoulder with pathetic helplessness. "Tell me the truth. I'm not crazy, am I?"

"Kinda funny way to ask a question, ain't it? Howsomever, I think mebbe I kin answer it, not definite-like, 'cause I wouldn't know, not bein' one o' them psychiatrists; but I will say this, I don't *think* you're crazy. An' I ain't the sort o' person as would take all this here trouble jess fer somebody I figgered was crazy anyway, an' didn't need help o' the sort I could give. An' Sylvia Jensen, I'm aimin' to help, but I gotta have help, too—yore help. Sorta give a hitch on yore halter an' git control. You cain't be goin' over the edge on me now."

"Over the edge . . ." Sylvia Jensen peered down curiously over her knees, into the pit of the car. "Over the edge . . ." as if she could see strange visions on the floor.

"Yessum. Ain't much a body kin do to help crazy folks—not my kind o' help, anyways, an' I'm plumb sot agin' wastin' my efforts. Don't like to go 'round exertin' m'self noways, an' effen I do, I wants it to 'mount to somethin'."

Judge Massie nodded to his left as the car passed a blaze of light behind a high hedge. "Figger Deedie and Pete in there kickin' their-selves up a gran' ruckus, an' mebbe strollin' out under the stars. Didn't have country clubs in my time, or mebbe I'd 'a gone strollin' under the stars, an' mebbe now I wouldn't be a sour ole bachelor. Heap o' comfort, strollin' under the stars, with sweet music playin'." At that moment the Club House Swing Rhythm Makers burst into *Chickery Chick* and the Judge snorted, "Effen it is sweet music."

Sylvia Jensen pointed right. "Between those stone pillars, and please watch my rhododendron bush. Wilks set it too close to the drive."

Judge Massie sighed happily. "Sylvia, that there is the sweetest thing I heared you say this here whole evenin'. Yessiree, sure is. A woman that kin worry 'bout her rhododendron bush ain't plumb lost her sense o' proportion, though pussonally I prefers azaleas."

Sylvia sat back in her seat with a sigh. "I was tense, wasn't? You've done a great deal for me already, Judge. Sometimes I get provoked because you are so busy hiding all your brilliant mind under that pretense of rustic language, and because you stay in this town when you could be a national figure."

"This here town," stated the Judge firmly, for he was on his favorite topic—next to reee-laxin', "this here town is same as any other town. Got people in it, same's any other, and the people is the same. Some of 'em mean as gosh-all-get-out, some of 'em kind as spring winds, some pore an' some rich. Yessum, this here is jess about every town there is, biled down into one little place. An' bein' as I ain't as spry as I once was, I sorta like my human-ity close at hand, so's I kin study it 'thout too much sashayin' 'round. 'Sides, I served m' state once in Congress, an' stood in imminent danger o' bein' 'lected Senator. Heap o' trouble bein' a Senator. A Senator's gotta look like a Senator, an' me, shucks, I ain't good at lookin' like nothin' but Judge Massie. 'Sides, I hear tell them seats in the Senate ain't so comfortable, an' I likes m'comfort. Sure do."

Willie nodded. "Yassum! Best thing the Jedge does is reee-lax-in', an' he's downright successful at it. Jedge an' me, we been thinkin' mebbe we'd sorta start a perfession of reee-laxin', on'y the Jedge says it'd take too much time from ree-laxin' . . . an' any-how, it's a state o' mind." Willie gave up, temporarily, his cham-pionship of the Judge, and slipped from his careful simulation of the Judge's accent and mannerisms into the enthusiasm natural to a sixteen-year-old-with-freckles. "Jees, what a house! I guess there must be forty-fifty rooms, maybe a hundert . . . an' there ain't a light anywhere! Gosh, it looks like a castle, a real castle, I mean, like in France, or on the Rhine . . ."

Sylvia pointed to the great black bulk, darker than the dark night. "It's copied from one in Scotland, I believe. Father called it Storme's Grote. It overlooks the river. It's quite nice in the daytime, Willie; you must come out and see it. However, it hasn't a hundred rooms, only about thirty-five. But I'm afraid you'd be a little disappointed in it. It has windows; oh, lots and lots of windows. Father was a sea-captain and he wanted fresh air, and Mother wanted a castle—they were very fashionable, then. So they compromised on a castle with big windows. It nearly drove the architect frantic, and the neighbors, too. In those days people didn't believe in fresh air, and built their houses with tiny windows and stuffy rooms. Most of those other 'castles' have been torn down, but not Storme's Grote."

"Yessiree!" The Judge waved a pudgy hand at the dark bulk of the house. "That there house, son, is a standin' monument to the sagacity, common sense, an' sanity of old Sylvester Storme. That there was one man that knew what was really good—what, in a world o' foolishness and fashion, was the sorta thing that a body could live with an' take comfort in, an' ain't a saner thing a man kin do."

"Was he a real sea-captain? Could he swear like a sea-captain?" Willie turned an inquiring face toward Sylvia, sitting, or bouncing—for the Judge's driving operated inversely to his speech—beside him.

Sylvia laughed. "He could, though I never heard him—much. He had a separate wing built in which he could see his employees—built separate from the house so he could roar and swear to please himself."

Judge Massie chuckled. "Don't reckon it pleased his listeners. Cap'n Sylvester could raise a middlin' fair breeze jess talkin', an' when he started swearin' it come up a gale. Hear tell once he worked a real good sweatin' rage an' bellowed—an' bust every window in the house. Ain't sayin' it's so . . . jess heard tell. Right fine man, yore paw was, right fine man, though he died sorta mild-like, cornsiderin' . . ."

Sylvia shook her head. "Why, Father burst a blood-vessel in a rage when he heard his dock-hands had struck!"

"Wellllll . . ." the Judge drawled dubiously, "yassum . . . but most folks was expectin' him to meet his Maker through explodin', so bustin' a blood-vessel was sorta mild-like."

"Father was a grand person, wasn't he?"

Willie nodded. "Jees! Folks still talk about Cap'n Sylvester, what a swell guy he was . . ."

Sylyja smiled into the dark, and laid her hand on Willie's arm. "You two, you beloved frauds, both of you. I do appreciate this and it has helped me. You have helped me to see Father as he really was, and that's helped me orient myself." At the Judge's cough of protest, she held up her hand, though he could not see it. "Oh, yes, I realize what you've been doing—getting my mind off what's to come . . . and what is past . . . trying to make me see that Father wasn't, well, eccentric . . . just a grand person too big for his times . . . and I thank you."

"Well, don't that beat the Dutch? So you figgered it out, did you, Sylvia?" Judge Massie drew up under the stone *porte cochere*. The dim headlights flared up as he raced the motor and coasted in, to pull up suddenly in a shuddering stop. "An' effen you kin figger that out, mebbe you kin figger this 'un out, too. Effen you're able, in yore present distress, to git soothed down by a mite o' talk about yore paw, an' effen that mite o' talk kin make you be somewhat reasonable, then how much danger is there, do you reckon, o' me figgerin' you're crazy? Not much. An' effen you're that reasonable, it mought not be any harm in askin' a few questions."

Sylvia sat forward, leaning over the back of the front seat. "Oh no. I can answer sensibly and without going to pieces now."

Judge Massie turned, and the car creaked under the shifting of his weight. "*Jessie Mae* ain't all she used to be. But this here house is plumb dark. Recommember turnin' off the lights? Or did the servants?"

"I don't know. I don't remember. I suppose I did, but it doesn't seem I would have bothered . . . I mean, I just ran out of the house, and down to the Country Club. I got a taxi there. So I must have turned off the lights, because this is the servants' night off. It's Thursday . . . I mean, I thought it was Thursday—and dismissed them."

"Even the chauffeur?"

"Chauffeur? Yes. Why?"

"Warn't it a mite odd to git rid of the chauffeur effen you was plannin' to drive to town to the theatre?"

"Why, no. Dr. Frederic usually takes the roadster and we go alone so we can stay the night. He didn't want me to be excited by the ride after the theatre. He always said the theatre excited me, but it didn't. It took me away for a while, so that I could forget—forget that . . . that he was there, if you know what I mean. I could forget he was tormenting me. I think it was part of his cruelty to let me feel that little escape, and then the bitterness of reality when he killed all the pleasure by being so *considerate* of my nerves."

"How come you didn't go tonight? 'Pears to me you went up to lie down instead. Didn't feel poorly, did you?"

She shrank back then. "I didn't cancel the reservations! I didn't! I don't care what the man said . . . I didn't cancel the reservations."

Judge Massie was easing his bulk slowly out of the narrow confines of *Jessie Mae's* front seat and he paused abruptly, swinging his leonine head around. "Cancel them reservations? You ain't tellin' me that after you went an' dismissed them servants you found out you warn't goin' to the theatre?"

Sylvia nodded dumbly, and then realized that in the darkness the Judge couldn't see. "Yes. Dr. Frederic suggested it. He said perhaps I'd better check on the reservations because I'd let so many things slip lately. I haven't really—or, at least, I don't think so. So just to prove to him I hadn't forgotten—I even remember the seat numbers, D 11 and 13—I called up the box office . . . and they said . . . they said I had cancelled the reservations this morning. It, well, it upset me . . . and then Dr. Frederic was so *solicitous*. He made me take my medicine and go up and lie down . . . to help my nerves . . . and after I'd been there a while . . . he came in . . . and . . ."

"Ain't a mite o' sense in goin' all over that again, Sylvia."

She whirled in the seat. "You too? Are you trying to save my *nerves?* Oh, forgive me, Judge, but . . . yes, I know you meant to be kind, but that's the sort of *kindness* Dr. Frederic gives me . . . protecting me from something I don't need to be protected from. I'm *not* crazy."

"Shucks," murmured the Judge affably, "ain't we jess been provin' that? Course you ain't crazy. Some sorta explanation's gonna crop up, sure as shootin'. Yessiree. But how come you didn't take this here roadster you been talkin' about?"

She shuddered. "The keys were in his pocket . . . and he was so cold . . . so terribly, deadly cold, I couldn't make myself touch him again, or even . . . even look at him. I couldn't."

"Yassum . . . 'spect you're right." The Judge sidled out of the car and held out his hand to Mrs. Jensen, the huge bulk of his rotund figure blocking a view of the front of the car. "Guess we got things down right smart, now."

Sylvia Jensen darted up the steps, fumbling in her bag for the key. Her fingers shook as she inserted it in the lock. Judge Massie leaned heavily against the great iron-studded door and it creaked open. Mrs. Jensen reached inside and flooded the hall with light.

Willie, close behind them, whistled as he viewed the tremendous baronial hall. It was an enormous thing, paved in stone, eighty feet long and twenty high. A great marble staircase rose at the far end, dividing at a landing to rise to a balcony that encircled the other three sides.

Sylvia Jensen shivered as she pointed to a door almost overhead, but to the right. "He's in there . . . dead." She started down the hall almost at a run, her sharp heels clicking hollowly on the stone paving. The Judge waddled slowly after her, and then looked with dismay at the staircase.

He complained to Willie. "Ain't much of a hand at sashayin' up an' down stairs . . . an' Land o' Goshen, look at 'em, will you? Wide enough to drive four horses abreast—effen I ain't forgot how to drive horses." Willie, goggle-eyed before such magnificence, nodded.

Judge Massie puffed up the stairs, Willie close behind, staring out across the great hall. He clutched the Judge's arm. "Look Jedge . . ."

Judge Massie turned ponderously. "Ain't a mite o' sense in givin' a body a jolt like that. This here house is plumb draped with ghosts, an' there's a dead man waitin' at the head o' these stairs." Judge Massie shook his head.

Willie was scornful. "Ain't scairt, Jedge? Ain't seen a man livin' or daid you was scairt of."

The Judge sighed. "Warn't a man I was referrin' to . . . 'twas a woman. An' look, Sylvia went up them stairs an' vanished behind that curtain. Leastwise, I hope she vanished behind that curtain, 'cause otherwise she jess vanished. An' what give you a start?"

Willie pointed down the hall. "I thought I saw that door open an' close." He glanced up to the landing where a tapestry still swayed slightly. "What's in vanishin' to startle you, Jedge?"

Judge Massie plodded on up the stairs. "Ain't the vanishin' that worries me, it's what she's doin' while she's vanished. Willie, I'm plumb worried she's called the p'lice an' I'm more'n worried 'bout what she's sayin' to 'em. Turn a woman loose with a telephone, an' th'ain't no tellin' what she'll say."

"Women!" stated Willie with the vehemence and knowledge of a sixteen-year-old. "Women are wacky, and this one is 'specially wacky. An' when women specialize in bein' wacky, they do a bang-up job. Let's you'n me be leavin'."

Judge Massie shook his head. "Cain't do it, son. Got three good reasons. Fust off, we cain't leave a woman to face this here corpse upstairs. Second, we was seen comin' in an' effen we run now, 'twon't look so good later, an' third, I'm plumb curious 'bout who killed that Pomeranian."

"What Pomeranian?" Willie looked in distaste down the vast spaces of the baronial hall. "I don't see no Pomeranian." He looked at the Judge with solicitude. "Jedge, you ain't feelin' bad, are you? I mean mebbe the heat . . ."

"Sure is hot," Judge Massie acknowledged with a sigh and fumbled under the voluminous tails of his frock coat. "Sure is hot." He drew out a battered palm-leaf fan that suggested Baptist picnics, droning flies and porch rockers. He fanned his broad, cherubic face and grinned at Willie. "Ain't feelin' the heat that bad, son. I really seen it. An' don't fergit, son, Sylvia Jensen ain't crazy, neither."

Willie looked dubious. "If she ain't crazy, Jedge, then she's been buildin' us up for the best out for a murder rap I've ever seen. Who'd ever convict her after they heard this here wacky story of hers?"

"You would," pointed out Judge Massie, and shook his fan firmly under Willie's freckled nose, "an' you've been seein' too many movies. Gittin' yore natchel language mixed up with *murder raps*

an' sech. Ain't right to spile a man's appetite fer his own language
that away."

But Willie was lost in the plot of a recent movie, or in some
fourth dimension of boyhood. "I figger she bumped off this guy
because he was makin' a pass at Deedie. Jees, she's one good-looker."

Judge Massie regarded his small confrere with affection.
"Make a swell movie, wouldn't it?"

"Yes *sir*," Willie agreed heartily and then flushed. "Well, it
would, Jedge."

"An' that still don't tell us who 'bumped off' this here Pomeranian."

Willie shook his head. "I don't like 'em."

Judge Massie shifted his bulk from one congress gaiter to
the other, and sighed. He fanned himself with leisurely strokes.
"Don't know's I like 'em, neither. Sorta look like animated floor
mops. Mebbe my pussonal choice would be to exterminate 'em
wholesale, but this here partickler Pomeranian's different. He jess
don't sorta fit into the picture, an' yet he's got to." He glanced at
Willie's puzzled face. "Seen him in that there *porte cochere* when
we druv up. Lights sorta flared up, and there was this here little
tyke. Mighty nigh run over him, but didn't. He's down there
now, under the front axel. Don't 'spect you saw it . . . you were
too all-fired set on gittin' to a murder."

Mrs. Jensen pushed open a door behind the tapestry and
came out, smiling a little timidly, a little defiantly.

"Been phonin' the p'lice," Judge Massie accused.

The woman nodded. "I had to. I had to do it myself . . . my
way. I told them we had just found the body of Dr. Frederic Jensen. Now, Judge, you'll have to help me. You're my lawyer, and
you'll have to help me. You're in it, now."

Judge Massie fondled his series of chins and eyed her over
the steel rims of his spectacles. "Don't recommember bein' in it.
Recommember a woman come to my office an' confessed to a
murder, an' recommember comin' out to see effen it's true . . . an'
to run spang up agin the truth, Sylvia Jensen, I ain't found out,
yit. No, ma'am. Don't look like Willie an' me are in this a-tall.

When the p'lice come, we jess tell 'em what we know, an' nuthin' more. Willie an' me, we got reputations in this here town, an' we got to uphold 'em."

"You wouldn't . . . you couldn't . . . you can't turn me over to the police like that. You're my lawyer. My confidences to you are sacred." She stepped back and peered up at him. "And it isn't for me. Please. I don't mind being tried for murder. I don't even mind dying. There hasn't been much for me in living recently, except Deedie. But I can't die and leave behind me a doubt, and if I'm ever tried that will have to come—that he was driving me crazy. Maybe they'll think I was crazy . . . and Deedie will always wonder. Besides," she added shrewdly, "you won't even have to lie. You've come home with me . . . you see me discover the body of my husband . . . and that'll be the truth. Nothing you heard at your office can be used . . ."

"Jess a moment . . . jess a moment." Judge Massie signaled her to silence with an imperative flap of his fan. "Mought be a meager miteness o' truth in what you've been sayin'. Jess a meager littlest bit of a mite o' truth . . . but have you got a Pomeranian?"

She looked up, puzzled, into the cherubic earnestness of the Judge's face. "Yes, his name is Chu Chin. Why?"

Judge Massie tilted her chin up with the tattered edge of his fan and studied her face, the drawn mouth, the tight planes of her cheeks, her wide, questioning eyes. He spoke slowly, convincingly. "Sylvia Jensen, effen you'll tell me the truth, effen you'll tell me why you killed yore Pomeranian, mebbe I mought help . . . by stickin' to yore story . . . near's I kin, you understand, 'thout deviating from the truth. Awful truthful man, I am . . . sometimes."

"Chu Chin? Me, kill Chu Chin? But he isn't dead. He's . . ." Her eyes searched the Judge's face. "So he's dead, too."

Judge Massie sighed. "Reckon that's an answer. I was lookin' spang in yore eyes, Sylvia, an' it were plumb news to you." He started slowly up the remaining stairs. "Don't know what's gonna come o' this, but, Sylvia, I'm stickin' to yore story. Let's git this here discoverin' over."

Sylvia Jensen stumbled along beside him. "But Chu Chin? Where is he? Who . . ." Her voice dropped to a scarcely audible mumble. "He's been the only comfort I had. Chu Chin didn't care if I was no longer beautiful. He didn't even care if I were mad . . . he loved me."

The Judge pointed down the long balcony. "Mebbe you better go on ahead an' git this here discoverin' over. We'll wait here, an' you kin holler at us, then we kin come arunnin'. Won't have to invent details then, an' when you're makin' up a story, the less details you got to invent, the better."

The Judge and Willie waited in an uncomfortable silence as Sylvia Jensen walked reluctantly down the long balcony. She glanced over her shoulder, half-turned back, and then went on. She paused at the entrance to nerve herself for the opening of the door. Suddenly she thrust it open, leaned in and switched on the light. She stood for an instant framed by the light from her bedroom.

And then she screamed!

It wasn't just horror at something she had seen, something she had expected to see. That scream was agony, sheer agony clawing at her throat.

The Judge lunged forward, his bulk tilting him rakishly, but he caught her just as she collapsed. Over her shoulder he peered into the bedroom where a murder had been committed.

The room was empty!

3

A CORPSE TALKS

The room was empty.

Judge Massie clumsily patted Sylvia's quivering shoulder with one hand. The other dangled limply, clutching the broad-brimmed, floppy panama and the palm-leaf fan, more by habit than conscious exertion. Suddenly he barred the doorway with them, cautioning Willie, "Don't go in yit." His fat, paternal arm encircled Sylvia's shoulders. "Right perty room," he said quietly. "Don't know's I've seen a pertier woman's room without doodads . . . not as I'm accustomed to goin' in ladies boudoirs. Ain't got no slinky, long-legged dolls, nor ladies' skirt kiverin' the telephone, an ain't no fancy pants on that there vanity-dresser thing. Right nice-lookin' wood, an' right shapely, too. Never did see no sense in kiverin' nice-lookin' furniture with fancy pants. It's agin nature. An' dad-burn me if that ain't a real, old-time crocheted bedspread, neat as all get-out. Cherrywood, that bed. Always did think cherry made a fine set o' furniture. Willie, yore jaw's hangin' slack."

The Judge was right about the room. Its dove-grey walls radiated the soft light of a bedside lamp, a pair of vanity lamps, and a single old-fashioned crystal lamp on a console by the door opposite the foot of the bed.

And it was in the space between the foot of the bed and that door that the body of Dr. Frederic Jensen should have been lying—and wasn't.

Judge Massie pushed Sylvia's trembling chin up with the hand that still clutched his panama and fan. "Right sure fer sartain this here is the room?"

Sylvia Jensen nodded feebly, and then buried her face against the Judge's ample shirt front, shuddering and crying, incoherently gabbling words that had no meaning. Awkwardly the Judge fanned the back of her neck with his hat and fan. "Land o' Goshen, Sylvia, ain't nothin' to git the heaves over. Fact o' the matter, ain't nothin' a-tall. Nary a thing. Yessireee. Jess ain't nothin'. An' *nothin'* ain't somethin' to git scared of, an' take on sech a pile o' to-do about. Now, effen there had been a corpse a lyin' there, there mighta been some sense in yore carryin's on, but shucks, its absence oughta be right comfortin'. Fact o' the matter, it's a right rare occasion I walk into a room an' find a corpse lyin' 'round."

Still the woman shuddered and shivered, and babbled meaningless sounds. The Judge's voice dropped to a soft murmur. "Sylvia, kinda pull yoreself together. This here ain't near so bad as you make out. Like as not it was jess a bad dream . . . nightmare, sorta."

But the Judge's voice held little confidence, for he was eyeing a shadowy depression in the deep pile of the carpet. It was very faint, so faint that the Judge had to reach carefully over Sylvia's shoulder to thrust his steel-rimmed spectacles into place for a clearer view. When it was obvious the woman was paying no heed he beckoned Willie over.

"Take her sorta easy-like, son, an' lay her down on that there chaise longue, over by the bathroom door. I gotta look around. An' take her close to the foot of the bed; I sorta want to keep this here space near the door untrompled on."

Willie, a little unsteady still from the shock of Sylvia Jensen's scream, took hold of the woman stiffly and turned her around. She offered no resistance and stumbled only slightly as he led her across the room. She dropped limply on to the chaise longue, burying her face in the tufted pillow. She didn't cry out; she just lay there shaking.

"Mought git her a dose of ammonia . . . in there, in the bathroom. Seems likely she'd have some," Judge Massie directed, laying his panama carefully on a chintz-covered chair and setting the fan up against it like a tattered sail.

Willie backed between the chaise longue and the bed into the bathroom, his eyes on the curious antics of Judge Massie.

Carefully, and with thought for his bulk and elderly knees, the Judge lowered himself to the floor, hands braced on the chair. He grunted and puffed, and the gold chain sagged, almost sweeping the floor. He was squinting along the carpet when he saw Willie still standing, fascinated, in the doorway. In a less serious moment Willie would have snickered.

Judge Massie grimaced. "Effen you're figgerin' on laughin' then git in that bathroom an' laugh where I cain't hear you. Ain't nowise dignified—nor comfortable, but it's gotta be done. When a corpse gits up an' walks away, somethin's gotta be done. An' quit gawpin', Willie, an' git that ammonia."

Judge Massie grunted heavily, and moved slowly. When Willie returned with a crystal goblet the Judge was hauling himself up by the jamb of the door, his fat fingers scrabbling at its smooth surface. Sylvia Jensen paid the Judge not the slightest heed. Only when Willie touched her shoulder and held out the glass did she raise her head, only to shake it dazedly in refusal.

Still leaning heavily against the door jamb and breathing unevenly, the Judge directed, "Drink that there stuff . . . do you good an' help you, too."

With childlike obedience she took the glass and drank gulpily, watching him over the rim as if waiting for his approval. When it was gone he smiled at her. "Warn't so bad. Come to think of it, lots o' things ain't so bad when we come spang up agin 'em. Feelin' better?"

She paused as if to take stock of herself, and then nodded. "I feel numb." Her voice was a flat monotone. "I can't explain . . . I was lying right here . . . in this . . ."

Judge Massie nodded. "Been wonderin' how come the bed warn't mussed up. Go ahead."

"He came through that door behind you, right at the foot of my bed."

Judge Massie stepped away from the door and regarded it thoughtfully. "From his room?"

She looked blank for an instant. "Oh no, his room connects through the bath. That's my own sitting room. He came through that way—he always did when he came to grin at me—and he was grinning tonight, looking at me and grinning. I reached out and grabbed the gun. It was on this little table." She started to indicate a place at her elbow, and then stared. There wasn't any table there. It was over by the bed. She looked wildly up at the Judge. "But it was there, and I did reach for the gun. It's true. He came through that door . . ." she pointed across the Judge's frock-coated bulk.

She froze into a horrid immobility, a gaping, terror-stricken caricature of a woman.

Then she screamed!

It was horrible—a wild, mad shriek coming from a fear-twisted, immobile face. And then it died into a bubble of choking laughter, and her face broke, like some wax mask melting, into a childish grimace. "So you came back!" Then she fainted.

"What have you done to my wife?"

The words were coldly furious, from a tall dark man who slammed the door of Sylvia's private sitting room and strode across the floor, brushing Judge Massie aside, kneeling beside the woman. "Sylvia, Sylvia!" He glared up at the Judge. "You stupid, stupid fools! What are you doing here? Who are you?" He rose and faced the Judge. "What are you doing in this house? In my wife's bedroom? Answer me. I demand to know what you have been doing to my wife that she should scream at the sight of me. I demand . . ."

Judge Massie nodded quietly toward the silent figure. "Effen you'd do less demandin', an' more lookin' after yore wife, Dr. Jensen, I figger it'd be more useful . . . an' look better."

The dark face flushed and the man turned abruptly, reaching for her pulse, glancing at a thin platinum watch on his wrist. He thrust past a white-faced Willie and went into the bathroom, returning in moment with a glass of amber fluid. He lifted Sylvia's head and poured the liquid between her slack lips. She gulped and gagged, fought feebly, and then sank back, eyes closed.

Judge Massie, with his unerring ability, picked the most comfortable chair in the room, eased himself into it, thrust his congress gaiters out before him and thoughtfully crossed them, regarding them with tolerant affection. "I gotta give 'em a rest onct in a while."

Dr. Jensen grunted at this affability, glared at the Judge, eyed Willie with distaste, and set the glass carefully on the bedside table before he turned back to the Judge. His face was still flushed, but he was making an obvious effort to be courteous.

"I regret my hastiness. Naturally I was worried that my wife should scream out at the sight of me, especially when she fainted immediately thereafter. And with two unknown men in her room, why I naturally thought . . ."

"Yessir, I was figgerin' that was the sort a' thing you'd naturally think, but two is jess precisely one too many fer the sort o' thing you'd be likely to think, 'specially since one o' them is a boy an' th' other an old man, mighty nigh to dodderin'. Not as I'm 'xactly sure o' what dodderin' means, 'ceptin' sometimes I feel like I must be doin' it."

Dr. Jensen flushed again. "I intended to imply nothing of the kind. I demanded, and I still demand, to know who you are, and what you are doing here."

Judge Massie glanced at the recumbent figure on the chaise longue, and then back to the doctor's saturnine face. "Jess an attorney, here on a matter o' business at yore wife's request."

"So late at night?" The doctor sneered. "I don't believe it. You have been hounding my wife to the point where, when she sees me, she screams. In her present nervous condition any disturbance is harmful, and yet you come here and badger her until she screams at the . . ."

"The sight o' you. You said that onct," Judge Massie remind him. "So it ain't 'xactly necessary to remind you that it was *you* that startled her . . . twarn't us."

"Eh?" The doctor glared at Judge Massie, and then sank in a chair, his arms limply hanging over its sides. "Yes, of course." The fury in his face was erased with a frown of worry. "Yes, of course," he repeated. "I'm sorry for my outburst. Very rude of me, but you can understand what a shock this has been. I'm scarcely myself."

Judge Massie smiled. "Effen you'd been most anybody else comin' through that door jess now I'da felt a heap easier." Willie blinked nervous agreement, and eyed the doctor as if he expected him to vanish in a puff of smoke.

The dark eyes questioned Judge Massie, and then dropped. "This has been very embarrassing. I've tried to keep my wife's condition, her highly nervous state, from becoming known, but you can see for yourself that she is, or was, quite wrought up."

"Been noticin' that. Been noticin' it pertickler these last few months, but 'special-like tonight." Judge Massie considered his boot affectionately, and made a tent of his fingers across his protruding paunch. "Yup, noticed it pertickler this evenin' . . . an' most pertickler when you come through that door. Gimme quite a start, m'self."

Dr. Jensen was making an effort at apology. "I trust, sir, you understand my actions."

Judge Massie folded the pink accordion of his chins in a thoughtful nod. "Yup, 'pears you done cleared up the situation, an' we accepts yore apology. It was an apology, warn't it?" he asked mildly.

"Of course . . . why, certainly."

"An' effen you don't mind my mentionin' it, I think the p'lice are at the front door."

"Police?" Dr. Jensen sat forward. "Police? But why should the police . . .? Are you sure?"

"Jess heared the siren screamin', and brakes squealin', but mebbe you warn't noticin'."

Dr. Jensen got to his feet slowly, as if he were thinking as he moved. He glanced at the Judge. "Could this young man answer the door? I don't like to leave Mrs. Jensen. She seems to bestirring and I don't want her to be frightened." He bent over Sylvia and touched her. She moaned faintly and turned away.

"Willie here kin answer the door, bein' as the servants is off fer the night. Me, I'm gonna reee-lax. Been right strenuous fer a man o' my age and general corporealness meetin' a walkin', talkin' corpse. Feel the need of a good piece o' reee-laxin'." Judge Massie closed his eyes and sank lower in the chintz-covered wing chair, his thumbs hooked into the sagging gold chain, his pink chins folding over his collar and black string tie. He opened one eye cautiously. "Effen you was aimin' to object, git it off'n yore chest now, but I'm still reee-laxin'."

Dr. Jensen glared down at the bulging contour of the Judge, at the congress gaiters, one locked firmly over the other with an air of permanence, and he shrugged faintly. He turned to Willie. "Will you admit the . . . er . . . police?"

Willie, still a little groggy from the rapid changes he had witnessed, nodded. He was not yet used to Dr. Jensen as a living man, and he tendered him the cautious respect usually reserved for the deaf, the mad and the dead. And he subtly managed to convey that Dr. Jensen might be all three of them. He backed slowly out of the room, fled along the balcony and down the stairs.

He opened the door to Detective Sergeant Emery's worried face, which always looked as though he hadn't quite caught up with the last thought he had, if any. But Emery wasn't dumb. In spite of mystery-story writers, policemen don't get to be detective sergeants by being dumb. Maybe they're slow and stick to routine, because routine keeps out a lot of blunders, but they are rarely dumb.

Emery stood there, his muscular bulk blocking most of the great doorway, and he peered down the huge hall as if he were afraid to enter. He wasn't afraid; he was sizing it up as a matter of routine—avenues of escape, places he'd have to cover, possible ambush for his men. Emery got sent places where he had to figure things like that more often than he got sent to mansions.

When he had finished his quick survey he eyed Willie skeptically. "What you doin' here?" He jerked his head toward Willie and bellowed over his shoulder, "Look, boys, the imp is here, the devil must be somewhere around." He frowned at Willie, and then mopped a suddenly beaded forehead. "I swear, I never knew it to fail; that old devil can smell trouble forty leagues off, or else make it come to him. How in hell does he always manage to crash in on my cases? Hardly through bustin' one in my face this afternoon, and making me feel like a fool on the witness stand, than he . . ."

"Mebbe you *were* a fool on the witness stand." Willie paused and then added, "Were you?" Confident of friendship from the big policeman, he planted himself in the doorway, legs straddled, fists to hips.

Emery made a mock swipe at his ear and Willie, from long practice, ducked expertly. Emery guffawed. "Listen, will you? That antiquated old hippopotamus is teachin' him a disrespect for the law."

Willie scanned the group behind Emery. He saw Benny, the diminutive cameraman who had a perpetual sniffle from living in damp dark-rooms, or so the squad maintained; Lew Legge, fingerprint expert, whose ham-like hands could work gentle marvels; and Garrison, Emery's right and left hand and boot.

Built for brute force, Garrison had never comprehended this permanent but amicable feud; in fact, there were many things Garrison had never comprehended, including timetables, his wife's temper when he appeared at supper without a coat, and least of all why his chief tolerated his consistent blunders.

Willie looked beyond Garrison into the night. "Where's Doc Cranshaw? Not missing a dinner at this time o' night?" For it was the coroner's standing complaint that his patrons invariably got murdered at his mealtimes.

"Doc's on a party tonight at the Carlyle's, but he's coming. Where's that old fossil, Judge Massie, and the corpse?"

Willie jerked a thumb upward and started an explanation but Emery thrust him aside. "He'll be destroyin' evidence first thing I know—or manufacturin' it." And before Willie could begin the tale of queer events, Emery was plunging up the stairs.

Willie scurried after him, trying to explain the abrupt change of status, dancing from side to side in an effort to stop Emery's wild charge up the steps. Garrison pounded along behind in a vain effort to catch the elusive Willie, with some vague idea that Willie ought to be caught and held, perhaps as material witness—not that Garrison had any particular ideas as to what constituted a material witness. Legge and Benny followed more slowly. Theirs was a routine job, slow and painstaking, and it would wait for them.

Willie was only a step behind Emery as he entered Sylvia Jensen's room and, contrary to mystery-story tradition, he removed his hat. He hesitated as he saw the inert figure. "Mrs. Jensen, are you well enough to . . ."

Dr. Frederic Jensen stepped forward to face Emery angrily.

"What do you mean by bursting into my wife's room? I demand . . ."

Emery, who topped the doctor's six feet by a good three inches, glared down at him. "Listen you, we don't ask permission to bust into houses when we're called on a murder. Go over there and sit down."

Dr. Jensen gulped, but stood his ground. "I will not be spoken to in this insolent . . ."

Emery pushed the doctor aside and muttered "Garrison!" Garrison caught the doctor's thrashing arms and pushed him into a chair where he sat sputtering ineffectually.

Judge Massie opened one eye and took in the scene. "Better keep yore shirt on, doctor. Dignity ain't what the p'lice want. They seen real dignity, an' they seen it split wide open an' spill some mighty ugly stuff. Course, I ain't sayin' Garrison there would recognize dignity effen it walked up an' bashed him on the nose."

Garrison glared belligerently around. "Who's gonna bust who on the nose?"

"I don't think Mr. Garrison wants anything to bash him on the nose, even effen it ain't 'xactly a beautiful nose." Judge Massie regarded Garrison's two-directional nose placidly. "It do seem like somebody's already bashed it."

Emery looked down at the Judge sprawled comfortably in the chair. "Yeah, I expected to find you settin' down. Must be a hot case if they've called you in already."

"Ain't nobody called me in . . . nary a soul. Jess came in with Mrs. Jensen over there." Judge Massie nodded toward the woman who now sat huddled in the chaise longue, her large, staring eyes fastened on the doctor. "But I gotta ask you not to disturb her. She's had a right smart shock."

"Yeah?" But he turned respectfully to Mrs. Jensen. "Like the Judge here says, ma'am, we don't want to disturb you, but we've got to get the facts quickly, because the quicker we get the facts, the quicker we can . . ."

Mrs. Jensen turned vague eyes on him for an instant and then turned back to her husband. Her voice was dull and lifeless. "There are no facts."

Emery shifted his hat to his other hand, and coughed uneasily. "Perhaps, ma'am, not facts to you, but sometimes the most insignificant things are facts to us. We got ways. So if you'll just tell us where the body . . . where your husband is . . ."

"There." She pointed listlessly to where Garrison was forcing the doctor back into the chair.

Emery followed the direction of her finger and stared at the once spruce but now considerably ruffled doctor. He frowned. "That ain't no corpse."

"Effen you don't call off your gorilla," observed the Judge mildly, "he soon will be."

"Who's a gorilla?" demanded Garrison truculently.

Emery still regarded the doctor with deep suspicion, as if he hoped perhaps he might turn out to be a corpse after all. "That ain't no corpse," he repeated.

"No, it isn't." Sylvia's voice was still toneless, still only half-alive.

Emery glanced around the room helplessly. Benny set his camera box down with a sigh, and Lew Legge leaned against the door jamb and fingered his print kit. Garrison stood over Dr. Jensen, one arm extended as if he intended to stiff-arm him. Willie stood in bright-eyed expectancy, awaiting anything up to and including murder—and rather hoping for that. Judge Massie shuffled his congress gaiters, wriggled comfortably in the chair, and waited.

The detective suddenly heaved a sigh. "Say, if I'm not crazy, who is?"

"I am." Sylvia Jensen's voice lifted a little, and she shuddered. "Quite crazy."

"This is monstrous, gentlemen; she is in no condition . . ." Dr. Jensen attempted to rise and Garrison casually thrust him back. "See here, you ruffian, I'll have your position taken from you for this."

"Quiet!" Emery bellowed in a voice that shook the windows. The doctor started to speak again and then hastily shut his mouth. Emery appealed to the Judge. "You've always been pretty sensible—or at least sometimes. What's this all about?"

Judge Massie carefully adjusted his glasses, and stroked his several chins. Dr. Jensen sat forward to hear him. "To tell you truth, I don't rightly know. Cain't say I'm caught up m'self on what's happened. I jess came here as Mrs. Jensen's guest an' attorney, but on somethin' entirely different. Cain't say I know much. Cain't even rightly say I know why you're here. I'm what you mought say corn-fused by the turn of events." As Emery started to question Willie the Judge shook his head. "What the old dog don't know, the pup ain't learnt."

Emery looked around the room then, and addressed it plaintively.

"Somebody phoned the department that Dr. Jensen had been murdered, and to come out at once. I want to know where he is."

"I am right here, Mr. Policeman," and once more Jensen attempted to rise.

Emery whirled on him then, and really looked at him for the first time. "Dr. Jensen! Well, I'll be damned. Why didn't you say so in the first place?"

"You didn't give me a chance, Officer. If you'll call off this person, I think I can clear this up in a moment." He didn't even glance at Garrison as Emery signalled him to step aside.

"Sorry, sir, but we're a bit touchy about people who interfere in murder cases. There's usually a reason." He looked at the doctor, watching him straighten his vest and tie and run a slender hand through a head of thinning hair. "You don't look murdered."

The doctor pulled himself together quickly and took over the situation. He smiled frostily and strode over to his wife, pretending not to see the shrinking of her frail figure.

"I'm not murdered. I'm quite alive and well. This is very regrettable. There has been some gross error committed. As you may see, I have not been murdered," he smiled more easily, "but on the contrary, am quite alive and well—quite alive and well."

"Then whom did I kill?" Sylvia Jensen spoke with a quaint earnestness, the puzzled note of an inquiring child.

"No one, my dear . . . no one. You simply had a bad dream." He touched her shoulder and she sank lower in the chair and quieted. The doctor glanced appealingly at Emery. "My wife is in a highly nervous state. She . . . she sometimes imagines that the things she dreams are quite real. It . . . it is a source of great worry to me and to her, but, until tonight, I have succeeded in keeping her imaginings a secret between us."

"He means I'm crazy." She said it stubbornly, naughtily, as might a child who wanted to say something shocking.

"Hush, my dear, you mustn't say things like that," and she subsided again as he touched her arm. "You'll have to excuse her, gentlemen, if she has given you any undue trouble. And I'll have to ask you not to question her further. Her condition won't permit it. As a physician, as a psychiatrist, I assure you she needs rest and relaxation. My wife is a highly sensitive person, exceedingly nervous and temperamental—an inherited characteristic, I might say." Dr. Jensen was assuming the lecture platform manner. "Doubtless you recall her father and his eccentricities . . ." He broke off, and began again. "In a moment of intense emotional excitation Mrs. Jensen called your office and informed you that I had been murdered. In view of these later events, this was a very regrettable but entirely understandable action—when you consider her case, I mean. Had I been here I could have given you the facts by phone and saved you this trip—and spared myself the exposure of my wife's condition."

Sylvia Jensen listened to this, and then, quite suddenly, sprang her feet. "My husband is trying to tell you I'm crazy—that I'm stark raving mad . . . and that's the one thing I wanted to prevent. But he's done it. He's told you I'm so crazy . . . I'm not responsible for my actions." She paused, glaring around the room with almost animal fury and then turned to stare long and hard at the doctor. Finally she laughed shrilly.

"I *am* crazy! I *am* crazy . . . and I'm not responsible for my actions," she screamed wildly and fainted.

Emery mopped his brow furtively. "Whew! What a look she gave the doctor. I wouldn't want anybody not responsible for their actions to hate me as much as that."

4

A SPOT OF BLOOD

Dr. Jensen shooed the men from the room with remarkable efficiency so that he could attend to his wife. He first ordered Emery to put her on the bed, and then hurried into the bathroom, returning in a moment with a hypodermic syringe. He herded Emery and Garrison to the door, and even routed Judge Massie from the comfort of the chintz-covered wing chair. Benny picked up his camera case wearily and stepped farther down the hall, there to lean against the wall and puff a cigarette, with Willie looking admiringly on. Lew Legge sat on the camera case, and when Benny started to protest, he muttered, "Shut up, I'm tired." Judge Massie sidled out the door and rested against the door frame.

"Ain't a mite o' comfort in leanin', but it's better'n standin'." He smiled affably at Emery and Garrison. "Ain't tryin' to figger out how you been done out'n a murder, are you?"

Benny glanced up. "The way I figure it, it's wish fulfillment. She's been thinking about getting rid of him for so long that bingo! she ups and thinks she done it . . . and phones the police. I don't blame her. He looks slimy to me."

Legge sighed. "Benny reads too many books. He's got beautiful hands . . . the doc, I mean."

"It's screwy," said Garrison, "but maybe Benny's right."

Emery glanced at Willie and the Judge. "Yeah, I'd figure it that way, too, if the Judge wasn't around. But wherever he is, there's apt to be somethin' crooked goin' on."

Judge Massie fanned himself with his broad-brimmed panama, having inadvertently left his treasured palm-leaf in Sylvia's room. "That there is skatin' perty close to slander, Inspector."

Emery snorted. "I ain't an inspector, yet, but if I could prove the things I'm thinking about you, you'd be behind bars and I *would* be an inspector."

"Joseph Aloysius Emery, you got a nasty mind." Judge Massie was beginning another of his amiable feuds with the big detective. He fumbled in his waistcoat pocket and produced two long, black, crooked stogies. "This'll take yore mind off'en your troubles—effen you got a mind other than a nasty one."

"Judge, you're a crowning insult to the law." He accepted the stogie, sniffed it and nodded. "That'll take the mind of a billy goat off his worries—if a billy goat has worries." He lit the stogie and began plaintively, "Judge, what you got against me? Every time I get a case sewed up, in the bag, you bust it wide open for me."

"Maybe you git it in the wrong bag, Joseph Algernon Emery . . ."

"My name ain't Algernon, and it ain't Aloysius," Emery cut in, biting viciously on the stogie. "And for ten-fifteen years you been calling me outa my name. There ain't no justice in you, Judge Massie. Leave my name be, and leave my cases alone. Last four cases you busted wide open right under my nose."

"Nose must be gittin' used to't by now, Joseph Abercromie Emery." The Judge considered his stogie mildly. "That don't sound right, neither."

Benny and Legge glanced up at their chief and snickered. Garrison looked as if he'd like to be belligerent but didn't know just where to begin.

"Take that Westmoreland case you finished up today." Emery aimed his stogie at the Judge. "I had that figured out months ago. Spent loads of time on it . . . and today, in court, you bust it wide open. It ain't fair. You been getting off fellers that are better off hanged."

"We don't hang 'em in this state, Joseph Aeneas Emery, but you gotta admit Westmoreland didn't kill his uncle." Glumly the detective nodded, and Judge Massie absently rubbed his spine along the door jamb. "Tried to tell you 'twarn't him but you wouldn't listen. I give you a straight tip on the Kinsolving case, recommember?"

"All right, all right. I'm just grousing, Judge. But I would like to know why you are here just when this murder turns up and then turns out to be a phony."

"Well, sir, I ain't the size o' man that's easy knocked over with a feather, but it gimme quite a jolt, some o' the things that's happened this here night. Now take me. I come here on a business matter an' run spang into a murder that ain't no murder. Mebbe you jess better write it off as a loss."

Emery grunted. "Don't figure it would be a loss if that guy had really got bumped off." He eyed the Judge speculatively. "You ain't the regular family lawyer, as I recollect. Seems to me old Fussbudget Willebrandt's been handling the estate, and you haven't been a particular friend of the family since old Sylvester died. If you are a special friend, stop me, but how did a girl like Sylvia Storme ever come to marry a middle-aged doctor with no special reputation—except with women—and how did old Sylvester happen to let his daughter do it?"

"Cain't stop you askin' questions, but it ain't essential I should answer effen I could, an' I cain't. Never could figger out what makes folks git married. Howsomever, I 'spect it's a right good idea. Heap o' folks been in favor of it a good many years. You married, ain't you, Joseph Annanias Emery? How come you got married to the gal you did?"

Emery scratched his head thoughtfully. "I often wonder . . ."

Garrison hastily covered a snigger, and Emery called himself hastily to the work at hand. "Come on, boys, let's get goin'. We got plenty work to do tonight."

Legge untangled his long frame from Benny's camera box and rose, rubbing himself vigorously where it needed rubbing. "Why do you put knobs on that thing?"

Benny swung his huge camera case under his arm and eased the strap over his shoulder. He glanced at Legge and spoke mildly. "To keep bohunks from sitting on it. Let's get back to that fellow at the morgue, at least if he's still there. I don't like corpses that walk out on me."

Legge nodded plaintively. "Used to do manual labor, but he's been going soft lately. Guess he was in the service."

"Gosh! Maybe he was a gangster." Willie almost wriggled with interest. "Did they take him for a ride?"

Emery shook his head. "Nup, sonny. This ain't a gangster killing. When we pick up gangsters that have been dumped in the woods like this guy—we just gathered him in about two hours ago—they're usually shot full of holes. This guy had only been shot once, close range. He had powder burns on his coat. We haven't checked yet, but it looks like a small-caliber gun, probably a twenty-five." He turned to his men. "Come: on, boys, we'll get back to our corpse without a murder and leave the Judge to figure on his murder without a corpse. So long, Judge; hope I'll be seeing you in jail."

Judge Massie peered over his glasses. "Figgerin' on bein' in jail, do you? Be right glad to come down, Joseph Ambler Emery."

"Guess that's Doc Cranshaw now." Emery leaned over the balustrade as the squeak of brakes sounded below. "Go down, Garrison, and let him in. But if it's reporters, shoo 'em away."

Before Garrison could lumber into action there came the babble of voices below, and above the male voice rose the thin cry of a girl. "A doctor? What's wrong with my sister? Is she ill?"

Without waiting for an answer the girl ran breathlessly up the steps. She stopped suddenly when she saw the group bunched outside her sister's door.

"What's wrong? My sister . . ." She ran to the Judge, tugging at his arm. "Please, Judge Massie, what's happened? Has there been an accident? Is she hurt? Is she ill?"

Judge Massie patted her reassuringly. "Ain't a thing wrong. Sylvia felt a mite upset an' is lyin' down. These here gentlemen come here by mistake. Dr. Jensen is with her and asked not to be disturbed."

She smiled then. "Oh, if Fred's with her it's all right." She glanced back down the stairs, and then turned again to the Judge. "But Judge, that man down there . . . that doctor . . . he said he came for the body." Her eyes pleaded with the Judge. "Please don't treat me as if I were a child. If something is wrong with my sister, tell me—don't try to be kind."

"Land o' Goshen, ain't sech a thing as a body 'round the house." Judge Massie led her gently away from the door. "These here men come up by mistake. Somebody sent 'em up here 'bout a murder that didn't happen, an' they're leavin', but it upsot yore sister a mite, an' Dr. Jensen is 'tendin' to her."

Emery nodded confirmation. "Yes, ma'am, somebody made a mistake, and we're leaving right now. Sorry to have worried you."

Relief showed in her eyes. "Oh, that's all right. And if Fred is with her, she'll soon be all right. She hasn't been at all well lately. She gets excited so easily. Fred says she needs a rest."

Pete Coleman came pounding up the stairs, evading a policemen's clutches by football dodges. He turned the corner, speaking as he came. "What's that swine done to her now? If he's laid a finger on her, I'll break every bone in his . . . What the . . .!" He pulled up short as he saw the crowd, straightening his dinner jacket as he came more slowly. "What's going on? Has that louse . . .?"

"Pete!" Cordelia drew away from the comfort of the Judge's arm. "I won't permit you to speak of Dr. Jensen like that."

"If that skunk has done anything to . . ."

Judge Massie sighed and went into the new fray. "Ain't a thing wrong Pete—less'n you might say yore tie ain't straight. Jess a leetle mistake that these here gentlemen made. Miz Jensen is lyin' down an' I reckon she'd prefer quiet."

The Judge's quietness calmed him, and Pete straightened his tie a little sulkily.

"Pete, you shouldn't speak of Dr. Jensen like that," Cordelia scolded, but she looked at him as if he were something on the top of the Christmas tree.

Suddenly Pete grinned. "At least you recognized him from the descriptions."

Deedie smiled around at the men. "I hope you'll excuse our little public love scene. We're uninhibited."

Pete grinned at the Judge. "She picks up nice long words and she has to use 'em. In a moment she'll say I'm an extrovert. She does it regularly."

"'Well, you are."

"Words . . . words . . . you pick 'em off that guy the way a monkey picks fleas," but he wasn't sore. He was looking down at her, Deedie being the sort of girl a man could look down at, especially if he ran to well over six feet like Pete Coleman. And in looking down at her his eyes were saying things that made the Judge cough firmly.

"I ain't been doin' my full share o' reee-laxin' lately."

Deedie started self-consciously. "Oh, do excuse me, Judge. Come down to the living room," she twinkled at Pete who was able to absorb a good hit of twinkling, "and we'll continue our exhibition of Peter Coleman being the masterful male."

Emery shifted uneasily and then nodded to his men, herding them down the long flight of stairs before him, gathering in the indignant Dr. Cranshaw as he went. The coroner's high rasping voice cut through the great hall. "When I go after a corpse I want a corpse, not an excuse. Damn your excuses; that was a good party. My wife wasn't on it. Judge Massie's up there, is he? Well, you can take it from me, he probably swallowed the corpse. Wouldn't put it past him. Judge, you're a reprobate," he squeaked over his thin shoulder.

Judge Massie leaned perilously over the balustrade. "Effen you could figger a way to make it pay better'n being coroner, you'd be one, too, Josiah Cranshaw."

The two ill-assorted cronies glared at each other with studied ferocity. "Judge Massie, if that corpse you ate ain't made you sick by Saturday night me and Prunellis Purdett can figure on taking some of your ill-gotten wealth at rummy . . . same as usual."

"Effen you've give up this gaddin' about to Amy Carlyle's parties an' kin keep yore eyes open after all this here night life, mebbe we'll let you play."

Dr. Cranshaw shut the door on further speech, leaving the Judge to interrupt a kiss. The Judge errumphed, and the pair broke guiltily. "Ain't a mite o' harm in kissin', 'specially when you figger ain't nobody lookin', but jess don't drag it out too long. I ain't awful good at waitin' 'round fer kissin' to be got over with, an' I kin wait a heap better effen I'm sittin' down."

"Of course." Deedie, still flushed, led the way downstairs.

Judge Massie frowned in concentration on the serious problem of picking the most comfortable chair. He was making for a large over-stuffed lounge chair when Deedie's question stopped him.

"Do you bite people when you frown like that?"

Judge Massie sank gratefully into the chair and sighed. "Bite people? 'Course . . . that's it . . . bite people." He peered over the rims of his glasses and puffed out his cheeks in a sigh of contentment. "Is the doctor fond of that there Chu Chin?"

Deedie looked puzzled at the abrupt change of conversation, but she answered, "Put it the other way around, and the answer is yes. The dog adores him."

Willie started to remind the Judge that Chu Chin was already dead, but he caught the Judge's oblique glance and remained silent. The Judge had his own methods of getting information, and some of them were devious. Now he wanted Deedie and Pete to talk, and he wanted a picture.

"Dog!" Pete snorted. "That's true if you can call it a dog. It's got perverted tastes . . ."

"When the coaching from the sidelines gets too objectionable, I can turn it off." Deedie tucked her arm through Pete's and smiled down at the Judge. "I can bring pressure to bear. Besides, he's ticklish. But about Chu Chin, Fred sort of, well, tolerates it. But you know how some animals just persist in hanging around a person who doesn't particularly care for them. Maybe they're just trying to make friends."

"Chu Chin wouldn't try to make friends with himself. He's a nasty tempered . . . Ouch!" Pete pretended he was going to slap her, and Deedie stuck out her tongue. Pete winked at the Judge. "I think he inherited his nasty disposition from Deedie."

"Chu Chin hasn't a nasty disposition. Just because he sees through your pretentions and despises you for the worm that you are isn't any sign he's nasty—just discriminating."

"One thing 'bout Poms," commented the Judge, "they may go 'round lookin' like animated floor mops, but they're good watch dogs—an' fer size cain't anything tech 'em fer general all 'round ferocity."

Pete nodded gloomily. "Ferocity is right. I shook my fist at the doctor the other day and that damned little thing nearly chewed my ankle off."

"It would have served you right, shouting and bellowing at Fred that way. And what if he did call you a worthless scamp after my money?" She dimpled at the Judge. "He is a worthless scamp, isn't he? But I don't think Fred was very flattering. I have other attractions besides my money, haven't I?" She pirouetted before the Judge, smiling at him.

Judge Massie chuckled. "Less'n my eyes is goin' back on me in my old age, you got a point here'n there I'd favor."

"They're not points, Judge, they're curves."

Willie looked embarrassed.

The front door groaned ponderously open. A tall big-boned woman stood there a moment, staring across the hallway to the living room. She bent and disengaged the key before she started heavily down the hall.

"Oh, Mrs. Hardecker, will you tell Benson to get us some . . . oh, what will you have, Judge?" She turned to, smile at Willie. "And you?"

"Reckon there's any o' Sylvester's brandy left? I mought be persuaded to take a drop, and Willie here is sorta partial to ginger ale."

Willie, his eyes still on Deedie, nodded.

Deedie checked the items on her fingers for Mrs. Hardecker. "Brandy for the Judge, ginger ale for Willie, sauterne for me, and since Pete likes his Scotch slightly diluted with Scotch, maybe you'd better bring him ginger ale."

"Deedie! Not ginger ale!"

Mrs. Hardecker smiled and was almost pretty in a big, horsy way, even if her hair was dyed black. "I'll get it, Miss Deedie. Benson is off for the night. And I know Mr. Pete's favorite."

"Right, Ann, and some of your toasted muffins, please."

Ann Hardecker withdrew with another brief smile.

Deedie shook her head. "He makes himself completely at home; and the way he has with women! Even Mrs. Hardecker unbends. She positively simpers at him, and her grim as a gyr-falcon."

"She's not grim—but I expect it is hard for her to have to act as a servant, and she's got that invalid son of hers to support. Besides, I'll bet you don't know what a gyrfalcon is."

"I do, too." She shut her eyes and recited hastily, "A large, sacred hunting falcon, particularly noted for its fierce glance." She opened her eyes, and thrust out her tongue at Pete. "There! I looked it up.

"Judge, I appeal to you. That man is corrupting her with in-formation. When she first came here three weeks ago she was a nice, ignorant piece of baggage, and now she talks like a mispro-nouncing dictionary." Pete dropped his bantering air and looked directly at the Judge. "What's this all about? Is there anything really wrong with Sylvia?"

Judge Massie folded his hands tent-wise across his paunch and considered his fingers with affection. He twiddled his thumbs as he were experimenting with their flexibility. "Don't know's there anything more'n usual, Pete. Sylvia Jensen is almighty fired up, an' the shock o' those men comin' here about a murder upsot her more'n a mite. Reckon a visit from the p'lice ain't sech a regular 'currence in this here house."

Pete became suddenly vehement. "If I had my way there'd really be a mur. . ."

"Pete!" Deedie shut him off effectively with a single word, his gay, childish face white and tense, and then she smiled faintly at the Judge. "Pete's so darned protective and possessive. He resents Fred's interest in me, and Fred resents Pete's attitude, which is natural enough. I know I wouldn't want an unspanked cub sit-ting around my house glaring at *me*. Yes, you do glare, Pete."

"Nuts! He's a . . . Oh, thanks, Ann."

Deedie accepted a glass and passed it to the Judge. "You shouldn' have bothered to serve. Couldn't Jessie bring it in?" Deedie offered Willie a glass, and he accepted it dumbly, eyes on the girl. Deedie helped herself to a gold-rimmed goblet and sipped. "Where is Jessie?"

Mrs. Hardecker held the tray awkwardly, as if she weren't quite used to handling it and wanted to put it down on something. She shifted it again before answering. "Miss Sylvia dismissed all the servants for the evening, Miss Deedie, and no one is back except Esther."

Deedie looked up from her drink in surprise. "Dismissed the servants? On a Wednesday? But why?"

Mrs. Hardecker's long, horsy face looked even longer when she furrowed her dark brow in a frown that called attention to the undyed, grey-brown roots of her hair. "I believe she thought it was Thursday."

"How silly! She must have known this was Wednesday—it's the night of the club dinner dance."

Pete glowered down into his glass as if he had discovered the unpleasant remains of a fly. "Perfectly natural. I've made the same mistake lots of times. People like Sylvia and me, with nothing particular to do, never keep dates straight." He raised his eyes to the Judge, and then lifted his glass in a hasty gesture that almost spilled the liquor. "Perfectly understandable, huh?"

"Land o' Goshen, yes. Effen it warn't fer Willie there I'd plumb fergit when Sunday comes. Sorta like to fergit it's Sunday, sometimes. Not that I'm agin church . . . no sirree . . . but a body cain't do no real reee-laxin' in one o' them seats." The Judge smacked his babyish lips thoughtfully. "That's mighty fine brandy yore paw laid down." He peered over his steel-rimmed spectacles at the housekeeper. "Mrs. Hardecker, reckon you won't mind effen I ask you did you kill Chu Chin?"

Mrs. Hardecker, a woman apparently virile almost to the point of masculinity, stared at him an instant, her lips working feebly. She dropped the tray with a clatter and caught at her side, swaying giddily.

"Her heart! Oh, poor Ann." Deedie ran to her and then stopped as the woman collapsed, sliding to the floor, her skirts ballooning around her. Deedie was staring where Willie's finger pointed.

There was blood on Mrs. Hardecker's skirt!

5

CALL IT MURDER

Judge Massie heaved himself out of the overstuffed chair with alarming rapidity and bent over the inert figure, forcing some of his precious brandy down the woman's throat. When she choked and sputtered and tried to sit up, the Judge handed the glass to a waiting Willie. He watched the color flood back into the sallow face as he squatted like an amiable frog on the floor beside her.

"Seems an all-fired shame to waste brandy like that on folks that's too unconscious to appreciate it." He twinkled down at the woman, his glasses sliding perceptibly down his nose. Deedie rubbed one of the woman's wrists distractedly.

Pete pranced ineffectually around in the background muttering, "Throw cold water on her . . . Hold her head down. . ."

Judge Massie peered upward from under ruffled eyebrows. "Cain't git her head no lower than the floor, an' you mought be gittin' the cold water."

Pete gulped once and hurried off down the hall. Judge Massie waved away Deedie's proffered help and Willie's solicitous wriggling. The girl stood aside looking down at the woman, her young face tortured by perplexity and a growing horror.

"Willie, git under that left arm," the Judge commanded.

As the two were lifting the groaning woman to the couch, Deedie blurted out, "Did she kill Chu Chin?" and then she gave a little cry of protest. "I don't believe it, even if she did hate him." She caught at the Judge's sleeve and almost pulled him around. "She wouldn't kill Chu Chin."

Mrs. Hardecker struggled to sit up, and then sank wearily back. "I'm sorry to be such a nuisance. I . . ." She shut her eyes and lay back among the cushions. "I didn't kill Chu Chin. I didn't even . . . know . . . he . . . was . . . dead."

Judge Massie eased his bulk onto the edge of the couch and took the woman's limp hand. "Jess who did you think was dead?"

Tired, dull eyes opened and fastened on the Judge's round, deceptively innocent face. The woman shuddered. "I didn't know. I didn't think . . . anyone was dead." She fought for control, her lips greyish white. "I'm sorry I'm such a nuisance."

"Said that onct before . . . figger you meant it." Judge Massie patted her dry-skinned hand. "Talk like a pusson that means what they says. Reckon you been 'round on yore own fer some time."

"Twenty-five years, Judge." She started to swing her legs down but the Judge pushed her gently back. "My son . . . he's delicate . . . has to have a nurse."

Pete came plowing through the door with a pitcher of water and was about to throw it over the woman when the Judge took it away from him. "Bring a glass?"

"Glass?" Pete glanced vacantly around the room and then started for the kitchen again, but the Judge stopped him. He tilted the pitcher against the woman's lips and she drank.

She started to get up, but when the judge pushed her gently back, she sank among the cushions gratefully. "You are all very kind. I thought I had gotten over these . . . these fainting spells. The sight of blood makes me faint. I studied to be a nurse, but I never could conquer this fainting, so I had to give it up."

Judge Massie pointed to the ugly stain on the woman's skirt, and Deedie shuddered into Pete's arms. "How'd you git this here stain?"

Mrs. Hardecker refused to look down at her skirt. "I'll never be able to wear it again. Oh, where? In the back hall, on the door that leads to the back stairs. I thought I heard someone on the back stairs and I opened the door. There was . . . it was on the step and the door. I didn't know I had gotten any on me. I think I would have fainted right then." She glanced at the Judge in sudden recollection. "Is Chu Chin dead?" As the Judge nodded, the woman shivered and lowered her eyes. "Poor little dog."

Deedie buried her head against Pete's shoulder. "Why should anyone want to hurt Chu Chin?"

"Jess been sayin' Pete would, an' so'd Pete." Judge Massie bent over to gather up the debris of the tray; and the deed of gift, hastily thrust into his pocket, slithered to the floor. When the Judge was careless there was usually a reason, and with calm speculation he watched Pete pick it up. The town's playboy held it a moment.

"Yes, Judge, I did say nasty things about the dog, but, well, killing it would be different."

"Yup. I been thinkin' 'bout that. Same as talkin' harsh about a man ain't same as murder, but effen there was a murder the p'lice would be lookin' fer the man that said harsh words. Mought hand over the deed o' gift. It's what I came here about." The Judge held out a broad, pink palm, but he did not hurry Pete as he glanced over it.

"Say, what's this? Sylvia giving Deedie a lot of money. Why on earth should Sylvia . . .?"

Judge Massie gently extracted the paper. "Reckon her reasons are her own. Hear tell, though, that Deedie's plumb sot on havin' a birthday in a week or two. Mought be a birthday gift." Judge Massie thrust the paper in his pocket.

"Oh, how sweet of her to think of it, as upset as she's been. But why money?" She turned to Pete. "What did you mean by a lot of money? How much is a lot?"

Pete pointed to the Judge's pocket, as if he weren't quite sure of what he had seen. "About two hundred thousand."

Deedie looked at the Judge. "That's an awful lot of money, isn't it? I mean just as a gift." She sat down suddenly beside Ann Hardecker and held her hand, but continued to address the Judge. "I've been wondering why you're here. I mean—of course, we're always glad to see you, but since Father's death you haven't been up to Storme's Grote often. You came about this . . . and then the police upset things so . . . and then poor Chu Chin. I suppose he is dead, or you wouldn't say so." She turned to the housekeeper. "Why, Ann, you're trembling! Poor thing, this has upset you. You'd better go to bed."

"Police? Why were the police here. Just about Chu Chin?" Mrs. Hardecker sat up.

Deedie questioned the Judge with her eyebrows. "About Chu Chin? No. It was some . . . some sort of mistake. I didn't get it clearly. Only it frightened Sylvia."

"Yup, jess a mistake. Now, Willie, effen you'd jess go take a look at that there door to the back stairs, mebbe we kin clear out and leave these here folks to a mite o' rest. Gittin' late as all get-out."

When Willie returned to report on the bloody door, the matted greyish-brown hairs and other gruesome details, Judge Massie held up a restraining hand. "They kin wait, son. Kin see you seen it. We'll be getting' 'long, Miss Deedie."

Mrs. Hardecker had better control of herself. She was sitting sturdily upright, her eyes held rigidly ahead as if she didn't care to look at the blood on her skirt, although her fingers plucked nervously at the pleats across her knees. "I don't believe I can ever make myself wear this again."

Deedie offered her a slim hand. "Can I help you, and then I'll go see Fred . . . see if there's anything I can do for Sylvia."

A faint buzz sounded somewhere in the back of the house, and Deedie started. "Who on earth could be calling at this hour? It must be after midnight." But she made no move to answer the door until Mrs. Hardecker spoke.

"I wonder, Miss Deedie, if you'd mind answering the door. The servants are still out, and I don't believe I can make it. No, no . . ." She waved away Deedie's quick offer of assistance and sympathy. "I'm quite all right, but my knees," the long, horsy face broke into a weak smile, "I don't trust them."

Cordelia hurried out to the door as Pete and Willie started to clear away the glasses. Judge Massie, after a last, reassuring pat, deserted Mrs. Hardecker for the comfort of the deep chair. He was settling himself with his careful attention to the important ritual of comfort, feet outthrust, congress gaiters precisely crossed, the pink folds of his chins melting over his collar, fingers interlocked in a tent across his paunch. He was just heaving his final sigh of satisfaction when there was a gasp from the door. Gasps from doorways annoyed the Judge when he was settling into comfort. He glared at the blonde, willowy woman who was swaying in the door, a dramatic red evening gown and white fur cape setting off her slender figure.

"Where are the police?" She searched the room with large, brown eyes, a gesture just a shade theatrical. "Where . . . where is poor Sylvia, poor, dear Sylvia?" She ignored the fact that Deedie was very obviously trying to keep her out by standing almost in front of her.

"Sylvia has gone to bed." Deedie spoke almost sharply.

"But of course! What a terrible shock! How ghastly! How utterly horrible! May I see him? Please . . ." There was hysteria back of her dramatic fluttering, and tears in her eyes, tears she was trying desperately to hide.

Judge Massie sighed, and heaved himself slowly out of his chair, grumbling feebly, "That Amy Carlyle's gonna put her foot spang in it. Does it every time."

If the woman heard him she gave no sign. She caught one of Deedie's hands and clung to it. "Please, may I see him? I know you don't like me, Cordelia, but now that he's dead, surely you won't be so unkind . . ." She sensed the incredulity in the room and glanced around.

Willie was frankly gawking. Pete looked as if someone had pulled a chair from under him and he was waiting for the bump. Mrs. Hardecker half-rose from the lounge and then sank back, her long face almost comical in its mixture of bewilderment and disgust. Deedie turned a look of desperate appeal over her shoulder. Judge Massie errumphed and waddled forward.

"Allus seems I gotta take people's troubles. Guess I'm hired to. Why should you see him, Amy?"

The woman left Deedie and swayed across the room to the Judge. "Judge Massie, help me!" She stood in front of him, arms flung out, rings and three-too-many bracelets winking. "Why?

Why? Because I love him. Now that he's dead, I don't care who knows it . . . I love him." She turned defiantly on the rest of them. "Yes, I love him, and I have loved him for a long time, and I've gloried in that love."

Pete and Deedie looked blankly at one another and drew together, staring at the woman. From the protection of Pete's arms—and he looked as if he were just waiting for something she needed protection from—Deedie spoke softly, almost as if she were frightened.

"But Mrs. Carlyle, surely you don't mean you want to *see* him . . . not all bloody and . . . and . . ."

Pete blinked at the woman. "How'd you know he was dead?"

Amy Carlyle whirled on him. "Does that make any difference?" Her chin quivered. "You're conspiring against me. You don't want me to see him, even now. You all hate me." She fought for control under the staring eyes. "All right . . . my maid told me. She overheard the conversation when they phoned for Dr. Cranshaw, and just reported it to me—just as my guests were leaving. I came right over . . . I ran."

Deedie stood away from Pete, holding herself erect, an almost arrogant little figure. "Mrs. Carlyle, you've said we all hate you. That's putting it a little strongly. However, I don't care for anyone who gets quite so dramatic over the death of a little dog. As much as we all loved him, not one of us has been so theatrically upset over the death of Chu Chin."

"Chu Chin?" Mrs. Carlyle's voice rose shrilly. "Chu Chin? But Fern said Fred was dead . . . murdered."

"Nonsense, Amy, nonsense." Dr. Frederic Jensen stood handsomely in the doorway. "Utter nonsense."

"Fred." The woman's voice was a thin wail. She stared wildly around the room, and then back to his face. "You aren't dead?" The flatness of her voice after so much histrionics sounded hollow and dead in the big room. Her eyes closed dazedly, and then opened "What a fool I've been." Without another word she fled past Deedie and Pete, brushed by the doctor and ran down the hall, her sharp, high heels clicking on the stone floor. The front door slammed heavily.

Dr. Jensen strolled into the room without once glancing after the woman. "What the devil brought Amy over here? And at this hour. Oh, do sit down, all of you. Hello Ann, what's wrong with you?" He walked quickly to the older woman and looked down at her. "You heart again?" He felt her pulse. "Nothing . . . er . . . worryin' you?"

"Oh, no sir, just my heart. Gave me a little turn." Mrs. Hardecker spoke quickly. "I'm quite all right . . . quite." She took the tray from Willie who had been holding it in awkward embarrassment during Mrs. Carlyle's little one-act drama.

As she left the room the doctor shook his head. "Ann oughtn't to let that run on. I have tried to get her to have a competent heart specialist prescribe for her. Oh, beg pardon, do sit down."

The Judge had long since anticipated the suggestion and was firmly settled in his carefully selected chair.

"Sorry to seem so preoccupied, but so many things have happened in the past hour or so." The doctor seated himself with an assurance that brought relief after so much hysteria. His calmness was soothing, almost hypnotic. Pete and Deedie sank down on the lounge. Willie stalked loyally over to stand beside the Judge.

Dr. Jensen nodded affably toward them. "You're Judge Massie, aren't you?" He held out a white-gold cigarette case, but the Judge refused. He passed it around and stuffed it in his pocket. "I believe you said you came here on business with my wife?" He made a question of it.

"Yup. Somethin' like that."

Dr. Jensen frowned. "I'm sorry all this confusion upset your plans. As you have seen, my wife is in a highly nervous condition. Such an exhibition is particularly embarrassing before strangers."

"Ain't a stranger," commented the Judge mildly. "Knowed Sylvia 'fore you did."

Dr. Jensen carefully simulated a smile. "Well, of course, I didn't mean it exactly like . . ."

"Is anything really wrong with Sylvia?" Cordelia leaned toward him, a worried frown making two creases between her dark brows.

The doctor smiled sadly. "Now, Cordelia, you know your sister. She's highstrung and very sensitive. Her nerves will not stand much shock, and tonight she's had a severe one, what with the police and all." He dismissed it with a wave of his long, thin hand. "Shock, but that's all. She needs rest and relaxation." He turned to the Judge. "I think you'll agree, Judge Massie—that's the name, isn't it? Massie?"

"Yup. Name's Massie. Reckon you're right all the way 'round. Sylvia 'pears to need a rest from the thing that's troublin' her effen she kin get it." Judge Massie nodded slowly and repeated, "Effen she kin get it."

"Exactly!" Dr. Jensen settled himself deeper in the chair. "I think perhaps if she could get away for a while . . . take a trip, or perhaps go to some quiet retreat . . ."

Pete, slumped on the lounge beside Deedie, glared at the doctor. "Are you trying to say Sylvia is nuts? Because she's not. She's got the clearest, finest mind I know and I . . ."

The doctor frowned. "I do not need you to champion my wife's mind. Mrs. Jensen has a very fine mind; in fact, she's been invaluable to me in some of my studies—but she is also fundamentally a nervous person, schizophrenic-paranoid type."

Judge Massie looked up from the contemplation of his boot-toes. "That there means folks that think they're mistreated, don't it? Folks that like to consult lawyers, too?"

The doctor looked surprised that Judge Massie should know the phrase. "Well, yes. Though I didn't mean it in its literal sense. Sylvia is, er, simply the type. She's very bright, really. She's been helping me in my psycho-neurological research." His thin face lit up. "In a few months I shall have the results of experiments that have taken years—results that will startle the world of psycho-neurology. I've gone a step farther than Jung and established, I believe, a new basis for revising his theories. Of course, it will take time and money, to convince the world." He sat back in his chair with a sigh. "But you probably aren't interested. You must excuse my enthusiasm."

Deedie had not been listening. She was puzzling over her own problem. "Fred, why should Sylvia give me money, lots of money?"

Dr. Jensen turned slowly. "Lots of money? Give you lots of money? I have no idea, unless it would be a birthday gift. You know you'll be nineteen very soon." He smiled paternally at the girl. "How much is a lot of money?"

"About two hundred thousand, Pete said . . ."

"Pete?" Dr. Jensen turned slowly to survey the younger man. "He enjoys a confidence of my wife's that I have not shared? Two hundred thousand dollars! That *is* a lot of money."

Pete flushed. "I don't happen to 'enjoy confidences.' I learned of it through an accident. Her attorney is right here. Why don't you ask him about it?"

"Her attorney?" Dr. Jensen frowned. "Oh, yes . . . Judge Massie, of course. Did my wife give Miss Cordelia quite a large sum of money?"

"Mebbe," stated the Judge with great deliberateness, "effen you ain't enjoyin' the confidences o' yore wife, she moughtn't intend you should know." Dr. Jensen flushed deeply and half-rose from the chair. Judge Massie waved him back, and he sank down, glaring. "On the other hand, it mought be only a rumor. Sech things have happened. Recommember there was a rumor goin' 'round these parts recent-like that you was daid. Warn't a mite o' foundation to it, were there?"

Dr. Jensen's mouth jerked sidewise. "Of course not, but . . ."

"This here is jess a rumor, Dr. Jensen, fer as you're corncerned." Judge Massie began the preliminary upheaval that would get him to his feet. "'Spect we stayed a mite over our welcome, but things sorta happened faster'n we calculated. Reckon we'll be leavin'. Howsomever, I 'spect we'll be seein' Miz Jensen in the mornin' an' conclude this here business I come here on." Judge Massie was erect.

Dr. Jensen slid to his feet, frowning thoughtfully. "I don't know, Judge Massie. She's had a terrible shock, as I need not remind you, since you were here and saw the whole thing. If not tomorrow, certainly within a day or two. Shall we say Saturday? She should be quite herself by then, I should think. Quite."

"This here business o' mine is right important. Don't know's I kin wait. Awful impatient man, sometimes."

Willie looked surprised to hear of the Judge's impatience, but he said nothing.

Judge Massie bowed with an old-world courtesy. "Good night, Dr. Jensen. Good night, Miss Deedie. Effen you need me fer anything, jess look me up. Got a spang new office, I have. Gotta do a heap o' lawyerin' to live up to it. 'Night, Pete."

Willie gave a creditable imitation of the Judge's courtliness as he bowed himself out.

Willie started to open the door of *Jessie Mae* but the Judge signaled him to the front of the car. "An' turn on the lights 'fore you come." Willie leaned into *Jessie Mae's* questionable innards and turned on the lights before he joined the Judge who was staring at the scuffed gravel in front of the right wheel.

"Willie, I ain't built fer stoopin'. Lean over there an' look close, an see if you see what I don't see . . . a dog."

Willie peered obediently. He bent down and looked into *Jessie Mae's* more intimate parts. He peered up into the Judge's puzzled face. "Ain't nary a thing, Jedge." He scrambled to his feet. "Maybe the little dog wasn't dead, an' crawled away."

Judge Massie pointed to the gravel, dimly lit by the lamps. "An' didn't leave a drop o' blood as he crawled? Ain't natural. I don't like it. I don't like it one bit."

Willie shook his head sadly in confirmation. "Not a bit." But he was also something of a philosopher. "Except that it's worth a thousand bucks, Jedge, less'n you dropped that, too."

"Ever see me lose somethin' I didn't want to lose?"

Loyally Willie shook his head. "Been wond'rin' 'bout that, Jedge. You done it plumb awkward, too."

"Did I, now? Ain't that too bad. But it worked."

"Worked?"

"We know how folks look when they git two hundred thousand dollars onexpected-like. We didn't know that before."

"Yeah," Willie commented, and then pointed out, "an' the cops know somethin' now, too. They know Mrs. Jensen's wacky, an' if the doctor should get bumped off, well, they'd never convict her now. It's a swell set-up fer a murder."

Judge Massie sighed and heaved himself into *Jessie Mae.* "An' effen what we heared tonight is all true, I'm beginnin' to think there's already been a murder—a murder without a corpse."

"Murder? Murder without a corpse?" echoed Willie.

Judge Massie settled himself behind the wheel. "Yup, son . . . jess that. Fer one thing, there ain't no corpse when you murder a person's mind."

6

IT IS MURDER

Judge Massie met his old crony, Prunellis Purdett, owner, editor, and chief reporter of the *Chronicle*, and the two glared at one another in amicable ferocity. Purdett blew up the ragged ends of a straggling mustache and eyed his old friend. "Hear tell you made a monkey outa Joe Emery last night."

"Cain't improve on nature, Prunellis," mourned the Judge. "Howsomever, I'd take it moughty much to heart effen you was to quote me—mought even go so fer as to sue the *Chronicle*. Mought even suggest Joseph Abernathy Emery sue the *Chronicle*, effen it was to make ridicule o' said Joseph Armstead Emery an' the part he played in last night's little fiasco."

Prunellis sighed. "His name ain't Abernathy, nor neither Armstead; it's . . ."

Judge Massie held up a massive hand. "Don't tell me! Take half the joy outen livin' effen you was to tell me. Been guessin' Joe Emery's name now nigh onto fifteen years an' ain't yet figgered it was Abner, like on his birth certificate. Joe an' me, we're jess like that . . ." Judge Massie put two plump fingers side by side and waggled them under Purdett's long, thin nose, "when we ain't like that . . ." and he crossed two fingers with difficulty.

Prunellis fingered the length of his threatened nose. "All right, all right. Wasn't aimin' to print a story about Joe Emery anyways, except in connection with this here actor fellow that was found shot. Printed a picture of him in this morning's edition."

"Did the *Chronicle* also interview the corpse? Reckon the corpse said jess about as much as that editorial o' yourn on the

disgraceful condition o' the old Edgewater quarry. Don't you
know you're jess incitin' the young folks o' this here town to go
out to that there deserted place fer spoonin' parties, tellin' 'em
how lonesome-like it is, an' how don't nobody go there no more?
Yessiree, incitin' to spoonin' . . . or mebbe murder." Judge Massie
shook his head solemnly in condemnation. "Even Willie here'd
know better. Don'tcher, Willie?"

Willie made an effort to look as if he were listening. "Oh,
yes, sir. Miss Deedie jess went into the department store across
the street," and Willie flushed under the Judge's thoughtful gaze.

Prunellis defended himself indignantly. "Mebbe so, mebbe
so, but least it's done is to have the State troopers promise to
keep an eye on it. And I'm not saying but what a little spoonin' would have kept your disposition a bit on the sweeter side,
Judge," and immediately regretted his lapse for he had laid his
hand on the Judge's arm and squeezed it affectionately.

Judge Massie looked away, up the steps of the courthouse.
"Reckon I better git this deed o' gift filed, an' deposit my fee,"
and the Judge lumbered heavily up the stairs, with Willie trailing
forlornly, his eyes on the door of the department store across the
street.

Prunellis Purdett stared after his friend and muttered to himself, "Derned old fool, that's what I am . . . and Mary's dead thirty
years or more." The two men had courted the same Mary Ames
those many years ago, and now the Judge was going up to see her
brother, Corporate Judge William Ames. Prunellis scurried away
to write an article on the intelligence of the local police.

Judge Massie filed the paper under Judge Ames' inquiring eye.

"Jim, I didn't know you were acting for the Stormes." He had
never thought of Sylvia as anything but a Storme. "Old Willebrandt will cackle and fuss over this—or send that grinning jackanapes down here to cite law at me—and, Jim, I hate a grinning
jackanapes citing law at me."

"Then, William, why'n't you cite a law right back at him . . .
or mebbe the Constitution. You could plumb floor him with the
Constitution." He flapped his broad-brimmed panama at Judge
Ames and moved off down the corridor, greeting friends through

open doorways, hailing one occasionally in the great open hall-way. The Judge loved the courthouse which, in spite of its inter-nal bickerings, was a great open house, a sort of civic fraternity.

Dr. Gresham marched in a stately procession of one down the hall and the Judge greeted him with the panama. "Elijah, how come you ain't up with yore rich patients? Don't see you so much these here days."

Dr. Gresham coughed importantly. "My time is rather well occupied these days, Judge Massie. And I really shouldn't be here today. Have an important appendectomy at noon . . . Mrs. Crispen, wife of James Crispen, the railroad magnate."

Judge Massie raised a quizzical eyebrow. "One appendectomy more important than another? Or jess richer? Then why ain't you at the bedside lookin' grave an' corn-cerned, an' issuin' bulletins? As I recommember, you issue a plumb elegant bulletin. They don't say much, but then, bulletins never does, does they?"

"Mrs. Crispen's condition is fair," stated the doctor, "and if that fool, Ambler Lee, hadn't called a meeting of the lunacy commission, I would be with her. But one's civic duty . . ." Dr. Gresham resumed his parade of one with a self-indulgent sigh.

"Civic duty!" snorted the Judge. "He's figgerin' it'll mean ap-pointment as the Governor's physician." Then he peered down at Willie. "Lunacy commission is meetin'?" He shook his head and moved on. "Cain't say's I like that."

He was still shaking his head and muttering as the two en-tered Mr. Lackey's bank which the Judge owned almost in toto. He waved his panama at the cashier and nodded affably at one of the vice presidents. Willie scowled, for sitting with the vice president was Peter Coleman. Pete answered the Judge's salute half-heartedly and turned to listen to the vice president. Willie scowled again; he was having a bad attack of love at first sight coupled with instantaneous jealousy. The Judge almost had to lead him out.

In the August sunshine the Judge expanded. He clapped on his panama and strode down the steps—or hoped he was striding. "Well, Willie, we done our duty. We filed the deed. We deposited the fee. Now we get the stock and turn it over to Deedie."

At the name Willie awoke from a scowling reverie. "Yes, sir
. . . It's good business for one day."

Judge Massie clambered aboard *Jessie Mae* and wriggled himself under the wheel. "Ain't never good business havin' a client
who ain't charged with a murder she didn't commit."

Jessie Mae's tumultuous awakening drowned the voice at the
Judge's elbow, but Willie saw her. He nudged the Judge's fat arm,
and flushed. "It's Miss Deedie," he shouted, and the Judge throt-
tled *Jessie Mae* to an amiable grumble.

"Oh, Judge Massie . . . and hello, Willie . . . I just wanted to
see you about that money . . . the money Sylvia was going to give
me." She leaned on the door and smiled up at the Judge.

Judge Massie grunted. "She's already given it to you."

"But I can't take it. Don't you see . . . Oh, officer," she turned
and twinkled at Mike Cassidy who was already reaching for his
hip pocket, "you mustn't give these men a ticket. They're going
right now." With some effort she wrenched open the rear door
and slid in. "They just stopped to pick me up." She smiled back
at Mike's grin. "Thanks."

Judge Massie leaned over the side of the car. "Leave six at my
office, Mike," and *Jessie Mae* lunged into traffic.

Willie screwed himself around in the seat. "Mike wasn't going
to give the Jedge a ticket; he was jess selling seats to the policeman's circus. I'm going to be part of a horse . . . the head end,"
he announced proudly.

Deedie nodded and then talked into the Judge's ear above the
roar of *Jessie Mae*. "If you're going to your office I'll tag along,
because, you see, I've got to get this straightened out."

"'Pears to be straightened out, far's I kin see."

"Oh, no. It's absurd for Sylvia to give me all this money. I
don't need it. I've got plenty. What do you suppose ever pos-
sessed Sylvia to turn this over to me? Especially when I know
Fred needs it so badly for his laboratory and some experiments
he's making. It would be so wonderful if he could continue his
work. I think psychology is fascinating, don't you?"

Judge Massie chuckled. "Jess reached that there corn-clusion
in the last three weeks, ain't you? 'Fore that it was jess a grind—
from ten to eleven under a stodgy old prof."

"Oh, you men! You all think it's because Fred is handsome and interesting."

Judge Massie glanced at the girl's flushed face. "Wouldn't be quotin' Pete, would you?"

"Pete!" She said it scornfully. "He's . . . he's callow. And besides, he broke a date with me because he had to go to Richmond . . . so I walked out and left them at home. Oh, are we here already? Oh, what a lovely building."

Judge Massie waited for Willie's usual request to be allowed to drive the car to the garage in the basement, but Willie was too engrossed in watching Deedie. The garage attendant, with the special scorn garage attendants have for dilapidated cars, said he would put it away, and the three went into the bright, modernistic foyer.

Judge Massie started up the single flight of stairs to his office, and waved a greeting to the blonde telephone operator who was doing her best to look like a combination of Hedy LaMarr and Lauren Bacall. She smiled up at Willie, once her devoted admirer but now blind to her charms. Susie Wilford, telephone operator, failed to notice his dereliction, for she became busy making mental notes of what the heiress to fifteen millions wore. Next week, Susie, the observant, would be wearing a strikingly accurate copy.

Judge Massie pushed open the door of his suite and held it open for Deedie. He shuffled angrily across the thick carpet, thrust open the door of his private sanctum, and grunted. "Don't like these here noiseless doors an' soundproof rooms. A body's meant to hear a certain amount o' corn-fusion an' effen you don't, it gits you plumb wrought up, like the poor man that spent a restless night waitin' fer the feller upstairs to drop the other shoe." He eased himself into the big, old-fashioned black leather chair, hooked out the second drawer with the square toe of his congress gaiter, and settled his feet in the drawer with a sharp clatter. He slid deeper into the chair, locked his fingers across his paunch and twiddled the chain with his thumbs. "Now git goin' at what's really troublin' you."

Willie watched her jauntiness collapse with dismay.

Deedie caught at her lace handkerchief, twisting its fragility recklessly. "It's about . . . about Sylvia, my sister. Is she, is she . . ."

Judge Massie shook his head. "Nup. She ain't crazy."

Deedie sank back in her chair with a sigh of relief. "Thanks."

"Understand," stated the Judge firmly, waggling a single finger above his paunch, "I ain't sayin' that jess to hand you a mite o' comfort. Coulda said it jess as easy an' meant it thataway, but I didn't. I sot here in this here office las' night an' talked with Sylvia mighty nigh an hour, mebbe more, an' there warn't nothin' wrong with her thinkin' apparatus. She done some right devious thinkin', an' she done it shrewd, too. 'Course, she was under a strain, an' a mite nervous, but that's natural, sort of. I been thinkin' mebbe she needs a good rest . . . away from . . . away from her present environment."

Deedie clasped her hands eagerly. "Oh, I'm so glad to hear you say so, too. It's exactly what Fred says. He wants her to go away, get a good long rest, and he feels she'll snap out of it. It's nice to hear someone else say the same thing, because of, well, because of Father."

"Land o' Goshen, child," the Judge's eyes flew open and he peered sharply over the rims of his spectacles, "what in tarnation give you any ideas about yore paw?"

"Oh, Fred said it wasn't anything to worry about, really, but I *do* worry, ever since he mentioned it. Sylvia *has* been acting strangely. But if both of you . . . But that isn't what I came here about. It's about this money."

"Wait jess a minute . . . jess a minute." The Judge disengaged one hand and held it up like a traffic signal. "Want to clear up one thing fast. Warn't nothin' wrong with yore paw, 'ceptin' he was smarter'n other folks—a dern heap smarter. Jess recommember that, any time you start doubtin'."

Deedie laughed. "I will . . . but about this money, I don't want it. I don't need it. I thought I might give it to Fred. He needs it so desperately for his experiments. The estate won't let him have any large sum, all at once. Couldn't I give it to him without Sylvia's knowing? I wouldn't want to hurt her."

"I wouldn't effen I was you," advised the Judge, slowly. "Leastwise, not right away. Wait until yore sister is more rested, or leastwise till she's gone fer a rest. Mebbe then we mought do somethin'. Take a little time, o' course. Fust off, we gotta git aholt o' that stock, on the basis o' that deed o' gift, 'fore we kin even turn it over to you. Mebbe then you kin start thinkin' 'bout this gift, or mebbe endowment to Dr. Jensen. Said anything about it to him?"

"Oh, no. Of course not. But an endowment would be a nice way of doing it, wouldn't it? And thank you so much." She got up to hurry away, and then stood uncertainly in the doorway. "I don't know about these things. Am I supposed to pay you a fee?"

"Already been paid. Howsomever, effen you was to git me to act in this here endowment, I'd sorta expect a fee."

Judge Massie watched her from under lowered lids as she softly closed the door. He heard Willie's long-drawn sigh.

"Willie, you jess been witnessin' the second act of a mighty sorry sort o' play, an' I don't know's there's anything we kin do 'bout it. I'm moughty much afeared Miss Deedie is stickin' her perty head in the same noose Miss Sylvia's in."

Willie's protest was instantaneous. "Not Miss Deedie. Gee, she's swell. Why that Miz Jensen is screwy. She's nuts, imaginin' she shot a guy."

Judge Massie frowned at his feet in the drawer, as if he had just discovered their trespass and didn't particularly like it. "An' 'sposin' I was to tell you she didn't imagine it?"

Willie was still leaning, chin on fist, gazing at the door through which Deedie had passed, and he didn't, at first, take it in. Then he swung around abruptly, and stared at the Judge. "Jedge, you ain't a mite tetched in the head? Why, I seen him with my own eyes, walkin' and talkin'."

For answer Judge Massie fumbled through his waistcoat pockets and laid a small packet of paper on the desk. Then he pulled open the middle drawer and took out the gun and bullets, spreading them on the desk around the packet. He tapped the gun portentously. "Willie, when she come in here last night that gun had jess been fired. An' in the wood frame o' that door at the foot of her bed where she said the doctor was standin'—well, in the frame o' that door, jess about where she said she aimed, was a bullet hole . . . an' it was filled with soap."

"Soap!" Willie inspected the Judge thoughtfully from the tips of his congress gaiters to the top of his domelike head rising out of the fringe of hair. "Jedge, you been eatin' mince pie agin."

Judge Massie sighed. "Willie, I wisht I could lay this here thing to a nightmare, but I cain't. It's there, an' it's monstrous. I don't 'xactly understand it m'self, but I kin see it's there." The Judge recalled himself with a start. "But that ain't nowise proof—effen there's anything to prove. But mebbe you kin recommember that there little table by the door? 'Member th' crystal lamp sittin' on it?"

Willie, always an appreciative audience for the Judge's soliloquies, shook his head. "Don't know's I do, Jedge, but if you say so, I reckon it's so."

The Judge carefully unwrapped the paper packet. It was a piece of toilet tissue. "Picked it up off'n the dresser," explained the Judge. "Effen you didn't notice the lamp, mebbe you also didn't notice somethin' funny 'bout it. Them lamps usually comes in pairs, an' that there was only one." From the toilet tissue little splinters of glass tinkled on to the Judge's old-fashioned desk. "These here are pieces of the lamp that ain't there, an' effen you was to fit 'em together, they'd fit right spang 'round a hole—jess sech a hole as a bullet would make." Judge Massie frowned over his spectacles past Willie. "An' effen you don't believe there was onct a pair o' them lamps, ask Miz Jensen. She's right behind you."

Willie hastily pulled himself out of the pretzel slump into which he had sunk to listen to the Judge, but Mrs. Jensen did not even glance at him. She didn't see anything, really—not even the Judge. She just stood in front of his desk ignoring Willie, ignoring the gun, ignoring the Judge. She spoke over his head.

"I want a divorce. I can't stand it any longer. I want a divorce. You'll have to file it for me. You've got to." If this were hysterics it was a new brand to the Judge, and he looked his surprise. She went on in her deadly calm voice, "I've left him. I can't live any longer in the same house with him. He can keep it. He's got his precious laboratory fitted up there. He won't even know I'm gone. Please file it immediately. I'm going down to speak to Judge Ames, and I'll tell him you're handling it. He'll understand why I don't ask Edgar Willebrandt, even if he is the family attorney. Good-bye . . ." And she walked out as quickly and as silently as she had entered.

Judge Massie half-rose in his chair, as if he were going to stop her, and then subsided. "Dunno but mebbe that's the right course." He fondled his pink chins. "Leastwise, it's better than murder."

Willie gawked at the Judge. "You don't think she was plannin' to . . . to . . . murder him?" Willie was horrified.

"Willie, jess cast yore mind back less'n twenty-four hours." Judge Massie watched the effect on his young assistant and adopted son. "Facks is sometimes hard to face, but you gotta learn to face 'em. Recommember the woman that come in here last night? Her eyes were bright of a fever, an' her face was pinched an' haunted, an' her mouth twitched, an' her fingers kept pluckin' an' pickin' . . . but on top o' that, mebbe you kin recommember the quick, keen way she follered ev'ything I said, an' played up to it. That there woman coulda thought an' done most anything."

Willie paused to consider. "You mean she was plannin' all along to . . ."

Judge Massie held up a cautioning hand. "Hold on, Willie. I don't mean anything. But facks is facks. Sylvia Jensen finds herself, or has fixed up fer herself, an ideal method o' committin' a murder—an' gettin' away with it." He sighed. "Howsomever, I'm right glad she decided on divorce instead. Ain't nigh as interestin', but a heap sight less dangerous fer all corn-cerned."

Willie nodded. "But what do you reckon made her decide on divorce so suddenly?"

"I can tell you." Pete Coleman stood in the doorway looking belligerent and slightly drunk. Not that he swayed, but there was a looseness about his arms and a slight forward roll of his head that told. "I can tell you," he said, as if defying the Judge to deny it.

"Land o' Goshen, then why don't you?" said the Judge mildly, flapping a hand toward a chair. "Set down."

"I won't sit," and he promptly sat in the chair the Judge had indicated. He stared at the Judge morosely for a long moment. "That bastard killed Chu Chin."

"I ain't claimin' no knowledge of his ancestors nor their moral standards, but I reckon you mean Dr. Jensen." The Judge shut his eyes and sank back in his chair, waiting. When Pete didn't say anything for a while he opened his eyes again, and coughed. "Pete, you ain't nigh as drunk as you'd like us to b'lieve, but you had enough drinks to put you up to sayin' somethin' you wouldn't say otherwise. Git it over with."

"Dr. Jensen is a bast . . ."

"Slander, Mr. Coleman." The Judge's mouth twitched in a suppressed smile.

"He killed Chu Chin. He said it was an accident . . . slammed the door on the poor little devil. Not that I particularly liked the brute; but Sylvia loved him . . . and Jensen lied."

"Ain't you gettin' it a mite corn-fused? But I reckon I kin foller you. Go on."

Pete looked up from his shoes. He spoke without anger but also without humor. "I'll bet you're way ahead of me. Anyway, Jensen admitted he killed him when the garbage men found the dog's body." He leaned forward on the Judge's desk, staring into the Judge's bland, cherubic face. "How the hell did you know Chu Chin was dead last night? They only found him in the garbage this morning." He beat one hand on the desk. "There's something funny as hell about this."

"Effen it is funny as hell—though I cain't say's I recommember hearin' hell was pertickler funny—that I shoulda' knowed it last night, ain't it jess about as funny you should know it this mornin' . . . when you're in Richmond?"

Pete grinned suddenly. "I knew you were way ahead of me. I had to tell her that to get out of a picnic date. Some business came up that, well, that I just couldn't stall. I went out there this morning to tell her. She gave me the devil for breaking the date. Said I wouldn't know business if it walked up and bit me—which it did—and then she walked out on me. That's when I found out about Chu Chin. Sylvia sent him to the vet for an autopsy. Thank the Lord Deedie doesn't know yet. But at least it'll revise some of her opinions of that . . ."

"Ah! ah! Pete." Judge Massie wriggled his interlocked fingers, and twiddled the heavy gold chain. "So Sylvia ordered an autopsy?"

Pete nodded. "And the poor little devil had been kicked and beaten to death with a stick."

Judge Massie wrinkled his nose in disgust. "An' that's how come Sylvia wants a divorce, is it?"

"I can readily imagine. The vet phoned his report while I was still there." Pete shook himself, and sat up straighter. "But what I came here about was to ask you not to mention to Deedie that you saw me . . . at the bank, I mean. She wouldn't understand . . . and . . . well, it's private, anyway." He shrugged. "Anyhow, it didn't work." For the first time he noticed the gun on the Judge's desk. "Say," he pointed, "did you get that from Sylvia last night?"

Judge Massie regarded the gun carefully. "How come you think I got that from Sylvia?"

Pete paused to consider. "Well, after you left last night, that scum said he couldn't find Sylvia's gun, and he was worried. Said in her condition she might . . . Ah, he's nuts; Sylvia wouldn't hurt a fly. Anyway, it was missing, and he was putting up a howl . . ."

"What makes you think this here gun is hers?" Judge Massie tapped it thoughtfully. "Ever see her use it?"

Pete laughed. "Sylvia shoot a gun? Not on your life. But it looks like one that came from one of those mail order houses. I happened to be there when it was delivered last week. That son of . . . that guy opened the package without even waiting for Sylvia, and it had a gun like that in it. I wish I'd had it this morning. I'd have punched holes in him with it, even if I didn't like the dog. And if he tries his little tricks on Deedie again, I *will* kill him."

"Pete, how come you don't marry the girl?"

Willie looked aghast. Pete stopped in the middle of his tirade and looked at the Judge, then he shrugged. "I couldn't . . ." Willie breathed easier, but Pete didn't notice, ". . . even if that rotten piece of tripe wasn't working on her to get rid of me. Poor kid, she doesn't know what to make of all this."

Judge Massie pursed his babyish lips and tapped his fingers together rhythmically. "What's to prevent yore jess walkin' in an'

askin' her, an' takin' her away?' Wouldn't she go? Last night I saw
her lookin' right starry-eyed . . . and it warn't at me."

Pete shook his head. "Even if she would, I couldn't ask her.
I'm broke." He grinned ruefully. "Yeah, the playboy is broke.
That's why I was at the bank—for the bad news. Deedie is too
nice a kid to marry like that. And some day she might wonder
about it." He stood up. "Hell, I didn't come here to weep on your
shoulder. Just don't tell her I'm in town. I've got to work this out
first." At the door he turned. "Know anybody who wants to hire
a thoroughly incompetent young man?" He was gone, completely
sobered of his brief drunk.

Judge Massie ruffled the fringe of his white hair. "Kinda liked
that there last remark. Mebbe we could use him." The Judge
flushed under Willie's calm regard, for Willie was well aware of
the Judge's habit of picking up strays. The Judge defended himself. "Leastwise, he's honest, an' he's got clean ideas."

Willie struggled manfully between the pangs of jealousy and
his loyalty to the Judge's opinion. "He ain't such a bad guy," he
finally conceded.

Judge Massie made a great to-do of looking at his ancient
turnip of a watch before he dared catch Willie's eye. He coughed.
"Sometimes, Willie, I make the mistake o' thinkin' you're one
o' the finest folks alive, but I kin guard m'self agin' sech senti-
mentality. An' I reckon I better git me my afternoon cup o' coffee." He hurried away from the look in Willie's eyes; an exquisite
blending of hurt and adoration. "I'll be at Luigi's," and the Judge
closed the door.

Willie was the Judge's self-adopted son—self-adopted at a
time when the Judge had needed friendship and reassurance and
faith. But long before that Willie had been a part and parcel of
the Judge's household. Willie, as the Judge had said, was less a
foundling than a lostling, though he had had no claim on the
Judge except the gameness of a lost, lonely kid with a grin a mile
wide. To have made it wider they'd have had to set his ears back
farther. The grin had got the Judge, and Willie had become part
of the Judge's life, for the Judge had "let him pay his way" by
learning to be a lawyer . . . at the Judge's expense. Only Willie

at the moment wasn't calling it *lawyer*. He called it *crim-in-nol-o-gist*, with all the syllables present and accounted for. Being sixteen, he ran to big words.

Some twenty minutes later the Judge was draining the last of Luigi's excellent coffee when Willie flung himself through Luigi's revolving door and breathed down the Judge's neck. "There's fifteen million bucks sitting upstairs in your office; spats, gold-headed cane an' everything."

Judge Massie didn't miss the last drop. He sighed with satisfaction before turning to Willie. "Spats an' gold-headed cane? Did you lock the safe, Willie?" He clanked a half dollar on the counter. "So Dr. Frederic Jensen come to see us, did he?"

"Shucks." The Judge had pruned Willie's earlier, more picturesque vocabulary to *shucks* and such homely phrases as the Judge's *Land o' Goshen*. Willie looked his admiration. "Howdja guess?"

"Willie, I figger that man's set himself out a pow'ful batch o' trouble, an' he's jess watchin' it rise . . . an' he's a mite worried. Yessiree. Come to think of it, I'd be a mite worried m'self effen my wife had murdered me last night. I'd seek comfort an' advice, Partickerlerly advice." He glanced at his watch. "Three-thirty. He sure found out quick."

"He warn't murdered, Jedge. He's walkin' an' talkin' jess like last night. I seen him."

Judge Massie was hurrying along, his panama tilted against the wind of his motion, and Willie was trotting alongside, backward, his freckles turned toward the Judge. Without missing a beat both waved at Pete emerging from the bank opposite, and Willie even negotiated the revolving door in reverse. At the elevator Judge Massie and Willie paused. The telephone operator was hidden from view but Willie did not crane his neck as of former times.

"Jedge, he warn't murdered," reminded Willie.

The elevator door slid open noiselessly and the Judge started in. "Yup, Willie, he warn't, an' that's what makes it so curious."

The silent elevator debouched the Judge and Willie at the second floor, and Willie flung open the Judge's door with a flourish,

as if he were about to announce royalty. He started to say something, and then stared at the Judge's outer office. There was no
one there to whom to announce his private god-head.

"He *was* here," Willie insisted, and offered a calling card to
prove it.

Judge Massie strode heavily across to the door of his inner
sanctum. Dr. Jensen sat at the Judge's desk, staring across its
battered surface with horrified eyes.

Judge Massie made an ineffectual effort to stop Willie, and
then he shut the door.

Dr. Jensen was very dead!

7

A CORPSE SINGS

Judge Massie fumbled at the end of the heavy gold chain, pulled out his watch, a massive, ancient affair, and stared at it. Except for the persistent buzz and thump of an August fly against the window, Willie's rapid breathing and the ticking of the Judge's watch, the room was quiet. Not even the traffic noises penetrated. It was, in fact, what the builder had promised—soundproof. The Judge snapped his watch shut with a decisive click. "Three thirty-seven . . . took us seven minutes to git here."

Willie continued to stare at the silent figure lounging grotesquely in the Judge's big leather chair. He walked slowly toward it across the deep pile of the carpet, looking back at the Judge, struggling against a childish quiver of his chin. "He's dead!" He looked down at the doctor's elegant gloves on the desk, and the gun beside them. He reached for it. "He done it with this."

"Don't touch that gun!" The Judge spoke sharply, and Willie drew back.

"You mean . . . it's murder?" The greyness faded out of his face, the sick, pinched look left his mouth, and a new light crept into his eyes. "Murder!" he whispered hoarsely. Murder, to a youngster of sixteen, was vastly different from death. Murder was a game, played with clues. The Judge could almost hear Willie's mind working. "Then we gotta look for clues?"

"Don't know's that's up to us, son." Judge Massie shook his head. "Reckon we better leave that fer the p'lice. You better run down to Luigi's and telephone Emery from there. Don't think

81

we better call up from here, bein' as Susie Wilford mought git hysterics an' give more wrong numbers than usual."

Willie looked hurt at being deprived of the privilege of watching his deity work on a real murder that had happened under his nose, so to speak.

"Tell Emery to rush it, an' bring his whole kit an' kaboodle with him. Only, Land o' Goshen, I don't want 'em tromplin' all over my place."

"Yes, sir!" Willie almost saluted, and turned to go. His eye caught something on the floor, and Willie sidled toward the desk, firmly planting his foot on a scrap of white that lay there.

Judge Massie had his back turned, looking down at Dr. Jensen's vacant, handsome face. He spoke quietly. "Willie, take yore foot off'n that there piece o' handkerchief. Mought be evidence."

Willie flushed, and reluctantly pulled his foot away. "Jees, Jedge, you've got eyes in the back o' yore head, same as my teacher." He stooped hastily and gathered up the white fragment, holding it out to the Judge with anxiety. "Jedge, that don't mean nothin', honest it don't. Jees, Jedge, she couldn't 'a done it. Honest, Jedge." Tears blurred Willie's eyes, and his voice caught. "Lissen, Jedge, mebbe she dropped it when she was talkin' to you . . . mebbe she did."

"Willie!" Judge Massie waggled the fragment of a lace handkerchief under Willie's nose. "Willie!" The Judge's voice was sorrowful. "You'n me kin both recommember Miss Deedie bein' here, an' we kin recommember she sorta twisted a lace handkerchief, but ain't neither o' us recommember seein' her tear off a piece. That there is evidence, Willie." He shook the bit of lace again.

"Yes, sir . . . but she's too nice an' perty, Jedge."

The Judge tucked the fragment negligently in his pocket, and sighed. "Howsomever, effen we don't recommember she didn't tear it, it ain't no real sign she didn't tear it then, is it, Willie? Mebbe she did an' we didn't recommember." Willie gulped and nodded, a smile beginning to crinkle the corners of his mouth.

"She might 'a tore it then, an' we didn't notice," he admitted happily.

"Yessiree. An' less'n somethin' else turns up that we cain't fergit recommemberin' so easy, I guess that's 'bout all, Willie." He turned abruptly away from Willie's shining gratitude and bent over the dead man, peering at his shirt front. "Mighty close range. Looks like a twenty-five calibre, Willie. Them bullets don't make much of a hole, and he ain't bled none. Musta kilt him right spang off . . . spang in the heart. Nup, wouldn't be much bleedin' from that." Judge Massie knelt ponderously and squinted along the desk top, and shook his head. He leaned forward and blew gently on the gun, and squinted again.

"Coolin' it off, Jedge?"

Judge Massie didn't glance up, but plowed industriously around the desk, blowing and squinting. Finally he sighed, and scrambled wearily to his feet. "Not coolin' it off, son, jess lookin' fer fingerprints. Sometimes, effen they're right fresh, like they'd have to be on this here gun, you kin see 'em by breathin' on 'em. Cain't make 'em out, but jess tell effen they're there. Ain't nary a one. Nor none on the desk, neither. Whoever done it, done a better job than th' cleanin' woman ever done sense we been here."

"Reckon Miz Jensen done it?" asked Willie in awed tones.

Judge Massie patted his paunch. "Willie, I come by my fat natchel . . . I never took no exercise jumpin' at conclusions." He herded the boy gently into the outer office. "Better git goin' on that phone call to Emery, an' do it quick."

Willie rushed down the hall, skidded around the newel post and shot down the stairs. The Judge could still hear the clatter of his feet when the elevator door slid noiselessly open and Sylvia Jensen strode toward him. Judge Massie hastily sidestepped her onslaught as she swept into his center office. He closed the door gently.

Sylvia stood in the center of the room, head high, her large eyes blazing with a terrible fury. Anger gave color to her thin checks and a regal, sweeping beauty to her figure. She held out her hand imperiously. "I came for my gun."

Judge Massie sidled between her and the door to his inner office. "Sylvia, I'm afraid I cain't give it to you." He took her arm, but she pulled away from him. "How come you'd be wantin' a gun, Sylvia? It's a heap safer right here . . . a heap."

Her mouth twisted in her effort to control the rage that was shaking her. "I don't intend it to be safe. I intend to shoot my husband."

This time the Judge's hand closed firmly over her arm, and he all but forced her across the room, into his law library opposite his private office. He closed the door and led her to a chair. She followed meekly enough, but the rigidity of her back was uncompromising. The Judge almost shoved her into a chair. "It ain't wise to make remarks like that, Sylvia. Folks'll think mebbe . . ."

She looked at him with scorn. "You mean . . . after last night? Or has he persuaded you, too, that I'm insane?" She shook her head at the Judge's frown. "Oh, I know he's been here. They told me down at the courthouse that he was coming here, but he can't do it. He can't! I'll kill him first!"

Judge Massie eased his big frame into one of the library chairs close to her and laid a comforting hand on her arm. "Don't know's I know what you're talkin' about. I ain't spoke to Dr. Jensen since last night. How come they tole you at court he'd come here?"

Her eyes met the Judge's fearlessly, a regal dignity adding conviction to her words. "My husband has applied for a lunacy commission to declare me insane. And he was coming here to stop you from executing my deed of gift. He's mad, crazy mad to get hold of money." She caught her breath. "Oh, God, what has he done to me? Even Judge Ames looked at me as if . . . as if he wondered."

"Sylvia, you ain't in no wise makin' things easier fer yoreself comin' here an' sayin' the things you said."

She broke then. It hurt the Judge to see her. She was such a poor, haunted wreck of a woman, held together by some force of will. But she just sat there, crumpled in the chair, her thin body shaken by sobs that were scarcely audible, tears running unheeded down her thin cheeks, her hands limp in her lap.

Judge Massie let her cry for fully a minute before he pulled out a large, old-fashioned handkerchief and thrust it under her nose, as if she were a small child. She took it dully and made

ineffectual dabs at her face. She didn't seem to care, really didn't
seem to know she was crying. She had withdrawn into some shell
of misery that was difficult for her to shatter, to give herself, up
to the emotional release of violent sobbing. At last, however,
she shook herself, straightened her thin shoulders, and tried to
smile. "I'm silly, aren't I? Please forgive me."

"Ain't gonna forgive," stated the Judge. "Heap easier jess to
fergit. Pow'ful good at fergittin' I am, sometimes." He caught up
the feather-light crepe jacket that had fallen drunkenly across
the arm of the chair and put it around her. "Effen you'll take my
advice, you'll go right back to Jedge Ames and talk things over
with him. Been my experience Bill Ames was a right understan-
din' man. An' in the meantime, I'll sorta talk to him on the
phone—sorta wise him up to how things really is. But you go
right back to Jedge Ames an' talk to him. It's pow'ful important,
pow'ful important." The Judge urged her gently out the corridor
door instead of sending her back through his center office.

She looked bewildered at this treatment, but she nodded. "All
right, I'll go to see Judge Ames, though what good . . ." She
shrugged and walked slowly down the stairs.

Judge Massie looked up as he heard the sharp staccato click
of heels along the corridor. Deedie, looking very young, and very
pretty, and very, very angry, came to a halt opposite the Judge. "I
was just coming to your office."

The Judge held open the door of his law library invitingly
and she strode in, whirled and faced the Judge as if she would
pinion him against his own door. "That beast! That dirty, rotten
beast!" She stamped her foot. "I could shoot him down like a
dog!"

Judge Massie waddled into her onslaught and patted her arm.
"So you been quarrelin' with Pete again?"

Deedie stared at the Judge for a moment as if she didn't quite
remember who Pete might be or why she should be quarreling
with him. Suddenly she burst out, "No, not him! That low, rotten Dr. Jensen. I could kill him . . . I could kill him!"

Judge Massie took her by the arm and led her—or rather
pushed her, for her slim little shoulders and straight back were

tense with anger—to a chair. Her trim little heels dug into the carpet at each step. She refused to sit, and the Judge urged her firmly. "Ain't no sense gittin' all flummoxed this here way. You jess set down. So you heared that the doctor ordered a lunacy commission to declare yore sister insane."

"What a dirty, rotten trick! He's a specialist, and what he says will have so much weight. Poor Sylvia, she won't stand a chance . . . not a chance. And he won't stop. I begged him . . . not half an hour ago." She glanced around the library as if she had just noticed it for the first time. "In your other office. Has he gone? I came back because I made such a fool of myself the first time. I cried all over the place, and simply couldn't be coherent. I thought maybe you could persuade him—make him see how cruel and unjust and unnecessary it is. Poor Sylvia! It will kill her when she finds out; it really will. I'm serious, Judge. She's sick, she's ill and nervous . . . but not . . . not that." She studied the Judge's face intently. "You do believe me?"

"Now, Miss Cordelia, you jess set an' ca'm yoreself a minute. This here ain't somethin' to go bustin' headlong into like a billy goat at a stone wall. 'Twon't git you nowheres a-tall, not a-tall."

Deedie held her breath a minute, and then asked slowly, "You . . . don't . . . believe . . . *him?*"

Judge Massie shook himself out of a dreadful reverie. "No, can't say's I do. But you tell me, slow-like, so's I kin take it in, jess what did Dr. Jensen say to you, an' you to him? Was he excited?"

Deedie shook her head so violently it threatened the safety of the little cup of a hat on her upswept hair. "He was beastly. He just laughed at me, nasty-nice, and spoke to me as if I were a child. I wish I hadn't cried. It makes me furious to cry, and I'll be doing it again in a minute if you don't stop me."

Judge Massie grinned; little crinkles broke out around his eyes, and little crescents deepened around his mouth. "You're a winsome brat. I hope Pete marries you an' beats you reg'lar-like."

"Am I winsome?" She almost smiled at him. "That's because I went to the ladies' room and repaired the damages. You have nice ladies' rooms in this building." She glanced around the room. "In fact, this is a nice office. If I ever have to work for a living

I think I'll ask you for a job." Then she put out her hand and rested it on the Judge's plump arm. "Thanks. That was a help. This has been so ugly, so messy, so horrible. I think I can talk sensibly now." She settled into the chair. "Do you think he'll go through with it?"

Judge Massie straddled one of the small library chairs and flowed over its sides. He shook his head. "Miss Deedie, he won't."

Deedie looked surprised at this ready assurance. "But . . . but what can have changed his mind? A little while ago he was . . . he was adamant. He even dared to say it was for the best."

"Would you recommember effen he mentioned that money yore sister give you last night?"

Deedie considered. "I guess he did. That's the deed of gift, isn't it? He said it couldn't be executed because she wasn't competent to handle her affairs. But I wasn't thinking of that. I was thinking of what he had done to my sister."

"A heap o' folks would do a heap o' things, Miss Deedie, fer two hunderd thousand dollars." He gauged the effect of his words.

"He could have had the money. I was going to give it to him anyway, remember? I spoke to you about it. In fact I was down at the courthouse to see Judge Ames about it when I heard about this lunacy commission. But now he won't touch a cent. I'll fight him at every step. I'll . . ."

Judge Massie gave up his scrutiny with a sigh of content. "Right glad to hear you say that, Deedie; it eases m'mind a heap. Not that that 'mounts to anything. Howsomever . . ."

Willie burst in from the center office. "Jedge, oh Jedge," and, despite soundproofing, you could hear Willie. He thrust open the law library door. "Emery didn't want to come. He said you pulled him in on one phony murder and, by thunder, the doc had better be dead this time . . ." He saw Deedie then, and halted abruptly.

Deedie scuttled around the bulk of Judge Massie and looked at Willie. "Is Dr. Jensen dead? Tell me the truth."

Miserably, Willie nodded, half-turning to Judge Massie in appeal.

"Was he murdered? You did say *murder* didn't you?" Willie nodded, half in confirmation and half from the shaking she was giving him. She released him and turned to the Judge. "And I thought you were being kind! You were setting a trap . . ."

"Jess a minute." Willie, regardless of his temporary infatuation, was loyal to the Judge. "You can't talk to the Jedge like that."

She ignored him. "Cheap lawyers' tricks." She stamped her foot childishly. "Oh, I hate you, and I'm glad Pete has an alibi. He's in Richmond."

Judge Massie raised his leonine head so that he peered directly through the lenses of his steel-rimmed spectacles at her. "An' how come Pete should need an alibi? Wouldn't be because he had a quarrel with the doctor last night over a lovely but very stupid young lady?"

"What makes you think so?" Deedie was defiant and very lovely. Willie sidled around for a better view.

Judge Massie errumphed. "Well, it's jess about the sort o' thing a gallant but somewhat stupid young man would do."

Deedie stamped her foot again. "He's not stupid . . . and it was a fine thing to do, although at the time I couldn't believe that Fred . . . that Dr. Jensen would ever look at that obvious, flashy Mrs. Carlyle. But, after what he's done to Sylvia I wouldn't put anything past him."

Detective Sergeant Joe Emery pushed open the law library door and stepped in. He frowned at Deedie, glared at the Judge and growled at Willie, "Did you call me up just now?"

Willie had a fundamental, small-boy gesture for cops. He didn't use it but his tone suggested it. "Yeah, an' you wouldn't believe me."

"I still don't. Judge, this young son of a gun—begging your pardon, miss . . . Say, didn't I see you last night? At the Jensen place? Sure, you're the kid sister." He looked doubtful for an instant. "Judge, is this on the level? Is the doc really dead this time, or are you nuts, too?"

Judge Massie waved Deedie into a chair in the far corner and, strangely enough, she obeyed meekly. "Yup, reckon it's real enough this time. An' dad-burn it, right in my office. Why cain't folks pick other places fer their murders?" He grumbled insincerely, for the Judge liked the intricate and devious ferreting of a murder case.

Emery glared. "Listen, I took one awful ribbing for that stooge play last night, so I didn't even bring Garrison this time. If it's on the level, I'll call the squad."

Judge Massie nodded. "It's on the level, but check on it yoreself. The body is in my private office, settin' in my own cheer, dad-gum." Judge Massie waddled across the center office and pushed open the door of his inner sanctum.

Six ice-cold centipedes crawled up his spine.

The body had been sitting in the chair facing the door. Now it was facing the window, and the body was humming softly and slightly off-key. Slowly the chair swung around.

"Oh . . . er . . . good evening, gentlemen. Er . . . ah . . . come in," invited a total stranger.

8

IS IT MURDER?

Emery gazed at the man who should have been a corpse, and blinked. He turned and eyed the Judge sourly. "This ain't even Dr. Jensen, let alone a corpse."

Judge Massie fumbled with his spectacles, sliding them along his nose trombone fashion, as if he hoped by this method to clear away the man who sat so placidly smiling up at them—a small man, with a baldish, domed forehead. "Why, this here is . . ."

"I don't give a damn who this here is. All I care about is who it ain't, and the fact that it ain't dead. Judge Massie, you'n me have been having our spats back and forth for the fifteen-twenty years I've been on the force, and we've tried to pull some mighty fast ones on each other, but damned if this don't take the pants off a pig. I ought to have you hauled before the state bar for this. You can't play murder with the police, like some kid game. Why, you . . ." Emery continued at length and fluidly, and, without regard for the presence of a lady, gave his complete, thorough, and unexpurgated opinion of the Judge, his antecedents, his co-workers, their antecedents, and was beginning on mere acquaintances before going back a couple of generations in the Judge's own family line, which he doubted was legitimate.

Judge Massie nodded at first feebly in protest, and then in growing amazement as Emery rolled on. "Joe, you left out splay-footed."

Willie murmured in awe-struck tones, "He ain't repeated once."

The mild little man in the chair nodded in time to Emery's perorations. He muttered audible comment. "Aphaeresis and apocope."

"Hunh?" Emery paused and glared. "What's that?"

Judge Massie tapped the flushed detective on the arm. "He's jess sayin' that when you git all het up you drop the fust syllables o' some words, an' the last letters o' some."

The little man beamed at the Judge. "Precisely. Remarkable example of the debauching of the English language. I must make a note of that."

Emery fumbled at his words before he could bring out, "Say, who the hell are you?"

"Who am I?" The little man jerked out a pair of pince-nez glasses and settled them on his long, thin nose. "Suppose you tell me who you are, bursting in here like this. I should call an officer, really I should." He looked blankly around and sighed. "Oh, dear me, I'm so sorry. This is not my office at all. I'm dreadfully sorry. Dear me, what a blunder! How frightfully stupid of me."

"Well," demanded Emery, "stupid or not—and we won't argue the point—who are you?"

The little man considered that thoughtfully. "Really, it is absent-mindedness rather than stupidity. You see . . . oh, yes . . . my name."

"This here is Dr. Royster Carlyle," Judge Massie put in.

"Thank you!" He gave a funny, ducking little bow at the Judge. "Precisely. Dr. F. Royster Carlyle. Is there anything I can do for you?"

"Yeah, plenty." Emery thrust himself across the desk. "What are you doing in Judge Massie's office? Especially at this time?"

The little man hastily glanced at his watch. "Four-five. Dear me. Is there anything odd about the time?"

Emery pulled himself reluctantly back. "Skip it. Just answer this—what are you doing here in Judge Massie's office?"

"Massie? Massie? Oh, yes, Massie. I remember now. I came here on an errand. I came here about . . . Oh, dear me, this confusion has completely driven it out of my mind."

"If you've got one." Emery turned on his heel and started out. "You're wacky, all of you . . . nuts." He glared at Willie. "Except you. I think I'll take you along to the station house and book you . . . calling the police station on fake murder charges." He laughed without enthusiasm at the Judge. "And how will you like that? Come along, you." He caught Willie's sleeve in a firm grip.

Judge Massie charged into action. He thrust the surprised detective out the door, pinned Willie against the wall with one hand, and all but butted Deedie out of the way before he lowered his bulk to his knees and peered along the carpet near the desk.

Emery turned in the doorway and looked down at the Judge scrambling along the floor between the desk and the door that opened directly on to the corridor.

Dr. Carlyle stood up, the better to peer over the bulk of Judge Massie's desk. "Did you lose something?"

Judge Massie, wheezing slightly, peered over his shoulder at the little man and saw Emery's grinning face. "I ain't 'xactly built fer this here snoopin' work, not havin' the cockroach type o' mind nor build."

He glanced at the little man. "Did I lose somethin'? A client. Or leastwise, I had sorta hopes fer him bein' a client." Painfully Judge Massie pulled himself erect, looking at his old leather chair where so recently had sat a man who was very dead. "He was dragged out."

Dr. F. Royster Carlyle adjusted his pince-nez at the Judge. "Dear me, are clients so valuable that you snatch them bodily from one another?"

Judge Massie leaned on his fists and spoke across the desk to the little doctor. "This here client was 'specially valuable, but not as a client. He was dead."

Emery guffawed and flapped a beef-red hand at the Judge. "It's a great act, Judge, a great act. I'll catch it some night at Loew's. I don't know why you're doing it, but it's still a great act. Mebbe you'll call it *The Three Bears All in One*." He turned to go as the telephone shrilled.

Something about the ringing of a telephone stops conversation and action until someone rushes for the phone. The little doc beat the Judge to it.

"Yes? Judge Massie's office? Oh, no, this . . . I beg your pardon, it is. Yes? Who? Dr. Jensen? No, he's not here . . . I'm quite sure, madam . . . Quite . . ." He glanced at the Judge indecisively.

"It's a Mrs. Hard-something. She says she can't find the papers Dr. Jensen asked her to get."

The Judge reached for the phone but the little doctor seemed unwilling to give it up. Judge Massie wrenched it from him. "Hello . . . Mrs. Hardecker. This is Judge Massie . . . Yes, yes, I recommember you . . . What's this 'bout papers? Say it slow-like, Mrs. Hardecker . . . Yes'm, I'm listenin' . . . Dr. Jensen jess 'phoned you fer some papers? Wanted 'em sent to my office? Yes'm, I got that. Now jess when did he phone? . . . Not ten minutes ago? . . . Jess at four o'clock? . . . No ma'am, he ain't here . . . Yes'm, I reckon I'm a lot sorrier'n you are . . . Good-bye, ma'am."

Judge Massie cradled the phone slowly and then mopped his brow. He stared at Emery over the steel rims of his spectacles. "He ain't dead. He jess called up his housekeeper an' ast her to send some papers to this here office . . . not ten minutes ago . . . at four o'clock." He pursed babyish lips and frowned at Emery. "An' you were here then."

"Right on the dot of four," Emery shook his head, and then added, for caution, "but I didn't come in here for a couple of minutes after that. You know, Judge, somehow, I'm beginning to think maybe you *thought* you were right." He swung at Willie. "But if I catch you telling any more phony stories to the police, I'll . . ." He made a grisly noise in his throat and stalked out.

Willie made a derisive noise—but not too loud.

Deedie crept from her place against the wall where the Judge had thrust her and perched uneasily on the edge of a chair. She blinked at the Judge, her very nice mouth twitching. "I don't know whether to laugh or cry."

"Must you do either?" inquired Dr. F. Royster Carlyle, settling back in the Judge's chair. The three of them gaped at him, and he looked bewildered. "Dear me, was that an odd question? I do seem to say the most unfortunate things quite unwittingly. But I merely inquired whether the young lady need either laugh or cry. The situation doesn't seem to call for either, but rather for careful analysis, a complete and thorough breakdown . . ."

Willie flopped into a chair. "I feel like I've jess had one, complete with pink elephant trimmings."

The little doctor ignored that. ". . . and when the analysis is complete, and we have the component parts and their interrelated values, we should be able to synthesize, to re-create . . ."

"Once was enough, without re-creating *that*," Willie suggested.

Dr. Carlyle eyed him through the pince-nez with a speculative gleam. "I have met your sort in my sophomore classes, and I appreciate the bon mot without condoning the interruption." He turned to the Judge and spread his hand invitingly. "Now just what are the elements?"

Judge Massie rubbed the second of his chins thoughtfully. "Well, fust off, you're settin' in my cheer."

Dr. Carlyle rose hastily. "I beg your pardon, so I was." He was a small man, fiftyish, running to a small paunch that pushed at the lower edges of his vest. His face was thin but not gaunt, the thinness of an aesthete, and he wasn't bad-looking behind the owlishness of his glasses and a mustache that hadn't been trimmed any too recently. His greying hair was probably a pompadour when he hadn't ruffled it into three separate horns across his forehead. He had nice hands. Legge, Emery's expert, would have liked to have finger-printed him, a suggestion that would have amazed and then troubled the doctor.

He moved around the desk with a vague swimming motion, intended to imply the chair was once more the Judge's. "Very careless of me."

Judge Massie sighed as he settled himself once more in his deep leather chair. "This here is the place fer thinkin'." His feet clattered into the second drawer, his fingers formed the little tent across his paunch, he let his head fall forward so the pink accordion of his chins overlapped his collar and black string tie, his spectacles slid to their customary perilous position at the tip of his bulbous nose, and he errumphed loudly. "The little doc, here, has mentioned the idee that mebbe we could do a little analyzin' an' synthesizin'. Me, I ain't sech a hand at big words, so I reckon we'll jess figger things out . . . from the beginnin'-like. Sorta helps, sometimes, figgerin' things out loud. An' the beginnin' is a good place to start, effen we knows the beginnin', which ain't likely. Nor the end, neither."

Dr. Carlyle pulled one of the metal-tube chairs fussily to the desk and settled himself in it. "Perhaps if we sort the facts we could arrive at X, the unknown."

"That'ud be most ev'rthing, Doc."

"Come, come. There are some pertinent facts, surely, that we have at hand."

"Oh, Dr. Carlyle," Deedie leaned forward, "it's so confusing. Judge Massie thought Dr. Jensen was murdered here in this room at, I guess, about three thirty or later—anyway, after I was here. But Mrs. Hardecker—that's our housekeeper—said he had just phoned the house at four and asked for some papers to be sent here."

"Sent here?" Dr. Carlyle's attitude suggested he was writing it down in a note book. "Then he must intend to return."

Judge Massie nodded thoughtfully. "Mebbe be did. Mebbe, if he kin wish, he's wishin' he could return right now. Trouble is, he's dead." Judge Massie pointed to the deep-pile carpet, near the door that opened directly on the corridor. "Somebody drug him from this here cheer to that door. Effen you look right close, you kin see where his heels scuffed the carpet."

Dr. Carlyle bent and peered at the faint traces. "Dear me, so I can, quite distinctly, now that you point them out." He glanced at the Judge. "For a man of your age, Judge Massie, you have remarkably keen eyesight."

"I was lookin' fer it. You see, I knew he was dead. But the p'int is, who'd want the body? Warn't many people wanted him even alive, an' he lost corn-sid'able in value dead."

"Ah!" Dr. Carlyle's eyes twinkled wisely behind his glasses. "The murderer might want it."

"Right onhandy thing, a corpse is. Cain't figger out why the murderer would want it, 'cept to conceal the deed, an' we already know this here Jensen is dead."

"Ah, but did the murderer know you knew it?" Dr. Carlyle made his point with almost childish glee, tapping firmly on the desk and beaming around for approval. When nobody responded to his amiability he coughed hesitantly. "Then who did know you knew?"

Judge Massie waved his hand. "Jess us, here in this here room. Me, Willie, and Deedie. Oh, Miss Cordelia Storme, this here is Dr. F. Royster Carlyle. That's right, ain't it?"

"Oh, I know him quite well," Deedie smiled at the little man, "but I expect he's forgotten me."

"Do I know you? Dear me . . . and have I forgotten you? Inexcusable. Possibly you are in one of my classes at the university?"

Deedie dimpled at him. "Flower girl at your wedding."

"Of course, of course. Round, chubby thing in pink, with yellow curls . . ." Dr. Carlyle beamed at his own cleverness.

Deedie chuckled softly. "You have a lovely, orthodox idea of weddings, Dr. Carlyle. I was skinny, and had braces on my teeth. You were too much intent on acquiring Amy to notice anything else."

Dr. Carlyle coughed and nodded, withdrawing his amiability perceptibly. "Quite stupid of me." He frowned intently. "Then you must be Sylvia Storme's sister."

"Yes . . ." As if this reminded her of the strange tragedy in the air, she sank back in her chair wearily.

Dr. Carlyle cleared his throat. "Were you aware that these gentlemen knew of the decease of Dr. Jensen? By jove, he's Sylvia's husband, isn't he? Of course."

Deedie nodded. "Yes, he is—or was. And I don't know yet that he's dead. Judge Massie said so, but . . ."

Willie, who had been practically goggling at Deedie, spoke up in defense of his idol. "Effen the Jedge says so, it's true. And I saw him, too, and he looked dead to me."

"Ahem." Dr. Carlyle drew them again into his imaginary classroom. "Perhaps if we approach this, as I previously suggested, in the scientific manner, by rationalization, by induction, and by deduction, we may arrive at the truth. Now, let us start with the known facts. Now, these are . . ." His classroom manner deserted him and he glanced confusedly around. "Er . . . ah . . . just what are the known facts? The known, pertinent facts, let us say."

"Effen we kin say," Judge Massie shifted creakingly in his chair, "th' ain't any facks. Never did see sech a case, effen it is a case."

"Come, come . . ." Dr. Carlyle rapped on the desk in repri-
mand. "Surely there are some facts. For instance, at what time
did you see this . . . this . . . er . . . alleged body?"

"Three-thirty-seven. Checked on it special, aginst jess sech
a question, an' . . ." The Judge held up his hand against the
doctor's next question. "I was down at Luigi's gittin' me a cup
o' coffee when Willie come in an' tole me this here Jensen was
upstairs. Looked at my watch then, too, wonderin' how come he
heared so soon that his wife was filin' divorce."

"Divorce?" Deedie nodded grimly. "I didn't know, but of
course it was the only thing . . ."

Dr. Carlyle nodded at Willie huddled interestedly in a chair.
Clues and investigations he understood and appreciated. "This,
I take it, is Willie. And you saw Dr. Jensen? Yes? He was alive?"

"He was swingin' a gold-headed cane an' talkin' down his
nose." Willie gave a recognizable imitation of Jensen's stately
arrogance, even to the tight mouth.

"And the next time anyone present saw Dr. Jensen he was
presumably dead. I'm correct so far? Good. Then this young man
was the last person to see him alive, if he was alive."

Judge Massie heaved indignantly. "Doc, th' ain't a mite o' use
accusin' Willie. He's a right nice boy when he has ter be, an' effen
he says Jensen was alive, then he was alive."

The doctor drew away from the Judge's mild but firm defense. "Of course, of course. I'm merely trying to establish the
time element." He glanced down as if consulting notes. "Now,
at three-thirty this Willie came into the coffee house and told
you Dr. Jensen was in your office, and you, Judge Massie, said
you reached here at three-thirty-seven. I wonder if Master Willie
would know how long it took him to get from the office to the
coffee shop."

"Took me about five minutes to get to the Jedge, so I musta' left here about three-twenty-five, an' I come back with the
Jedge."

Dr. Carlyle nodded at this precision. "Now we have it, I
think. Between three-twenty-five and three-thirty-seven—a matter of twelve minutes—someone presumably entered the office

and killed Dr. Jensen. Shot him presumably with the gun that belongs with these two shells." He pointed to the remaining two of the six shells that had been with the gun when the Judge took it away from Sylvia Jensen. The gun was gone.

"There was a gun here when Willie an' me come in an' found Jensen, an' there warn't but one bullet fired then, so fer's I could see. An' that come out o' the empty shell lyin' at yore feet, Dr. Carlyle. Ain't got a likely explanation handy o' how a corpse walked away with a gun an' five extra bullets, have you?"

Dr. Carlyle retrieved the empty shell at his feet and peered at it before answering. "Yes, this shell has been fired. And I haven't any explanation. But whom did you inform of this . . . tragedy?"

"Willie, here, went down to Luigi's to telephone the p'lice. We only got a switchboard telephone now, an' Susie's right handy at listenin' in on conversations. I didn't want her havin' hysterics all over the buildin', or spreadin' a general news bulletin." Judge Massie peered from under his shaggy brows at the little doctor, and smiled grimly. "You doin' right good, Doc."

Dr. Carlyle bowed his head at the compliment and went on, "And he returned when?" Dr. Carlyle was almost judicial.

"Willie come in jess 'fore Emery come—jess 'fore we walked in here on you . . . four o'clock."

"And what did you do between three-thirty-seven and four o'clock? Not that I'm implying . . ." the little doc hastened to assure the Judge.

Judge Massie sighed. "Doc, mebbe you warn't implyin' like you said, but you got me right spang where the hair's shortest. I slipped up right there. Never figgered on a corpse gittin' up an' leavin'. Somehow corpses, once they's genuine corpses, has a habit of stayin' put. But I shoulda knowed better. Nothin' seems to keep this corpse down. Howsomever, that ain't the p'int. I neglected him. Mrs. Jensen come in jess as Willie shot down the stairs. I figgered it jess warn't the thing to take her in sudden-like on Dr. Jensen, so I took her into my law library. She was more'n a mite upsot about this lunacy commission. You may not 'a heared, Doc, but Dr. Jensen had jess ordered a lunacy commission to hear Sylvia's case."

"Bless my soul, no! Sylvia is as sane as I am," he gave the Judge a brief, quizzical smile, "though I dare say there are some people who would not consider the comparison a recommendation for Sylvia."

Willie hastily stifled a laugh and Judge Massie snorted quietly. "Howsomever, I took her in this here other office an' talked to her fer a spell, mebbe ten minutes, got her a mite ca'm down, an' sent her off to see an old friend, Judge Ames. An' that reminds me, I better call him in a minute an' git him to break the news. Figgered he'd do a better job'n me. An' I'd scarcely got shed o' Sylvia when up pops Miss Deedie. Met her at the door o' the law library, in fack."

Deedie nodded confirmation. "I wondered at the time why you were standing in that door."

"I took her into the law library, too, fer the same reasons as I took Sylvia. She'd been in here a bit earlier, an' I wanted to ask her some questions."

"Let's get the times straight." Dr. Carlyle appropriated a sheaf of paper and the Judge's favorite pen. He hastily scored off a small diagram and filled it in. He murmured as he wrote, "Jensen arrives, three-twenty-five, and Willie leaves; then there's a gap of twelve minutes, during which the murderer arrived . . ."

"Wait a minute." Deedie leaned forward and pointed to the diagram, disregarding the Judge's gesture of protest. "I was here then. I came in right behind Dr. Jensen . . . I saw Willie run out. I wasn't here but two or three minutes . . . I started crying, like a fool, and ran out."

Dr. Carlyle wrote that into his diagram. "Miss Cordelia Storme with Jensen from three-twenty-six to three-twenty . . . shall we say nine? Three-twenty-nine?" Then he looked up sharply. "But my dear lady, do you realize what you've just said? That makes you . . ."

"The perfect suspect, doctor." Deedie's chin was up. "You're quite right. However, I didn't kill Dr. Jensen. I have nothing but my word for it."

"Bless me! Most distressing . . . awkward . . ." and the little doc looked quite upset. "Dear me, I don't know what to do."

"Mought as well write it down, Doc. Got me down fer a matter o' thirty minutes or so in which I mought 'a kilt him an' got rid o' the body, too. Do it up fair an' square, an' the truth'll come out. Bound to." Judge Massie nodded his convictions. "An' put down that Miss Deedie and I was talkin' in the law library 'til four o'clock, when Emery came. An' Willie . . . don't fergit Willie."

"Hmmmm." The doctor stared at his crude chart and frowned. "According to this, for eight minutes, between three-twenty-nine and three-thirty-seven, Dr. Jensen was alone except for the presumed murderer, and again, for approximately twenty minutes, between three-thirty-nine, or, let us say, three-forty—allowing three minutes for your inspection—and four o'clock, the corpse was alone in this office while you were two offices away, talking with two different young women for approximately ten minutes each." He handed the chart to Judge Massie who adjusted his spectacles and then peered over them to read the sheet. Using the fountain pen as a pointer he explained in his best classroom manner, "As you will see, the murder presumably took place prior to three-thirty-seven, and from three-forty until four we have these conditions. First, Miss Cordelia Storme is in the building but a free agent for the first ten minutes, while for the second ten minutes, while you are with Miss Cordelia, Sylvia Jensen is a free agent. And during the entire time Master Willie is free to do as he pleases, aside from the telephoning."

Willie nodded. He appreciated the need for charts as well as clues. "Took me 'bout four-five minutes to get to the phone, mebbe ten minutes talkin' to that cop to get him to see his nose, an 'en I waited in front of the building 'til I see Emery comin' an' beat it for here."

"Hmmmm . . . very satisfactorily accounted for." Dr. Carlyle took back his list and added something to it. "But dear me, this completely upsets our calculations. How could he call his home at four o'clock if he was already dead at three-thirty-seven?"

Judge Massie groaned his chair forward and took the chart. He pondered it a long moment. "This here Mrs. Hardecker coulda made a mistake in the time, but it ain't likely she'd be a whole twenty minutes out. Less'n the murderer called up an' pertended to be Jensen. But why should he?" The Judge flapped away the little doctor's intended speech. "Reckon he wanted us to find the body? At a certain time? Mought want to establish an alibi; but in that case I figger he'd want to delay findin' it."

Willie frowned in excellent imitation of the Judge's concentration. "Mebbe not. Mebbe his alibi needs a . . ." his hands went out in a vaguely measuring gesture, ". . . a limit."

Judge Massie rubbed the fringe of hair, and sighed. "What for do you reckon he stole the body? It was already gone when the call to Mrs. Hardecker was put through like she says at four o'clock. Emery was here then."

"Gentlemen," Doctor Carlyle stood up as if he would conclude his lecture, "all this presupposes that Dr. Jensen is dead, and that there is a murderer. Last night I was informed that Dr. Jensen had been murdered, and he was not. Perhaps . . ."

"He's dead all right." The Judge hesitated. "Otherwise, how'm I gonna trust my own eyes agin? if we could jess establish the times closer . . . when the body was stolen."

"Dear me . . . how stupid . . . but of course. *I* can." Dr. Carlyle tapped his rumpled vest. "Of course I can," he hesitated, "but not much. I arrived at four minutes to four, and I'm a very precise man. Four minutes to four, and there was no body in here then."

Judge Massie nodded. "Been waitin' fer that. Been wond'rin' when you'd bring that up. An' how come you should be here at all?"

"Dear me," Dr. Carlyle fumbled with the string of his pince-nez and stammered, "o-oh m-my. All this talk has just reminded me."

"Well, Doc, why'd you come?"

"I resent that tone, Judge Massie."

"Git off'n yore high horse, Doc. Jess tell me why you come here to see me."

"Why, I didn't come here to see you at all. I came here to murder Dr. Jensen!"

9

A CORPSE GOES DRIVING

Judge Massie closed his mild blue eyes for an instant, and exhaled a soft "oof." He fingered his upper left waistcoat pocket and produced one of his long, crooked, black and villainous stogies. He bit off the end carefully and lit it with deliberation. He whuffed out a dense cloud of smoke and then swept it away with his hand. "That's downright astonishin', Doc. So you come here to murder Dr. Jensen?"

Carlyle adjusted his glasses and stared at the Judge. "Yes. Why not?"

Judge Massie coughed on his smoke and peered over the steel rims of his spectacles at the little doc. "Why not? Off hand I'd say there's a couple o' good reasons agin it. Fust off, murder is apt to be onhealthy fer the victim, an' second, it's jess as apt to be onhealthy fer the murderer. Ain't feelin' onhealthy, are you? Sposin' you jess tell us why you come here to murder Dr. Jensen."

"Really, Mr. . . . er . . . Judge Massie . . . that's a very personal question."

Judge Massie hit heavily into the stogie. "Figger the victim would think murder was right pussonal. Why did you come here to murder Dr. Jensen?" The Judge emphasized each word.

Dr. Carlyle smiled guilelessly. "Because I heard he was here, and it seemed quite convenient."

"Oh, my sainted Aunt Mehitable's purple hat!" Judge Massie leaned forward from the comfort of his big chair, a rare act, and rested fat elbows on the desk. He aimed the stogie at the little doc. "So you wanta play games?"

"I assure you, Judge Massie, I am rarely frivolous."

"An' neither is murder, Doc. But mebbe I'll jess ask questions, an' you answer 'em. Fust off, how did you know Jensen was here?"

The little doctor considered that a moment. "One of the attendants at the court where I went to see about my divorce told me."

Deedie murmured in surprise, "Not you and Amy?"

"Er . . . ah . . . yes. You see, last night, when Amy heard of Dr. Jensen's death, she, well, rather in hurt and desperation, I suppose—Amy's quite temperamental—she told me of their . . . ahem . . . their . . . er . . ." He flushed deeply, and the Judge took pity on him.

"We already heared o' that, Doc, so's no need to repeat what's best fergot." He glanced over the little doc's immaculate person. "How'd you figger on killin' him? Got a gun?"

"Gun?" The doctor looked shocked. "Oh, dear me, no. Guns make me quite nervous."

Judge Massie snorted. "Reckon it would. But how'd you expect to kill him? With a knife?"

Dr. Carlyle looked puzzled. "You know, I hadn't quite got around to methods. I mean, I had the primitive impulse, and . . ."

Judge Massie concealed his smile behind a cloud of smoke. "You ain't 'xactly got the look of a man burnin' with primitive passions, Doc."

The little doctor smiled weakly. "I dare say I do not give the appearance of virile emotions, but I assure you . . . However, I did not get the opportunity for exercising them. Someone else seems to have murdered him first. You know, it seems to have got to be a habit with someone. First, last night, and now, today—and both times he gets up and walks away." Dr. Carlyle dragged at the loose ends of his straggling mustache. "It gets discouraging."

"Mebbe," Judge Massie grunted, "only this here time he didn't git up an' walk away. He was dragged, an' I'm a natchelly suspicious ol' codger, an' I'm wonderin' if mebbe it wasn't you that dragged him."

"If it *weren't you*," corrected the little doc, and then consulted his little chart. Quite impersonally he remarked, "Dear me, I could have done it. Except, of course, I should have run into the person who was really doing it had I been here when it was being done . . . if you see what I mean?" He queried the Judge through those twinkling glasses of his.

Judge Massie's mouth twitched, his craggy eyebrows wriggled with suppressed amusement. "It sure sounds reasonable the way you put it, an' somewhat on the riddle side, too, like you was askin' *How old is Ann?,* an' I'm afeared the p'lice would want a stronger alibi than that."

Dr. Carlyle's eyebrows went up in surprise. "But the police don't want an alibi. In fact, it's quite apparent that they don't want anything to do with the case. But . . ." the doctor's eyebrows wiggled with excitement, "but I do have an alibi. Quite a good one, I should think." He began to pat himself all across the chest and around his pockets, murmuring, "Bless me . . . bless me . . ."

Judge Massie eased himself back into the comfort of his chair and eyed the doctor as if he were something recently added to the aquarium. "Make a habit o' carryin' yore alibis in yore pocket?"

"Eh?" The little doc was peering down into his pockets as if they were gopher holes. "Ah, here it is." Triumphantly he flourished a tattered, crumpled piece of paper.

Judge Massie reached for it. "A parkin' ticket." He smoothed it against the edge of the desk. "Yup, a parkin' ticket."

"You see, I was parking my car to come up here. I saw what appeared to be quite an adequate space, and parked there. Unfortunately, there was a fire plug on the curb. The officer and I had quite an altercation which ended in my receiving that. I believe there is a time written on it—three-forty-five. I then had to park my car and come up here. Under our schedule, that would not allow time for me . . ."

"Yup." Judge Massie slid the paper across the desk. "Didn't figger you was a likely suspect."

Deedie scrambled to her feet. "I hate every one of you . . . you, just sitting around here playing with this as if it were a game

of cards or . . . or a railroad timetable. Don't you realize what
this means to my sister? She's somewhere eating her heart out
over this monstrous thing Dr. Jensen has done to her . . . and if
he's dead, then she's the one that has a right to decide what's to
be done."

Judge Massie looked up mildly over the rims of his spectacles.
"Miss Deedie, ain't you fergittin' the possibility that mebbe she
knows an' has already decided what's to be done . . . an' done it?"

Deedie started to strike him, and then froze—except her face
which flashed from incredulous anger to terrible, searing doubt,
and then to childish agony. "Oh, *no!*" She slumped into her chair,
covering her face with her hands. Willie tucked a miraculously
clean handkerchief into one clutching fist, and she dabbed at her
eyes. "You can't mean it! You can't. She didn't. I know she didn't
kill him."

Willie was patting her shoulder and looking accusingly at the
Judge.

"Mought help a little effen you'll git a good cry out'n yore
system. An' mebbe you'd like to know I don't think she did, but
ain't a pusson I know ever had a better excuse fer killin' another."

She shook off Willie's consoling pats and glared at the Judge.
"You can say *that?* And not even *know* he's dead. You can't . . .
and even if you do know it, you can't prove anything, because
the body is gone."

Judge Massie regarded her for a moment in silence, and then
heaved a deep but unsatisfactory sigh. "That there is jess what
the murderer would think, if not say."

That held her in horrid fascination while the Judge picked up
the phone and called a number.

Deedie walked slowly toward him. "Do you think I did it?
You do, don't you? And suppose I did? Suppose I picked up that
gun and shot him instead of crying like a ninny. Suppose I ran
out and hid, and then came back and put on an act for you."

Judge Massie regarded her calmly over the lip of the telephone. "That's jess precisely what I been 'sposin'. Hello. Gimme
Judge Ames' office . . ." He turned back to the girl. "But I've also
been wond'rin' effen you had strength enough to carry him out—

and the time to do it. Oh, hello Bill, this here is Jim Massie. Is Mrs. Jensen with you? No? . . . No, nothin' important . . . Oh, yes, of course . . . Of course we'll fight that there black-hearted rascal's charges. Never did like that there Jensen, noways . . . No, ain't a thing to fear. Certainly could make things look awkward, but he was here in my office 'bout half-hour ago, an' somethin' come up that'll change things . . . Oh, yes, definitely, Bill. An' she's not there? Haven't seen her since she got the news o' the sanity commission? . . . So long, Bill." He clattered the phone into its cradle. "She didn't go to see Bill. Mebbe we better go out to the house."

Dr. Carlyle spoke up. "My car is downstairs, and I live out that way; perhaps I could drive you? No trouble . . ."

"That's sweet of you." Deedie accepted the invitation, and the four walked down to the doctor's car, a conservative sedan.

Willie looked it over. "We got a rattle-trap . . ." The Judge's car was a sore point with Willie.

"Shall I drive?" Deedie offered, remembering the doctor's absent-mindedness.

"Dear me, that's what Amy always says, and I haven't had an accident yet." He climbed under the wheel and started with a roar and a jerk, then settled to a placid twenty.

The little doc swung the sedan into the long drive, narrowly missing the rhododendron bush, and drew up under the *porte cochere* just as Mrs. Hardecker came around the corner of the house. She waved briefly and hurried into the open French window, a bunch of bronze gladioli clasped in one arm.

Judge Massie nodded toward her. "Right perty woman when she's got her color up an' a sparkle in her eye. An' them flowers help; mighty perty shade."

Willie, who had been surreptitiously smoothing his rowdy hair, leaped out and offered his hand to Deedie who, after a startled glance, accepted it with a ravishing smile. And Willie was her squire for life . . . or at least until something blonde and blue-eyed should smile at him across a school desk.

Deedie called out to Mrs. Hardecker, "Is Sylvia home?"

The dark, intense face appeared again at the French window. "I wouldn't know; I've been out gathering flowers. Is Dr. Jensen all right?"

Judge Massie, who was struggling to get his bulk through the car door, popped himself out suddenly. "So fer as I know. Anything s'posed to be wrong with him?"

The dark brows drew together in a frown. "Well, sir, your voice sounded rather queer—hesitant, sort of—over the phone. When I asked for Dr. Jensen about the papers. I never did find them."

"Don't reckon he'll be needin' 'em. Probably twarn't important, or he'da called back. Or did he?"

"Why, not that I know of; but I've been out in the garden." Mrs. Hardecker returned to her flowers in the library, and Deedie went to look for Sylvia.

In a few moments she returned to report that none of the servants had seen Mrs. Jensen, and Deedie frowned. "I don't like it."

"Screwin' up yore face ain't doin' nobody a mite o' good. Not that I'm askin' fer a Pollyanna, but there's a heap o' very good reasons why she mought not be here. Mebbe she went to buy a hat. Heared tell effen a woman was plumb downhearted, warn't nothin' like a new hat to cheer her up."

Deedie smiled wryly. "I'd need a dozen new hats and an evening gown to cheer me up right now." She perched on the arm of the Judge's chair. He had, with his unerring instinct, picked the most comfortable chair in the room and was lounging back in it.

"Reckon we mought as well face facks, Deedie. We know fer certain-sure that Jensen is dead. What we need now is more facks, to sorta round out the picture."

Deedie clasped her hands around one knee and swung her foot in an excellent imitation of nonchalance. "Why? Isn't this the best way? He's gone. Nobody knows where, or how, or cares . . . except that he's gone."

Dr. Carlyle fidgeted. "My dear, that's a very callous attitude, I'm sure."

Deedie whirled in her chair. "Callous attitude! He's tried to wreck my sister's life. He's tried to steal my money. He's done you the nastiest trick . . ." One hand clapped over her mouth, and she shook her head. She spoke, her voice muffled by her hand. "I'm sorry; I shouldn't have said that." She took her hand away and swung around so that she sat on the arm facing the Judge. "You see the mess he'd have made of our lives if he had lived. Isn't it better this way? Think of my sister."

Judge Massie took her shoulders in rough affection. "Child, that's jess what I am thinkin' of, an' what the p'lice are gonna say when they find the body . . . an' I'm figgerin' they will. They ain't fools, though mebbe I do call Emery that ev'y now'n then. But supposin' they don't find the body. They're gonna find out he's missin', sooner or later, an' they'll start askin' questions an' some of 'em will be mighty awkward to answer. Fust off, somebody'll wonder why he ain't continuin' this here lunacy hearin', an' that'll raise some all-fired unpleasant questions. An' then they'll recommember I said he was dead; an' then they'll recommember yore sister said she killed him the night before, only he warn't dead; an' they'll add them things up an' the answer won't be pretty."

"Quite so, quite so." Dr. Carlyle edged himself into the conversation. "May I suggest that we attempt to discover some clue to the person who might wish to do away with Dr. Jensen—other than myself, of course, and the two young ladies."

Willie shook his head. "It's gangsters. I'll bet they took him for a ride, and gave him the works."

"Willie has seen too many movies." Judge Massie shook his leonine head. "Don't fit the facks, son. Nup, twarn't gangsters. They wouldn'ta cornered him like that an' shot him down with jess one bullet; that is, 'cordin' to the best gangster standards I'm familiar with. We gotta figger out somethin' else, less'n, o' course, we want to corn-sider the possibility that Sylvia . . ."

"She didn't!" Deedie leapt to her feet. "I know she didn't! You've got to do something . . . anything."

Judge Massie nodded. "That there is a mite different tune." He held up one plump hand and checked on his fingers, "Fust, we gotta find out all we kin about Jensen. Next we gotta look up his case records, his patients, where'd he see 'em, what he treated 'em fer."

"His laboratory and office are right here. His lab is upstairs, between his room and Sylvia's. When Sylvia had the house done over after Father's death she fixed up the room adjoining her bedroom and bath as a laboratory. It used to be a store room opening into the hall, but she had that door plastered over and a new one cut into his bedroom. But the office is entirely separate. Father built it for conferences. He sometimes met queer people he didn't want to have us know socially, so he built a little apartment wing off the library. I suppose most of Dr. Jensen's records are there. Would you like to see them?"

At the Judge's nod Deedie led them across the living room and down the great hall where a door opposite the stairs led into the library. Mrs. Hardecker was trying a vase of the bronze gladioli against the mulberry drapes. Deedie walked swiftly across the room to a door concealed behind a portiere.

Mrs. Hardecker called out sharply and scurried across the room, "The doctor isn't in there. He doesn't allow anybody in his office when he isn't there."

"Ann," Deedie spoke brusquely, "I'd rather you didn't speak to guests that way."

Mrs. Hardecker stubbornly barred the way to the door. "He doesn't let anybody in there and you know it, Miss Deedie."

Judge Massie touched the woman's arm and she turned to face him. "Mrs. Hardecker, Dr. Jensen is dead. We're aimin' to look after his effects. As his wife's attorney, I have that right."

"Dead?" She frowned at him, puzzled. "But you didn't say anything when I asked how he was just now . . . and you didn't say anything when I called your office."

"An' we wouldn't be sayin' anything now, on'y you won't let us git into his office. Course, effen you want to git technical, we could git the p'lice, an' a warrant."

The gaunt woman stood aside, more as if to think it over than as a gesture to let them through. "It's all very queer . . ." She almost mumbled it, ". . . all very queer."

Judge Massie started on through the door. "When we git through here I reckon we'd better look over his laboratory. Mebbe we'll find some evidence there, though 'tain't likely . . . nor here neither. Be mostly records, I reckon. Howsomever, we kin gather 'em up an' put 'em in a safe. There is a safe, ain't there? Recommember yore paw had a fine one."

"It's still here." Deedie ushered them into a lavishly furnished apartment and pointed out a business-like filing cabinet in a small office cubicle. "He was a specialist in nervous disorders," explained Deedie with a sniff, "and I imagine most of his pa- tients—women—liked to have nerves so they could get him to hold their hands."

"Kinda reversin' yore opinion, ain't you?" inquired the Judge.

"My eyes have been opened. I've been a terrible fool."

"Wellll," commented Judge Massie, "I been reservin' judg- ment on that. An' I jess 'bout decided mebbe when comes a time a body admits mebbe they're a fool, that there is jess 'bout time they quit bein' one. Willie, lock up that there filin' cabinet. We ain't got time to look now. We'll jess sorta mosey 'round, an' git the lay o' the land."

Willie resented being shut away even temporarily from his new idol, but he set to work. Deedie led the Judge through the apartment wing. "This is his reception room."

Judge Massie peered at the taffeta curtains and low divans with distaste. "Reckon ol' Sylvester would have a rip-snortin' fit effen he could see them doo-dads. Don't seem moral."

"Probably weren't intended to be, Judge," and Deedie escort- ed them through the rest of the lavishly furnished suite and back to where Willie was finishing his job of locking up the filing cases.

"Reckon I'll take charge o' the key. That there stuff is a mite bulky fer the safe. An' now let's see this here laboratory, though I cain't figger what a psychiatrist does in a laboratory."

Dr. Carlyle, eager to help, volunteered the information. "Dr. Jensen was working in sensory perception and reaction. He had some very fine machinery, very delicate recording instruments, a high-speed camera, and a most intricate spectroscope, quite the latest thing. I've envied him that spectroscope."

At the door of Jensen's room Deedie held back. "I don't like to go in there, but I suppose I must. He never allowed anyone in there." With reluctance she pushed open the door and pointed.

"There, that door on the right—nearest us. The one near the window leads through the connecting bath to Sylvia's room."

Judge Massie waddled across the room, Willie and Carlyle at his heels. He pushed open the door Deedie had pointed out and reached in to fumble for the light switch. The light clicked on.

"Land o' Goshen!" Judge Massie held the other two back with massive arms. "I never see sech a sight. Somebody sure wrecked this here laboratory."

Dr. Carlyle whimpered. "The spectroscope, its smashed. Everything is ruined. Oh, what wanton destruction!"

Just at that moment the telephone shrilled.

Deedie pointed out the instrument, and Willie picked it up reluctantly. It was Emery. Willie handed the sputtering telephone to the Judge with relief.

Emery was almost gleeful. "You can be glad I had that Wolfe trailing you all afternoon, Judge."

"I been wond'rin' what that truck was, follerin' us. What you so set up about?"

"Listen, Judge, and be glad you ain't in on this. Wolfe just reported you safely out of it, so that's that, but your little playmate won't fool anybody any more. Yeah, and this is official! Jensen was just killed in a motor accident about fifteen minutes ago!"

10
METHOD OF MADNESS

Judge Massie clutched the telephone closer. "Automobile accident? Joseph Anthony Emery, you ain't a drinkin' man or I'd swear I could smell it from here. Jensen killed in an automobile accident?"

"Yeah, and it's official this time: He was killed when his car went through that flimsy guard rail at the Edgewater quarry—the one your friend Purdett's been writing editorials about. A state trooper just reported it. They had orders to watch the place, and he'd just passed it about fifteen minutes before and the fence was all right. When he went by again it was broken, and he investigated. He saw the wreck in about five feet of water, and fished up the body. He's identified him by his driver's permit and insurance cards. What I called about is to ask somebody from the house to go down to the morgue and identify him."

"Morgue?" Judge Massie regarded the telephone with distaste, and then clapped it back to his ear.

"Yeah. Even if a state trooper did find him, the quarry's still in the city limits, so he sent the body to the morgue. Get some member of the family to go down and identify him officially, and we'll turn over the body to 'em. And send Wolfe along, will you, Judge? I need all the men I can get on this other case—the actor-fellow murder."

"Heared tell o' that. Seems the *Chronicle* interviewed the corpse . . ."

"Damn the *Chronicle*. That damned Dutchman, Eddie Ertz, took a candid camera shot of the corpse and published it, and

113

now nearly every damned person in town has been down to the morgue to get a look at him. Well, get Wolfe off your tail and send him along."

Judge Massie clucked forlornly. "Joe, it's been nigh onto fifteen years since I had a p'lice escort, an' I'd sure hate to give this'n up. Howsomever . . ." Slowly Judge Massie lowered the phone to its cradle and stared at it.

Deedie clutched his arm. "Judge . . . Judge . . . Is it true? Is it really true that Dr. Jensen was just killed in a motor accident?"

Judge Massie turned slowly. "Reckon so. Reckon that there really was Emery. Warn't a soul but Emery woulda knowed that was Charlie Wolfe follerin' us out here, an' Joe Emery don't make useless jokes. An' he don't call off his shadows less'n he's sure."

Willie glanced delightedly behind him, as if he expected to see a full set of black whiskers. "Dees, were we really follered? By a real detective? Gosh!"

"Willie, effen yore eyes hadn'ta been glued on someone I could name, you couldn'ta missed him—big as a Mack truck an' jess about half as smart."

Deedie tugged at the Judge's sleeve. "But if he was killed in an automobile accident . . . don't you see . . . oh, it's marvelous! It's wonderful! I feel so free . . . I could kiss you . . . I could . . ."

"Jess let it go at kissin'—an' you'd better reserve that 'til there ain't so much audience. Howsomever, I cain't see that Dr. Jensen would figger it's so marvelous—but I reckon he didn't have much say in the matter."

Deedie pirouetted around the room and back to the Judge. "But don't you see . . ." She was suddenly solemn, like a child stopped at play by the schoolteacher. "Don't you see, we don't have to worry about Sylvia . . . she didn't kill him. It was an accident."

Judge Massie nodded slowly. "Thought mebbe that was eatin' yore heart out. 'Fraid all along yore sister done it . . . even when you was denyin' it loudest, warn't you?"

"I suppose I was, Judge, and yet I knew she didn't. She couldn't. She is too sweet, too gentle. Oh, she just couldn't!"

"Yet you went on doubtin' right up to jess now," reminded the Judge gently.

"Things did look awfully black, Judge. Oh, I do hope she comes in soon. It may be a shock, but she'll be so much better off. Oh, I'm so glad he's out of the way . . . and that it was an accident . . . such a fortunate accident."

Judge Massie clicked open his ancient timepiece. "Five-ten. Fifteen minutes ago would be four-fifty-five. Let's see. You'n Willie an' the little doc an' me were in the doctor's office then. Reckon that counts us out. Wonder effen we could fix it any closer'n that? The trooper went by fust time about four-thirty-five, an' the fence was all right. Guess that fixes the limits o' this here *fortunate* accident."

"That would just about give him time to leave your office and phone Mrs. Hardecker," commented the little doc timidly, "and then drive out to the Edgewater quarry."

"Plumb fergot Mrs. Hardecker. She was here."

"I don't like that woman," announced Deedie flatly. "Sylvia only keeps her on because of her son. He's an invalid, or something."

"Tutt, my dear, tutt. Nobody ever likes a housekeeper." Dr. Carlyle shook his head solemnly. "I've been afraid of mine for ten years, and I'm blessed if I know how to fire her."

Judge Massie stowed his watch away, and moved deliberately toward the laboratory door. "Won't be gittin' Jensen ready fer anybody to see fer an hour, mebbe more. Reckon we mought as well git at this here mess."

The little doc craned his head between the door jamb and the Judge's broad back. "Dear me, such vandalism! Oh, dear, that beautiful spectroscope, utterly ruined. Oh, dear me." He pushed by the Judge and knelt among the wreckage, touching the black enameled machine with almost maternal care.

Nearby lay a bent and battered home movie projector, once a very fine, expensive machine, and around that lay the glittering of shattered retorts and broken test tubes. Other intricate machines lay at grotesque angles around the room, and over and under and across it all, like streamers of black confetti, were hundreds of feet of home movie film. Dr. Carlyle shook his head sadly and wrenched his neck around to look up at the Judge. "It's a crime—a miserable, devilish crime." He caught up a strand of film, peering through the minute pictures. "Those precious experiments of his! Oh, dear, whoever could have done it?"

"Jess what I'd like to know," Judge Massie hauled the little doc to his feet with a tug at his arm, "an' what I'm aimin' to find out. Deedie, reckon you could round up the servants? Got some questions I'm jess bustin' to ask."

"But Judge," began Deedie, "it was an accident."

Judge Massie jerked a thumb over his fat shoulder. "Right pow'ful accident that come 'long an' happened in there. Aim to find out the name o' that accident."

"Oh, that." Deedie dismissed it with a shrug. "Certainly. I'll have Mrs. Hardecker round them up. Where do you want to talk to them?"

"Noticed a right comfortable lookin' cheer in the library . . ."

Judge Massie usurped the most comfortable chair. "There's sech a lot o' me that when I gits oncomfortable I'm awful oncomfortable." He looked vainly for a handy drawer into which to slip his feet, and gave it up with a sigh. He turned to Mrs. Hardecker. "Let's git yore story fust, an' then take the others as they come. Been in Dr. Jensen's room today?"

Mrs. Hardecker sat straight in her chair. "No, sir. Esther tends to the doctor's and Miss Sylvia's rooms. I seldom go there except to check up about once a week, Mondays as a rule."

"Anybody come to the house today?"

"I wouldn't know, sir. Benson might. I checked supplies with cook until eleven. Then I went to market—I do most of the ordering direct—and then came home to lunch. After lunch I ran over the accounts. Cook has been complaining of missing things, sir, but she always does. About four Dr. Jensen called up—you'll remember I called your office—and then I went into the garden for flowers. You came about then, sir, with the others, and went into the doctor's office. What you told me knocked me all of a heap. I just sat and waited for you, sir, to see that no one else would come in whilst you were searching for . . . whatever you were searching for." She hesitated. "I think that's all. And he wasn't dead at all," she shook her head slowly, "wasn't dead at all. It's very queer, isn't it?"

"Right peculiar, ma'am, right peculiar. Reckon we kin talk to this here Esther?"

Mrs. Hardecker produced Esther, a plump girl with tendencies toward giggling.

"Howdy, Esther. Didn't know you was workin' here." The Judge waved her to a chair. "How's Bill?"

Esther eased herself into the carved oak chair with caution and glanced quickly around at Deedie, and then back to the Judge. "He's been doin' fine since you got him that job at the repair shop. He ain't been in trouble once since."

"Now, Esther, this ain't a court. We're jess tryin' to find out what happened in this here house; who come in, an' who went out. See anybody as shouldn'ta been here?"

Esther considered that. "I wouldn't, sir. I had five rooms to do besides Mrs. Jensen's and the doctor's."

"Clean up the laboratory?" Judge Massie asked it mildly, but watched her from under shaggy brows.

"Oh, no. Nobody's allowed to touch anything in there. The doctor tended to that himself."

Judge Massie regarded his tented fingertips, watched the twiddling of his thumbs. "Don't reckon you'da noticed any glass when you were cleaning Miz Jensen's room?"

"Now, that's funny, Judge, 'cause I did. From Mrs. Jensen's boudoir lamp, it was. The garbage men complained when they found the rest of it, along with Chu Chin's body."

Dr. Carlyle, who had followed the questioning with interest, coughed. "Dear me. Chu Chin dead? That will distress Amy." He turned to the Judge. "She gave him to Sylvia. I tried to explain to her that Chu Chin is a Chinese name and Pomeranians are . . ."

Judge Massie was waving away the girl, and didn't hear the explanation of what Pomeranians are—if anything other than Pomeranians. The other three housemaids could add nothing. They had done their chores and retired to the servant's wing at the back. Wilks, the gardener, had little to say and less to add, and that surlily, while he eyed the flamboyant gladioli with a distaste that said such things weren't for the house.

Benson, the butler, could recall no one who might have called, and descended so far from his vast and pontifical dignity as to admit having corns that required occasional resting. "Sometimes my feet hurt me fair to kill, sir, so I wasn't by the door the entire day, sir."

To which the Judge nodded in sympathy. "Me, I got bunions . . ."

Mrs. Meaney, who presided over the kitchen and a platoon of lesser help, flatly denied knowledge of anything and demanded immediate release, as the angels-on-horseback required her undivided attention or there would be the devil to pay. With this quaint bit of contradiction, she huffily withdrew. Her assistants were no more helpful beyond corroborating the story of the finding of Chu Chin and the lamp, although one gangling youth reluctantly admitted sneaking out back for a smoke.

This was confirmed by Leonard, one of the chauffeurs, who had spoken to him from the upper window of the garage, cautioning him against smoking near the gas tank. He explained to the Judge. "We was playing a friendly-like game of poker, me and Ed and Forbes, here, and the club steward from across the road."

Judge Massie glanced over the three smartly uniformed men. "Which one o' you drove Miz Jensen to town this mornin'?"

Leonard twisted his cap. "Reckon you got a good reason for asking, Judge, or Miss Storme wouldn't allow it and I wouldn't say otherwise. Mrs. Jensen came out of the big house mad as hops—about the little dog, I expect, sir—and took the roadster. The doctor came out a little later and asked for it. Ed told him Mrs. Jensen took it, and asked if he could drive him in, but the doctor wanted to drive himself and took the light Lincoln."

"Were you in the garage last night—in yore rooms over it, I reckon I should say?"

"No, sir. Leastwise, I wasn't. I got a wife in town and I stays with her when I can. Mrs. Jensen give us the evening off, though it was Wednesday. Ed and Forbes ain't married, but they sometimes spends the night out, sorta." He flushed uncomfortably, and the other two shifted nervously and nodded.

Judge Massie errumphed, and then apologized in advance with a glance at Deedie. "Ever take the doctor on a . . . a night out?"

All three shook their heads and left Leonard to act as spokesman. "If he was going on a night out he most generally took the light Lincoln and drove himself. He was very discreet, the doctor was. But he liked the ladies . . . begging your pardon, Miss Deedie."

"Reckon you wouldn't know any of these . . . er . . . ladies?"

"If you mean *know* 'em, well then, it's no; but if you mean do we know *who* they are, well, then it's no, too—but we could maybe guess pretty good: the ladies that come to his office. He had mostly ladies that come there, except some of the bums. He did experiments, sir . . ."

Dr. Carlyle interpreted that for the Judge. "You see, Dr. Jensen was studying time-reactions—emotional reactions to various stimuli. He had a new hypothesis that he thought would upset the current theory of emotion. I can't say I agree with him wholly, but perhaps I am reactionary. However, he was making some progress, and he used some rather odd subjects occasionally—men from the Union Mission, beggars, anyone whom he could persuade to come for a dollar or two. On occasions he used students from my classes at the university. Some of his slow-motion pictures quite possibly could be interpreted to indicate that time-reaction was secondary to emotional response. He made this particularly clear through the relationship of cardiographic records, photographed simultaneously with the subject. I'm of the opinion he relied too much on fear as a stimulus, although he occasionally used the sex impulse. Of course, fear is perhaps the easiest reaction to induce and record."

Judge Massie jerked a thumb upward. "That would be the film we seen." He turned to the chauffeurs. "Reckon you'd notice effen any o' these men come back recently . . . or sorta hung around?"

Leonard shook his head. "Most of 'em seemed glad to get away . . . all except the 'queer one'. He come back pretty reg'lar."

"Queer one? Reckon most of 'em were a mite queer."

"That they were, sir, but this one especial; though come to think of it, I can't jest lay my mind on what it was." He appealed to the others and then went on, "I guess it was the way he changed. Sloppy when he first came, and he was shabby—but most of 'em were. Later on he sorta perked up and dressed decent. But the really queer part was his face. It sorta got better looking—straightened out, if you know what I mean." He appealed to Ed.

Ed was more certain. "It was mostly his nose, sir, and his mouth, and I guess his eyes. They got more sorted out, sir, and matched his face better, instead of being loose and sloppy-looking."

Dr. Carlyle nodded. "Sounds very much like cretinism. Doubtless Dr. Jensen was treating him with glandular extracts." He questioned the chauffeur. "Did you notice his walk? Was it first uncertain and shambling, and gradually became progressively firmer and steadier?"

The chauffeurs nodded general agreement, and Leonard said, "In a way we did. And after a time he got so he'd imitate the doctor—his walk, you know, and his gestures, and even, sometimes, his expressions. It was kinda pitiful-like, sir, if you know what I mean, him being so grateful and hero-worshipping. We figgered maybe the doctor had got him off liquor. Ed and me said it was the first decent thing the doctor had done." He looked startled and apologized to Deedie. "I hope you don't think we discuss the family, Miss."

Deedie nodded wearily. "I dare say you know us better than we know each other." She frowned. "This man who stayed on—is that recent? I don't know of anyone who . . ."

"I don't think you was meant to, Miss. The doctor was sort of secret about him. I don't think anybody knew." Leonard saluted and started to leave.

Judge Massie halted him with a gesture. "Now this here 'queer one', you say he come back reg'lar-like. Seen him today, maybe?"

"Not today, sir, not that I recall. He's been staying nights, lately, but I don't . . ."

Mrs. Hardecker sat forward in her chair. "Leonard, what's this? Staying nights? How can you be sure?" She explained hastily to the Judge, "I think I would have known . . . but, of course, the doctor may have . . . I mean, I don't know how anyone could stay all night without my knowing it."

"Well, ma'am, me and Ed saw him in the garden a couple of times along about six, or maybe earlier. Mornings, I mean. I'm a light sleeper and the milk truck mostly wakes me up. We didn't say anything, figgering the doctor didn't want us to know."

Mrs. Hardecker nodded. "I suppose you may be right, Leonard. Several times Mrs. Meaney has complained of things missing from the pantry but with the amount of food we keep on hand I was never really convinced that she knew. She rather likes to complain."

The Judge signaled the men to go and they left hurriedly, edging each other out the door. Judge Massie settled back in his chair. He puffed out his cheeks and exploded a little "whoof" through babyish lips. "On'y decent thing the doctor ever did. That there is a mighty poor epitaph fer a man jess dead." He sat forward. "That cover everybody? Ain't the doctor got somebody to greet the customers?"

Deedie nodded. "Miss Quiller—but I doubt if she could tell you more than what those rooms and the chauffeurs already have—that Fred was a beast. Besides, she's gone. He dismissed her when she came this morning."

"This mornin'? Got her riled up a bit, didn't it?"

Deedie smiled. "I don't think so. He paid her a month's salary in advance in place of notice. Besides, I think she was relieved. At least she said she wouldn't have any more gruesome work to do. I could phone her to come over if you wish. She's a sweet little thing."

"Mebbe we better . . ." The Judge crooked a finger at Willie, who hopped up with alacrity and all but came to attention. "You, Willie, had better call Emery an' tell him about the laboratory."

Some of Willie's enthusiasm vanished. "Aw, Jedge, that cop don't like me pretty good already, an' if I was to . . ."

"Figgered mebbe this would help square up that last. That's why I want you to do it. Use the extension in the hall."

Willie left, but without any noticeable buoyancy.

Judge Massie settled back in his chair. "Seems like we ain't learned nothin' 'cept practically anybody coulda got in an' out'n this house 'thout nobody seein' 'em. Dad-gumdest thing I ever run across."

Slowly the door between the library and Dr. Jensen's private wing opened and the portiere slithered back with a soft hiss. Judge Massie turned slowly. "Great Land o' Goshen, Mrs. Carlyle, you like to made me bite m' tongue. Don't never creep up behind a body like that. M'stomach jess tried to crawl up m' backbone."

Amy Carlyle stood in the doorway, clutching the edge of the portiere and smiling a little uncertainly. Then she saw the little doc and gave a low soft cry and ran toward him. "Frankie . . . Frankie . . ." She clung to him. She was a bare inch taller than the little doc but, being willowy and in an advanced stage of blondeness, it made her appear much taller and as if she had swooped down on him. He peered over her shoulder at the Judge, a puzzled frown frizzing up his stubby eyebrows and wrinkling his bland and dome-like brow

"Amelia, my dear, whatever is the trouble?" As if he had just seen her free hand, he clutched it and patted it clumsily.

"Frankie, Frankie! I've been such a fool—such a terrible, heartless fool," and, in spite of the gummy make-up on her lips and a certain Eleanor Duse gesturing, she sounded sincere. "I came over to leave this key." She flung the thing she had clutched across the room, and it tinkled against the glass of the French window. "I never want to see it again . . . or him." She caught Dr. Carlyle's hand in both of hers and held it tight. "Please, Frankie, don't hate me. I never meant to hurt you, I really didn't. Oh, I've been a fool, but I know better now." She dropped into the chair the little doc had leapt from to meet her onslaught, and sat with bowed head. The little doctor just stood looking stupidly down at her.

Finally he smiled, first a wispy, thin shred of a smile that gradually spread over his whole pink little face. "Amelia, Amelia! Do you mean we . . . I mean . . . can we . . . start . . . Oh, my poor Amelia, how you've suffered." The little doc knelt at her feet, though he must have known that it made him look like a very badly stuffed rabbit. "My poor Amelia, I never meant to hurt you."

Judge Massie blew his nose very firmly into a large snowy handkerchief, and looked at Deedie. "Don't know's I've seen a man in years as could do sech a stupid thing—and be so damn good and gallant at it." The Judge waved Deedie and Mrs. Hardecker ahead of him as he started out of the room, but Mrs. Carlyle stopped them.

"No, don't go. I want you to share . . ." She caught the little doc's hand and clung to it, ". . . to share in a brand-new happiness." The woman was radiant, clutching the little doc and smiling through a moist soot of mascara and tears. "You never know quite how dear a thing is until you've lost it . . . and been fortunate enough to find it again. Oh, I could sing."

The little doc smiled uncertainly. "But Amelia, dear, you never could sing."

Amelia Carlyle flung back her blonde head and laughed, not shrilly, but with fine, full enjoyment. "Frankie, you're priceless." Then she saw the bronze gladioli and rushed to them, smothering her face in them. "They're lovely . . . beautiful." She turned briefly to Deedie. "But I didn't know Sylvia had any Evans' Bronze Beauties. I could steal them." She scooped them up and then dropped them back in the vase and almost pirouetted back to the little doc, catching his hand and smiling at the others. She was the first to see Sylvia Jensen in the doorway.

"Sylvia, where have you been hiding those lovely, lovely Evans' Bronze Beauties? You must let me have some bulbs. I didn't know they were on the market yet."

Sylvia Jensen walked slowly into the room, not, as if she were tired, but more as if she were burdened with many thoughts. Her voice sounded strangely flat after Mrs. Carlyle's vivid tones.

"You'll have to ask Wilks. I haven't kept track of the garden for
months."

Deedie hurried to her and put her arm around the thin shoulders. "You must be tired, Sylvia, it's been a hard day. Perhaps
you'd better lie down."

Sylvia Jensen shook her head. "No. On the contrary. I've had
a very pleasant day. I've just seen Frederic."

"Just seen Frederic! But . . ." Deedie was aghast.

Sylvia nodded dully. "Oh, yes. I drove out the Edgewater
Road to our summer place—I wanted to be alone—and I saw
him. He had just been killed in a motor accident. I drove away
when I saw who it was. He was quite dead . . . quite." She smiled
wryly.

Judge Massie waddled across the room and caught her shoulders, forcing her to look at him. "Sylvia Jensen, were you on the
Edgewater Road this afternoon?" At her nod he groaned. "An' I
reckon not more'n half the county saw you. Of course. More'n
likely the State trooper took your license number, too. He did?
My sainted Aunt Mehitable's purple hat! Now we're in fer it."

"Why?" she asked with the simple, disconcerting directness
of a child.

Judge Massie stepped back and picked up his limp panama. He fanned himself slowly, regarding the woman. "Sylvia, I
knowed you sense you warn't more'n a twinkle in yore daddy's
eye, an' dad-gum if I kin figger yet whether you're plumb smart,
or jess plain, goshall-fired dense, sudden-like. When the p'lice
gits to figgerin' on how come Dr. Jensen got kilt today, they're
sure gonna recommember last night . . . an' somethin' that happened this afternoon ain't gonna help none. An' by the great
lord Harry! I jess sent Willie to phone fer the p'lice about that
wrecked laboratory."

Sylvia smiled calmly at him. "You needn't have. I wrecked the
laboratory. You see, I just found out this morning how he was
making me think I was crazy."

11
A CORPSE IS VERY DEAD

"Sylvia!" Deedie stared at her sister. "He was trying to do that? Make you think you were . . ." She shivered. "How ghastly!"

Judge Massie shook his head unbelievingly. "Sylvia Jensen, how come you wrecked the doctor's laboratory?"

"Dear me." Dr. Carlyle adjusted his glasses and peered at her. "Such wanton destruction! My dear Sylvia, don't tell me you smashed that spectroscope. It was a rare instrument." Then the little doc recalled the rest of her statement. "Driving you crazy? That's . . . why that's ridiculous, preposterous. I mean, after all, Frederic Jensen was a doctor."

Mrs. Hardecker shook her head. "He was a beast," and then, as if even this were more than she intended to say, she snapped her thin mouth shut.

Deedie took her place beside her sister defiantly. "Judge Massie, now is not the time to hound my sister. She's upset. She . . ."

Sylvia patted her shyly. "No, Judge Massie is right. If there is to be an investigation, I have so much to explain . . . so terribly much—things that even you don't know. But I've convinced myself that I'm not crazy, and that's something."

"Tutt, Sylvia, tutt-tutt. No one ever thought you were crazy. Perhaps a bit depressed lately, but not . . . er . . . no, of course not." The little doc glanced at the Judge. "But you seem to take this seriously."

"'Pears to me it is right serious. Come to think of it, it's generally right serious when a man dies sudden-like." He eyed Sylvia speculatively. "How come you figgered the doctor was usin' that there movie machine to make you think he was in the room?"

Sylvia glanced up in surprise. "So you guessed it! Well, perhaps I could show you more easily than I could tell you." She led the way out of the room and past Willie who was still trying to convince someone that he wanted to speak to Emery and no one else.

The Judge tapped his arm. "Leave it be," and Willie hung up.

Upstairs in the bedroom Sylvia Jensen pointed to the chaise longue. "I was lying there, remember that." She sat on the edge and looked at them plaintively. "For a long time I've wondered if I weren't going insane. Oh, yes, Deedie, I really did. But after last night, I could stop and think—I had to—think clearly, and remember details. I remembered looking up as Dr. Jensen came in, but he didn't look quite right—flat, or twisted, or something. At least, that's the way I remembered him . . . and I thought perhaps the distortion was inside me, the way you see things strangely through a fever. But he was solid and real and cold when I knelt beside him on the floor. . . and those two things didn't fit. He must have run very cold water over his hands just before I found him there, to trick me. But I didn't figure that out until I remembered I had seen him from here instead of from my bed. And a moving picture would look a little flatter from here than from the bed, from which I had usually seen him come and vanish. That's what made me look for it . . . for a place from which he could throw a natural-colored movie on the wall by that door. And I found it right above my bed, a small hole almost concealed by the tester. His laboratory is in the room at the head of my bed. I went in there, found the machine, and pulled it down."

"When did you do this, Sylvia?"

"I came directly home from your office. When I discovered Dr. Jensen was trying to put me in an insane asylum, I had to think . . . hard . . . search for something that would save me, and the motion picture idea came to me. You see, he never spoke during these 'visitations' and that set me thinking, but I couldn't be sure until I looked." She went toward the door. "I'll show you the machine he used. He was very clever with a camera."

"My dear," rebuked the little doc, "he made a science of the camera."

At the door of the laboratory she paused and stared at the wreckage. She raised startled eyes to the Judge's bland, round face. "But I didn't do this. I just pulled down the machine that was up there." She pointed to a shelf about eight feet up on the wall next to her room.

"Didn't figger it was you. This here is more calculatin', more purposeful, 'pears like."

"I really didn't destroy all that." She said it plaintively, like a child explaining some minor naughtiness that went disastrously wrong.

"Isn't it true, Mrs. Jensen, that you were so furious that you didn't know what you did?" Emery bulked large in the bedroom door. "Isn't it true that you hated him so much that you wrecked anything you could lay your hands on . . . and then you followed him out to Edgewater Road, and there you murdered him?"

Sylvia Jensen whirled. "No, no, no! It isn't true! I didn't wreck this room . . . and I didn't even know he'd gone out the Edgewater Road." She paused. "And I didn't know he was murdered!"

Judge Massie shoved himself between his client and the detective. "An' neither does Joe Emery."

Emery grinned sheepishly. "You're right, Judge. Sorry, Mrs. Jensen, but we police run up against some queer cases, and you've told us one phony story and the Judge here has told another, so you can't blame me if I try to get something by surprising you." He edged around the Judge's bulk and glanced into the laboratory. He whistled and scratched his chin. "Boy! that's a thorough job. Who done it?"

Judge Massie motioned them all to sit—but not until after he had selected the most comfortable chair. Emery and the little doc elected to stand while the Judge repeated the story of Mrs. Jensen's discovery of how she had been tricked into believing she had killed her husband, including even the discovery of the bullet hole and the shattered lamp, and her subsequent destruction of the projector.

Emery listened carefully. "What an old devil! We can check the bullet hole in a minute, but if what she," he jerked his thumb at Sylvia, "says is true then the picture of Jensen coming into the room ought to be in there, somewhere. Right? That ought to clinch it for Mrs. Jensen."

Sylvia and the Judge nodded. The others had listened in fascinated interest, Willie hunched forward, chin on knotted fists; Deedie with one foot curled under her; Mrs. Hardecker impassive and aloof, nodding from time to time. Only Amy Carlyle seemed restless.

"It's horrible . . . it's beastly! Has anyone a cigarette?"

Dr. Carlyle began patting himself in a rhythmic, unhurried order, and Amy smiled. "Please, someone get me one. Frank will never find his."

Emery offered her one and she accepted it gracefully, and acknowledged his offer of a light with a smile, casually provocative, as if she were so used to them they were automatic. Then Emery turned to the laboratory and stared at the mess. After his marriage to Mary Blosset he had become promptly blind to all other women. He groaned. "Guess we'll have to run all this stuff through a projector."

"All that? Look at every one of them?" Amy asked with an unbelieving catch in her voice.

Emery grunted. "Every damned one of 'em." He signaled Willie. "Might as well get started gathering 'em up. Give a hand."

Judge Massie glanced down at the ribbons of celluloid tangled through the wreckage. "Reckon I ain't so good at stoopin', but I'm pow'ful good at standin' by an' suggestin'. Look out!" he shouted at Amy. "Great Jumpin' Jehosaphat!"

Amy had knelt among the tangled skeins of film, and there was a flash and then the acrid smell of smoke billowing up. The room was full of smoke and flaming film. Amy stumbled from the laboratory, coughing and gasping. Emery, shoving Willie ahead of him, came out swearing. Judge Massie glanced into the swirling inferno of crackling flames and smells, counted hastily and then slammed the door shut.

Dr. Carlyle nodded approval. "It's quite fireproof, Jensen assured me. However, I think we'd better go elsewhere as the smoke is offensive." In the brief instant the door was open the bedroom had filled with the sickish-sweet odor of burnt film.

Emery bundled them all into the hall belligerently, and then he turned to face the group. "Who done that?"

Amy Carlyle caught the, little doc's arm and shivered. "I did. That cigarette . . . I don't know just what happened. I picked up a piece of film, meaning to help, and I guess my cigarette touched it. Anyway, it flared up, and I threw it down."

Emery thrust out his lantern jaw at her. "Right among my evidence! I ought to have you locked up."

"Come sir," Carlyle bridled and faced the big detective sergeant like a bantam rooster. "I defy you to lay a hand on my wife. She has confessed to what was, perhaps, an error in judgment, but it was intended as a gesture of aid, in no way meant to harm."

Amy looked at him gratefully, and tightened her grip on his arm, clinging to him with pathetic eagerness.

Emery almost laughed down at the little man. "Okay, Doc. I don't guess any great harm's done. We was just checking up on the lady's story about the picture. Even if it's never proved it won't hurt none, if she can show where the film was shown through the wall—and then it's only for her own satisfaction. I can't arrest a guy that's just driven over an eighty-foot cliff and killed himself. Oh . . ." He recollected his mission and became ponderously official. "Excuse me, ma'am. I came to inform you of the death of your husband."

Sylvia nodded smilingly at the detective. "Yes, I know. I was there and saw him."

Emery stared at her. "Well, why the . . . I mean, why didn't you . . . well . . . speak up? Identify him?"

Sylvia seemed to think that odd. "But the trooper already knew who he was, and he was arranging everything. You see, I wasn't interested, except to know that he was dead."

The detective started to say something and then nodded. "Yes ma'am. I guess if somebody had been doing the things he seems to have been doing to you, that's all I'd worry about too." He became almost pleading. "But you could come down and identify him, just to make it official."

Deedie spoke. "I'll go. I don't think Sylvia ought to be subjected to any more . . . any more of this than she has to. Judge Massie, you'll take me down, won't you? And Mrs. Hardecker can put Sylvia to bed." Sylvia nodded placid acceptance and Mrs. Hardecker took her arm.

Deedie hurried down the balcony. "I've simply got to fix up a bit."

Judge Massie looked after her. "Land o' Goshen, I ain't got my car here."

"I'll drive you down, both of you," volunteered the little doc, looking from the massive Judge to the equally massive Emery as if he were calculating the effect of their combined tonnage on his springs.

"Thanks . . . and I don't know but what I ought to pick up that young lady who started the fire. Say, where the devil did she get to?" Emery whirled to look back, for Amy had vanished.

Dr. Carlyle looked embarrassed. "She has gone to the . . . er . . . ahem . . . she will return in a moment. I think the fire is burned out by now." He scurried back into Jensen's room and returned in a moment. "It's out, but there's quite an odor."

Emery turned to the Judge. "Can you show me the bullet hole you were talking about? And you," to Mrs. Jensen, "the place where the doctor projected the films?"

The inspection satisfied the detective. "I'll send a man out here to get the bullet out and check it against the gun. Just a formality, Mrs. Jensen. By the way, where is the gun?"

Judge Massie errumphed. "Joe, it's kinda queer. I had that gun—Mrs. Jensen give it to me last night—but somebody stole it today . . . off'n my desk."

"Say, what is this, a run-around?" Emery started to be belligerent and then shrugged. "Oh, well. But if this was a murder case, Judge, I'd handle it a lot different, especially after last night and what I've heard today." They were walking slowly down the stairs, with the little doc hopping birdlike alongside the big detective. "Confidentially, that woman had the swellest reason for bumping off a guy I've ever heard of, and I'd come close to wanting to help her do it—unofficially, of course." He glanced over his shoulder. "Reckon it's a good thing that housekeeper's putting her to bed."

Judge Massie was very casual. "Anybody examined the body yet to see what caused his death?"

"After a tumble like that there isn't much difficulty in deciding how he died. Pick any of a dozen reasons: broken neck, fractured skull, internal injuries, crushed chest—any or all of 'em. No, we haven't yet. They'll look him over at the morgue. Haven't seen him myself. Been too busy with this actor fellow's case."

"That there would be your 'corpse without a murder'? Who is he? Ain't so many actors hereabouts."

"Don't know yet. Mebbe jest an amachoor out with somebody's sweetie and got bumped off. We'll work it out, though."

"Then how come you're so all-fired sure he's an actor?"

"Grease paint. They found some in his hair and the pores of his skin. He even had a little pellet of nose putty in his mouth."

"Dear me, how slovenly," commented the little doc, and then wilted under Emery's glare. "I meant the personal habits of the . . . er . . . actor." The little doc smiled. "Perhaps he wasn't a very good actor. I've often felt I could shoot some of the actors I've seen. I recall one who quite butchered *King Lear*. He . . ."

"Ain't the doc a sketch?" Emery was becoming jovial. He nudged the Judge in the ribs.

Somewhere downstairs a woman screamed shrilly and in terror!

Emery plunged on down the stairs, the Judge, for all his bulk, close behind—before the little doc was aware he had lost his audience. At the foot of the stairs Emery almost collided with Amy running from the library. He caught her in his arms. She pointed back.

"He glared at me. He . . . oh, what a horrible face!"

Emery thrust her on to the Judge and charged into the library. He glanced around, peered hurriedly behind the portieres and dashed back. "Where was he?"

Judge Massie had succeeded in disengaging himself from Amy's clutches and transferring her to the little doc. Amy shuddered. "He was looking in the window."

Emery jerked a thumb toward the library. "What was you doing in there? Weren't you going to the . . ." he coughed and reddened.

"I was in there. I mean, I just stopped to look at the gladioli. I was looking at them when I saw his face at the window."

Mrs. Hardecker, who had run in from the kitchen, sniffed, "Hysterics," and glared at Amy.

But Emery bellowed, "Outside!" and started for the front door. He had not quite reached it when it swung open as two figures reeled into the hall. Emery pulled them apart, yelped, "Wolfe," and let that one go and turned to the other. All the fight had gone out of the man. He dangled from Emery's arm and squirmed feebly.

"Wallaby Jo." Emery shook the man once more and set him on his rubbery legs. "What the hell are you doing here? Didn't know you'd taken to house-breaking!" He dragged the little man before Amy and forced his chin up. "This the man you saw?"

Amy laughed nervously. "Yes, but he doesn't look very dangerous now."

"He ain't dangerous—or didn't used to be. Frisk him, Wolfe."

The bedraggled little man protested more from habit than from sense of injury. "I ain't done nothin'. I was jus' lookin' in." The search of his shabby clothes continued with implacable thoroughness. Suddenly Wolfe thrust his hand deep in a pocket and pulled out a little Spanish automatic.

Sylvia, descending the stairs with Deedie behind her, stopped. "Why that's the gun. I . . . I mean it looks very much like the one I had . . . but the Judge has it now, so it couldn't be."

Judge Massie stroked his uppermost chin thoughtfully. "Jess reported it stolen, Joe, recommember?"

Emery nodded. "Possessing stolen property, carrying concealed weapons, attempted housebreaking . . . or maybe we could make it armed entry," he grinned evilly at the little man, "with intent to kill. That'll net you about twenty years, Wallaby Jo."

"Wallaby Jo . . . wallaby . . . dear me, that's a species of kangaroo, a small, hopping animal of Australia." Dr. Carlyle peered at the derelict as if he expected something definitely marsupial.

Emery chuckled. "Jo, here, is small, he's an animal, and he's hopping whenever he can get it; but he ain't from Australia, or are you, Jo?"

The rat-like little man shook his head.

"Hopping?" Dr. Carlyle looked more closely at the man.

"Sniffing," explained Emery, "coking, taking a shot in the arm," and as the doctor still looked blankly at him he added, "dope fiend, hop-head."

"Ah! Oh yes . . . curious bit of punning. I must make a note of it for my chapter on 'Nicknames.' I'm writing a dissertation on popular etymology. Hmmm, curious. I hadn't thought of the underworld as having so precise an analytical sense of etymology. Hopping—wallaby. Probably some of the lawless element shipped from England to Australia picked up the word and . . ."

Emery ignored him and turned to Jo. "All right, let's have it—the whole story. Or shall we add attempt to shoot an officer? With your record that ought to give you life."

"Lissen, sarge, you can't railroad me. I ain't done nothin', see. I was jus' walkin' by, thass all. Jus' walking by. Lemmie go."

Emery weighed the automatic thoughtfully. "Just walking by, huh? With a gun in your pocket, in the wealthiest section of town? Sure, I believe it." Emery's sarcasm was heavy. "By the way, Jo, where've you been getting the stuff lately? Haven't seen you around your usual dives."

Wallaby Jo's eyes shifted uneasily. He wet his lips and shook his head.

"Ain't sayin', huh?" Emery turned ponderously to the only slightly less ponderous Wolfe. "Maybe you'd better take him down to the sweat box for a few days. Maybe a week from now he'll be needing some of the stuff and he'll talk. We got plenty of time."

The little man darted venomous eyes around the great hall.

"There's no good trying to make a break, Jo. It's the sweat box for you." Emery's voice deepened dramatically. "When it gets real warm and your tongue starts getting dry, and your head starts hammering, you'll be needing some . . . needing it bad . . . real bad."

The little man squealed like a stuck rat. "Don't! Jesus, don't! I need it now, honest, sarge. I need it now. I gotta have it. Jesus, even what he does to me, I gotta have it . . . now . . . right now."

"That's better." Emery sighed happily and began conversationally, "Where did you get the gun?"

"I don't know . . . but I gotta have some. Honest, sarge, you gotta fix it so I can get some. I'm . . . I'm all shot . . . honest, sarge." His pleading eyes faltered away from Emery's. He mumbled hastily, "I found it just now. I was walking up the back way, and I found it."

"Yeah?"

Jo nodded miserably. "Honest, sarge. I seen this guy poke it under a rock, and I sneaked up and copped it. I thought maybe he was hiding money, but that there gun was all. I thought maybe I could hock it."

"You're a liar, Jo. You know a guy has to leave a weapon thirty days before he can collect on it. So your story is still that a guy hid it under a rock. What sort of a guy?"

Jo shook his head. "Just a guy. I was up on the next ridge when I seen him hide something, so I went and took a look. Honest, sarge, I'm telling all I know. Can't you get me a sniff . . . just a little one? My nerves are shot, honest, sarge."

"Notice that it's generally the dishonest folks that uses *honest* the most," commented the Judge.

Feet pounded on the gravel outside, and then thundered up the stairs. A fist pounded on the great door.

"That's Pete." Deedie skirted the group and opened the door.

Pete Coleman stood in momentary surprise, and then strode forward, his muddy shoes tracking the marble floor. "You poor kid. I just heard the news flash over the radio. I had stopped at the club to change my clothes," he added hastily. "When I got in from Richmond I felt dirty, but I came right over as soon as I heard. Is Sylvia . . . oh, hello Sylvia. Excuse me for rushing in like this, but I just heard the news about Fred."

Deedie spoke coldly. "Neither Sylvia nor I are heart-broken, but thank you for coming." Evidently the memory of the broken date still rankled.

Pete looked down at her with a curious frown, and then shrugged. He eyed the shivering little man. "Who's he? Say, haven't I seen you before? Around here somewhere?"

Esther appeared in the door. "Are any of you gentlemen here named Emery?" She looked doubtful about the *gentlemen*. "He's wanted on the phone."

"There's one right here on the table," pointed out Deedie, "or if you want privacy . . ."

Emery reached the hall telephone and muttered into it. He listened, nodding, mumbling an occasional "yeah" into the instrument. Finally he cradled it with surprising gentleness and lumbered back along the hall. He stood looking down at the little hop-head before speaking to the others.

"At the morgue they examined Jensen's body. He was murdered before the wreck. Shot with a Spanish automatic, twenty-five." He patted the gun taken from Wallaby Jo. "Wolfe, take him away and book him for suspicion of murder of Dr. Jensen."

Wallaby Jo's squeal of protest was cut short by a hand that gripped his tattered, tieless collar.

"'Pears somebody wanted to make certain-sure that Dr. Jensen warn't gonna live. Where was he shot?" inquired the Judge mildly.

"Where?" Emery shook his head and growled. "Where? Somebody liked that guy so well they shot him full of holes. Four times in the chest."

"Four times?" Judge Massie shook his head. "Great Land o' Goshen, an' I only knew about one . . ."

12
MONEY SPELLS MURDER

"So Jensen was shot four times?" The Judge asked the question more of himself than of Emery.

"Yup. That's the report from the morgue. Four times with a Spanish twenty-five. And Mrs. Jensen's was stolen from your office, huh? And then this bird turns up around the Jensen house with a Spanish twenty-five." Emery turned the gun over in his hand. "Fingerprints will be just about useless—too many people handled it. However, we'll try to check. Why the hell do people buy these things, anyway? Nobody sells them any more, except phony pawnshops and mail-order houses. Well, what you got to say about it now, Wallaby?"

The little man shivered until his teeth chattered, and he rubbed one arm painfully, slowly. "N-n-nothin', sarge. Honest, I found it. I wasn't gonna hurt him none . . . honest, I wasn't. I just hadda have some snow, and I didn't care what he did to me. I only meant maybe to scare him a little but I didn't . . . I didn't . . . I didn't . . ." His voice squealed off into a shriek, and he clawed at Emery's lapels. Slobbering and whimpering he turned from the detective's adamant face, appealing to the Judge, to the rest. "I gotta have it . . . I gotta. I can't think . . . I can't eat. Lemme see the doc . . . lemme talk to him. He'll fix me up. He'll gimme . . . Oh, Jesus, he's dead."

"You oughta know." Emery signaled to Wolfe who collared the whimpering little man. "You killed him. You killed him because he wouldn't give you dope, and then you beat it back here, so's you could steal . . ."

"I didn't." He writhed frantically in Wolfe's grasp. "Gimme a chance. Oh, God, gimme a shot. I gotta have it . . . I gotta . . . I'm going nuts . . ." Suddenly his wrigglings subsided and he sagged against the officer limply.

Sylvia turned away and Amy covered her face with her hands. Deedie buried her face against Pete's protective shoulder. "He's so miserable, so wretched." Willie was striving to match the Judge's judicial calm instead of being sick.

Judge Massie peered down at the little man. "Don't reckon there's much more'n a good healthy sham in him. Figgerin' on sympathy, I reckon."

Dr. Carlyle nodded. "I agree that it is perhaps a pose. However, I believe I could lay my hands on Jensen's supply of cocaine and, while I am not a practicing physician, I hold a medical degree and a license to practice and administer narcotics. If I can be of help . . ."

Emery looked down at the limp little man in disgust. "I think maybe he'll talk a bit if we could use the cocaine."

The little man came to life. His bleary eyes fastened hungrily on the little doc. "Jus' gimme a shot. I'll talk . . . I'll talk," he whimpered softly, "but I didn't kill the doc . . . I didn't."

"Well, effen you didn't mebbe it 'ud be best effen you was to talk. Tellin' the truth mought help more'n a little. Generally does, I figger. S'posin' we all go in the doctor's office an' set a spell. Ain't had a speck o' reee-laxin' sence Sylvia come to my office last night. Been sech a heap doin' sence then. I'm awful good at settin' still an' listenin'." He waddled across the library to the doctor's private wing, and lowered his bulk into the biggest, most comfortable chair there. "An' I'll let the little doc do the talkin', now."

The little doc directed the seating and rather pompously took charge, as if he were directing a classroom. "I believe Mrs. Hardecker was formerly a nurse and can prepare the hypodermic. I will show her where the apparatus and drugs are kept. And in the meanwhile Mr. Wallaby Jo can tell his story. I think at it's conclusion we might help him."

Judge Massie twinkled up at the little doc, but the derelict, slumped between Emery and Wolfe, attempted to get to his feet. "You can't do this to me. You can't. I ain't gonna say a word. I ain't talking till I get a shot . . ." Wolfe's arm jerked him back.

Emery started to rise. "Okay. Take him away, Wolfe, and put him in the sweat box. I can't waste any more time. When I get there, oh, maybe tomorrow or the next day, he'll be crying to talk."

The little man shivered. "Don't, sarge, please. I'll talk." His eyes sought Dr. Carlyle. "On'y get goin' with that snow, will yu? Git me a needle so's I can see it . . ." He wet his quivering lips. "Jus' lemme see it."

Emery nodded and the little doc disappeared a moment and reappeared with a needle, a small phial, and a spirit lamp. "Mrs. Hardecker, can you prepare a hypodermic?"

The gaunt woman nodded and accepted the layout.

Emery prodded the little man whose bloodshot eyes were fastened on the glittering instrument. "All right, Wallaby, we're giving you a break. Let's have the story, and it had better be good—damn good."

Slowly the story came, between protests, curses, pleadings for the needle, and punctured by Emery's calm, unemotional threats.

Wallaby Jo was a bum, and he had heard of a doctor who would pay you to let him take pictures of you. Yeah, he'd thought they meant dirty pictures, but they were pictures of being scared outs your wits by a snake, being soothed by music, and being excited by pictures of women. Once there had been a real woman—Jo licked his lips—but there was always a little dope if you wanted it. Not much, a little; and in spite of the rattlesnakes and tarantula and hot irons thrust at him, Wallaby Jo had come back—because of the dope. And then there wasn't any more dope. Jensen wouldn't give him any more. He didn't need him any longer. Wallaby Jo whimpered, "He wouldn't even talk to me. On'y this morning he told me to go to hell." Wallaby Jo leapt up suddenly. "I hope he roasts there! Oh, Jesus, gimme that shot!"

Emery thrust him back. "When did you steal that gun?"

"I didn't. I tole you how I got it; I found it." And Wallaby Jo went repetitiously over his story. He had seen Dr. Jensen downtown that morning near the courthouse, and the doctor had brushed him aside. He had walked out here hoping he could see the doctor, maybe make him give him some dope. He had come the back way, like the doc had always made him, and he'd seen this guy—he was too far away to see plainly—and then he'd found the gun. Maybe it had given him ideas, but he hadn't used it . . . he hadn't killed Jensen. As Emery scoffed at his story he began drearily, hopelessly again, as if he, himself, no longer believed it.

Finally Emery signaled for the little doc to give him the shot and Wallaby Jo scrambled to his feet, baring his arm eagerly, sucking in his dry lips. He followed the little doc and Emery into the receptionist's office and then, after an interval, a heavy sigh—and Wallaby Jo came out almost swaggering, a disdainful curve to his lips.

"You cops! You ain't got a thing on me. You won't hold me ten minutes. Why, I got influence that will take your shield away for what you done to me. Why jus' for laying your hands on me, I could break you. I got friends that will take care of me."

Emery nodded easily. "Sure, you and the Governor are old school buddies. Come along, Wallaby, and meet your old palsy-walsy, the desk sergeant. He'll give you a big welcome and fix you up with a nice quiet room in the east wing." Emery shoved the shabby little man roughly toward Wolfe and came back to the group in the reception room. "Sorry you folks had to hear some unpleasant things, but we did get something. And thank you, Dr. Carlyle and Mrs. Hardecker. You've both been a great help. And thanks, Judge, for your . . . er . . . passive cooperation."

Judge Massie flapped his palm-leaf fan at him—he had recovered it on his second trip to Mrs. Jensen's room and was happily waving it under his several chins. "Figgered the little doc could fix things fer us."

"And now, Miss Storme, if you'll just come down and officially identify the body we'll try not to bother you too much. The coroner hasn't set the date for the inquest, but I'll have to ask you to hold yourselves ready for that. Possibly tomorrow. I've got to take Wallaby Jo down to the station and book him, or I'd go with you to be of any help I can. I guess I'll be able to join you there." He waved a general salute. "I think we've got our man. Goodbye," and, well pleased with himself, he left. At the door he turned. "I'm glad this one isn't your client, Judge Massie. You couldn't get him off but you'd be sure to try to make me look like a monkey."

"Nature were a jump ahead o' me there. Howsomever, I reckon I could smash holes a mile wide in your case, an' one of 'em would be how come he got from Edgewater Road plumb to this place in less'n half an hour 'thout any autymobile?"

Emery shook his head sadly at the Judge and shut the door.

Mrs. Hardecker again led Sylvia unprotestingly off to rest. Pete volunteered to drive the Judge and Deedie down in one of the Jensen cars, but the Judge had already accepted the offer of Dr. Carlyle, and the little doc looked so wistful at being cut off from the last act of the drama that the Judge shook his head. "Reckon we'd be sorta crowdin'. Me, I'm pow'ful good at crowdin', seein' how prodigious I got to be. Mebbe, Pete, you could drive Miss Deedie down."

Pete grinned. "Sure. We can take Deedie's roadster," he turned to her, "if you don't mind."

Deedie looked her surprise. "But where's your car?"

"Oh, I traded that in." Pete grinned down at her. "Took a taxi out. The new car isn't quite ready." Pete didn't add that he wasn't quite ready for the car, either.

"What? Why Peter Coleman! That car was practically new. You've only had it since you got out of the army." Deedie sighed. "Some day, Peter Coleman, you'll learn that money . . ." She glanced at his rumpled suit and soiled shoes, and then scanned his beaming face. Suddenly she capitulated. "Oh, we'll use my roadster." She turned a grin on the Judge. "I expect Dr. Carlyle will be crowded."

They watched Deedie and Pete drive off in her little green Buick, and then clambered into the little doc's stately sedan. Dr. Carlyle turned from the operation of starting. "Really, that boy is most extravagant. Dear me, turning in a car three months after he bought it, and I've had this five years. It seems a shame."

"'Pears to me he put a right gay face on it. Y'see, Pete didn't turn that there car in. He sold it. I guess I ain't sayin' what won't be known all over town tomorrow, but Pete's broke. I reckon if this here death of Jensen hadn'ta come up today he'da sorta faded out o' Deedie's life. Leastwise, he gimme that impression this morning."

Amy was outraged. "She has more than enough for both . . ."

"Don't reckon Pete figgers thataway. He's afraid mought come a time when she'd be wonderin' effen he didn't marry her fer her money. So I've been right glad to see him standin' by in this here trouble, and not lettin' his pride . . ."

"Pride!" Amy was indignant. "If he's really in love . . ."

The little doc lurched the car into motion. "I think it shows some character for the boy to refuse to live on her money. I'm glad someone in the younger generation can stand on proprieties. This younger generation . . ." The little doc was off on his favorite topic, but Amy silenced him with a touch on the arm and a smile.

At the edge of town the Judge suggested that they stop and let him pick up his car. "After you git me delivered we kin separate. I gotta git in a heap o' reee-laxin' fer all this time I put in sashayin' 'round." The Judge eyed the reunited couple up front. "'Sides, I reckon you two got things that want sayin'," he added not too subtly.

Amy smiled at him across the back of the seat. "Thanks . . . and shall we have some music? At least the radio isn't five years old."

Music swelled and died. A flat, precise voice announced with spurious excitement, "We break into this recorded program to announce the sudden, tragic death of Dr. Frederic Jensen, noted psychiatrist, who was killed this afternoon on the Edgewater Road . . ."

Amy snapped it off. "I don't want to hear any more of that."

She was silent for a while, but her mercurial temperament had changed almost to gayety by the time they drew up in front of the Judge's office. "Oh look, Frankie, those flowers in that florist shop—the Bronze Beauties. Frankie, I must have some; I must. Sylvia was mean not to tell me where she got the bulbs for her garden. I won't be a minute. Wait for me in the Judge's office." Almost before the car had stopped rolling she was out and across the sidewalk.

The little doc twinkled at the Judge. "We'll never get her away. She really loves flowers." He glanced at the *No Parking 4-6* sign. "It must be after six. I think I will just run up to your office for another look around if you don't mind. I haven't the situation clearly in mind. Perhaps directly on the site I might visualize it better and thereby work out the details."

He trotted along beside the Judge's bulk, and Willie sulked on the other side. Deedie had paid him scant heed after Pete had arrived. Willie again ignored the telephone operator, his former favorite.

At the central door to the Judge's offices the little doc stopped. "Now the murderer apparently could go in through this central door, but he must have brought the body directly from the left-hand room to the corridor." He pointed to the corridor door of the Judge's private office. "But where did he go from there? He took considerable risk carrying a body through an open hallway."

"Warn't so much of a chance, come to think of it. This here's a brand, spankin' new buildin', an' I'm the on'y tenant on this here floor. Ain't many folks comin' an' goin' here yit, an' the murderer could git from my office to most any o' these others, an' stow the body. An' the service elevator is jess around the corner a step. It's one o' them automatic gadgets. Goes down to the basement entrance and the garage. Goin' down now to git m' car. You kin mosey 'round this here office 'til Miz Carlyle comes fer you."

"Right here in this building? A garage?" Dr. Carlyle clucked faintly. "Dear me, what will they think of next? Though I dare say it's a very practical idea."

Willie rushed into an explanation. It was a favorite topic, with inexhaustible possibilities. The little doc was interested, and the Judge followed Willie's guide-talk around the corner, counting slowly as he walked, "Ten, eleven," and watched the tips of his congress gaiters rise and set along the horizon of his belt. "Twenty-seven," he announced triumphantly and bumped into the little doc standing in fascination before the glowing green light. "It's jess twenty-seven steps from my office door to this here service elevator. Man could make that in less'n thirty seconds, even carryin' the doctor."

"But what a thirty seconds, Judge, for the murderer fearing detection. It must have seemed an hour. Dear me, it almost seems to force a belief in Einstein's theory of relativity—certainly of the time-perception sense."

Judge Massie shook his head sadly. "Mought 'a caught him at it effen it hadn'ta been fer that phone call makin' us wonder effen the doctor was still alive. Howsomever, I figger the murderer musta got clear o' the buildin' 'fore he'd put in a call to the house that 'ud be checked back, an' it was ten minutes or more 'fore Mrs. Hardecker did call back." The automatic door opened and they stepped in.

"An' the telephone call was meant as an alibi to prove the doctor was still alive." Willie nodded at his own astuteness.

"Then that there should mean we gotta look fer a feller that ain't got sech a good alibi fer 'round four, but has got a swell one fer the time o' the accident."

"What a coldly premeditated crime. The murderer must have familiarized himself with the building, driven his car in, walked up and killed the doctor, taken him out . . ."

"Hold yer horses, Doc. That there woulda taken lots o' plannin', an' the murderer didn't even know 'forehand that Jensen was comin' to my office. An' then there's the gun. Effen he'd been figgerin' on killin' the doctor, he'da brought his own. He used the one on the desk, recommember?"

"Ah," Dr. Carlyle accepted the challenge that wasn't given. "The murderer used the one on the desk, but he also may have had his own gun and not used it."

"Then you're gittin' away from the little feller, Wallaby Jo, Doc. He didn't have anything but a Spanish automatic. A murderer ain't gonna throw away the gun he didn't kill nobody with, an' keep the one he did—effen he was gonna throw away any. 'Course they's always the possibility that this here dope fiend is tellin' the truth."

The little doc's eyes twinkled. "Surely you aren't seriously considering this Wallaby Jo as a suspect."

"Mebbe I'm jess hopin'," and they emerged into the gloomy, cavernous reaches of the basement garage.

They were still talking when Willie made the startling dis-covery.

"Jedge, the car's gone!"

In fact, the garage was bare except for a new and shiny coupe.

The Judge glanced around the garage. "Doc, looks like yore theory of a premeditated crime sorta goes up the spout, don't it? The man that done this was jess grabbin' things as they come. An' I even left the keys in it so's the garage man could git some-one to put it away. Great Jumpin' Jehosaphat! I reckon it's plumb smashed at the quarry."

"You been needin' a new car, Jedge, come Christmas nine years ago," added Willie philosophically and with a gleam in his eye. He was already picturing the new car.

"Better git upstairs an' report this here theft to Emery. Dad-gum it, somebody's rung up the elevator. Willie, you hunt up that there Jim Farney and see effen he seen anything. Know he didn't, but you mought ask. Reckon I gotta climb these here stairs." The Judge sighed, and then went up them with an agility that left the startled little doc some distance behind.

Dr. Carlyle emerged into the lobby just in time to see the Judge's coattails whisk through the revolving door. He walked over to the telephone operator who was watching the Judge's rapid departure with interest. She nodded brightly toward the door, which she could see by craning a very lovely neck. "Ain't the Judge a scream? I just told him about that guy, and he yelled something about jumping Jehosaphats, and started after him."

"Who is this . . . er . . . guy?"

"Him? Oh, he's a slicked-up lily in pants. He was here earlier this afternoon but the Judge was out getting some of Luigi's cof-fee. About three-thirty, I'd say. I sent him up to the Judge's office but he didn't wait long. And you should've seen the Judge when I told him that that beautiful blonde that was here about the same time just went upstairs with an armful of flowers."

The little doc glanced up the stairs. "Blonde? Armful of flowers? My wife was going to get flowers and meet me up there." He frowned slightly. "You say she was here earlier? About . . . about three-thirty?"

The girl hesitated. "This girl is young."

Dr. Carlyle smiled vaguely. "My wife is young . . . very young."

Just at that moment the Judge pushed through the revolving door with difficulty, thrusting ahead of him Charles Detweiler, assistant to Mrs. Jensen's attorney. He was one of those watered imitations of the type of Englishman that makes you wonder what holds the British Empire together. He suggested a drawl. He did drawl—and just missed lisping.

"Judge Massie, this is very kind of you. I appreciate the courtesy. I . . . Oh, howja do," he greeted Dr. Carlyle coldly. He looked hurt. "Judge, I had expected to see you alone . . ."

"This here is Dr. Carlyle. He's jess waitin' fer his wife, an' then he's goin'. We kin go up to my office."

"Amy is up there now, Judge. I'll get her and we'll just drive on and tell them you're coming right away."

"Land o' Goshen, I jess recommembered Susie said the woman who was here about three-thirty jess come back." He broke off and hurried Detweiler upstairs. Carlyle followed, a frown of perplexity furrowing the blandness of his forehead.

Amy Carlyle greeted them at the door, her face radiant over an armful of gladioli. "Frankie, I got them. But he won't sell me any bulbs. He insists they're not on the market. Isn't he nasty? Oh, Frankie, darling, I'm so happy, so terribly happy."

Judge Massie hurried his thin young man across the central office and into his private sanctum, as if looking at so much happiness shining in a person's face made him uncomfortable. As he remarked to Detweiler, "This here bein' Cupid ain't suited to my pertickler figger, but I gotta go back. See you in a minute."

When Judge Massie returned Amy was still standing there with those flowers in her arms, smiling at the little doc. Judge

Massie extracted one of his immaculate handkerchiefs and blew his nose firmly before breaking in on the tableau.

"Miz Carlyle, Susie tells me you come here to see me 'long 'bout three-thirty. Anything I kin do fer you?"

A little frown creased her forehead and she looked at him blankly. "To see you? Oh, no . . ." Then she flushed. "Oh, yes, I did ask her for your office number. I . . .well . . . oh, please Judge, I don't want to think of it ever again."

Dr. Carlyle nodded. "Yes, Judge, it's best forgotten. My wife is trying to say that she came to see you about our divorce. Isn't that it, dear?"

She sighed with relief. "Yes, Frank . . . it was. But please, let's not talk about it." She smiled at the Judge. "I'm glad you weren't here. I might have said things that would hurt people . . . but me especially. Frank has . . . has been more than sweet." She caught the little doc's hand and squeezed it.

Judge Massie caught the agonized plea in the little doc's eyes, and he made his next question as easy as possible. "Was anybody else here?"

"Why no. That's why I left. Oh, yes there was—that man who just came in. He came in in a terrible hurry just as I was leaving. I hardly stayed a minute."

"Hear anybody talkin', say, in my office?"

"Not that I remember. I think I would have waited if I'd thought anyone was around."

"But this here Detweiler come in, did he?"

"That man?" She nodded toward the Judge's inner office. "He came in but I didn't wait. You see, I was considerably upset, and I wanted to walk . . ."

The little doc laid a quiet hand on the Judge's arm. "Please, Judge, my wife didn't . . . I can't let you . . ." He hastily apologized. "I didn't mean it quite so sternly as it sounded, Judge. I quite understand your motives and your idea. But if she had killed him here, she wouldn't have come back to be readily identified!'

Amy Carlyle stared over her flowers at the little doc, a new horror in her eyes. "Then . . . then . . . he was killed . . . here?"

She glanced slowly around the room. "But the accident . . . how
could he . . ."

"The doc an' I were jess figgerin' on how he coulda got away."

"Was it . . . did it happen while I was here? I didn't hear anything . . ."

"Jess about then. Now you let the doc take you out to that
there car, an' effen you don't mind I'd be plumb obliged effen
you'd wait an' take me to the morgue. Willie an' me will be 'long
in a minute."

Dazedly she let herself be led away, clinging pathetically to
the little doc's arm. At the door she glanced over her shoulder.
"You'll begin to wonder if I did it, won't you?"

Judge Massie made his head shake a bluff negative. "Ain't
even corn-sidered it."

She shuddered. "I knew you'd think it because I thought of it
myself. I wanted to do it."

"You git downstairs with the little doc an' start figgerin' on
that there new honeymoon you're goin' on."

He marched in to where Detweiler was sitting stiffly upright.
The young man glanced up petulantly and then smiled tight-
ly. "My dear fellow, nice of you to see me at this hour. I just
dropped by to see about a letter we sent you this morning. An
unimportant matter, really, but I was passing by and I thought,
well, fact of the matter is, I rather wish you'd . . . er . . . ah . . .
disregard the letter. It was . . . ahem . . . well, written in the heat
of the moment and . . . er . . . such things sometimes do . . . er
. . . irreparable harm . . . disrupt friendships, what?"

"Don't recommember we was sech friends, Charlie. Anybody
else ever call you Charlie? Didn't think so. Oh, yes, that there
letter. Now, come to think of it, I don't jess see how I kin ignore
sech a thing." Which was quite true, since the Judge could hardly
disregard something he hadn't read, and he hadn't seen his mail
all day.

Detweiler gnawed at a fragile mustache, and reddened.
"There's very little to be said, eh? But of course, the doctor's tragic
death puts a different light on things, eh? The absurd charges will

be dropped, assuredly. After all, our firm is too well-established to make such ridiculous inferences possible. As you are well aware, we have been handling the Storme estate for more than ten years—and very well, I might add." Some of his unctuous assurance was returning. "There were no complaints until Dr. Jensen suddenly demanded . . ."

Judge Massie errumphed loudly. "So somebody's been pilferin' from the Storme estate?" Judge Massie walked around the desk and eased himself into his big leather chair. He reached in the desk drawer for one of his palm-leaf fans and waved it gravely at Mr. Detweiler. "How much is missin'?"

Detweiler's silly little mustache twitched as he tried to smile. "Don't be absurd, Judge Massie. Nothing is missing. Nothing. I only resent the implication that such a thing could happen. I . . ."

"Lots o' folks has called me lots o' things, but don't recommember nobody tellin' me not to be absurd. Ain't sayin' I ain't absurd, but folks generally knows better'n to mention it." The Judge was mildly warning the young man. Then he leaned fat elbows on the desk and stared at him with a curious, bland smile. "How come ol' Edgar don't come to me? He's head o' the firm," and Judge Massie managed to imply that that was a very good thing for the firm.

"Mr. Willebrandt? Why such a suggestion would . . ."

"Sorta thought the ol' boy woulda pitched Jensen outa the office fer jess mentionin' it, but you listened. Wonder why. Ain't the sort o' thing a man what is a man would listen to effen it warn't the truth. You kin jess climb off'n that high horse o' yourn. We are aimin' to go through with this here investigation, but fer an entirely different reason than Jensen had. *We* really want to know an' *he* didn't."

Detweiler stared at the Judge, his undertucked jaw swinging slack. He snapped it back with an effort. "You mean he didn't intend to go through with it?" He stood up suddenly.

Judge Massie sighed. "I got my doubts. Figger he jess wanted to put the wind up you, so's when he took over the estate income there wouldn'ta been a squawk. Howsomever, we figger we'll jess take a look at them assets an' stocks an' bonds an' sech, an' I reckon we'll find some skullduggery. Are you very good at skull-duggery, Mr. Detweiler?"

The fine shell of Detweiler's dignity was collapsing. His chin, what there was of it, was trembling. His knees buckled, and he sat down abruptly. "But . . . but . . . surely I . . . oh, my God, it's so useless, so utterly useless." He buried his face in his hands and cried.

The Judge looked across at him. "Detweiler, it's a mighty good thing fer you that you ain't got the guts of a rabbit. Effen you had been man enough to stand up under it, then I'd be won-derin' then you didn't kill Jensen. Now I don't believe you got guts enough fer the job cause that there job took real nerve."

Detweiler leapt to his feet. "You can't pin that on me! You can't! I didn't do it!" His mouth jerked crookedly. "But if you want to know who did do it, why don't you ask Miss Cordelia Storme? She was here in the building. I saw her, and she was crying."

Judge Massie sank back in his chair, his chins lapping down over his collar, his spectacles sliding down the pudgy incline of his nose, his mild blue eyes closed, and he almost smiled as he tented his fingers across his paunch.

Detweiler hesitated, then his voice suddenly squeaked, "Haven't you anything to say to that?"

Judge Massie nodded slowly, and his spectacles slid again. "I'm reee-laxin' . . . so's I kin figger on the best way to hate a man that hides behind a woman's skirts. 'Course, I'm also wonderin' how come you know Jensen was murdered in this here buildin' when the papers say he died in an autymobile wreck . . . an' don't slam the door as you go out."

Detweiler stared across the desk at the recumbent figure of the Judge. He started to speak, and then turned and bolted.

"Gotta open me a winder," commented the Judge to himself, "an' air out the smell." He opened the window and went slowly downstairs to pick up Willie and rejoin the Carlyles.

13
PATTERN FOR MURDER

The little doc was waiting patiently, and Amy was huddled down in the seat, peering cautiously, frightenedly out at the Judge as he and Willie climbed into the car.

Willie reported on his interview with the garage attendant. "He don't know nothin'."

"He doesn't know anything," corrected the little doc.

"That's what I said—he don't know nothin', an' he don't."

Amy turned half around in the seat. "Judge, do you really think I did it?"

Judge Massie, struggling to make himself comfortable in the rear seat, grunted. "Don't 'pear that you did, Amy. Certainly don't look like it. You see, this here Detweiler . . ." and the Judge told her of his encounter with the spineless Mr. Detweiler.

"And you let him get away?" There was definite relief in her voice.

"Git away from what? We ain't catchin' murderers, even effen he is a murderer. Me, I got a client to perteck, an' I'm perteckin'. Any time we want Detweiler we kin git him, an' effen he tries to run away it's jess as good as confessin'. Howsomever, I'm thinkin' o' swearin' out a warrant fer embezzlement—that'll kinda hold him—but jess now we want a card or so up our sleeve."

The little doc was still working on his time chart. "Then that narrows the time margin somewhat, doesn't it? For the murder was evidently committed between the time Miss Deedie left him and the time . . ." He saw where his reasoning was leading him, and stopped abruptly.

Amy gave a little cry. "Oh, you see, it doesn't let me out, because I was there ahead of Mr. Detweiler. I only glanced in the
center office, but you can't be sure of that." Her eyes pleaded
with the Judge for reassurance.

"Twouldn't make much difference what you did effen this
here Detweiler feller killed him after you left. 'Course, this here
thing is gonna take a lot o' figgerin' an' a lot o' untanglin', an'
don't fergit, this here Joe Emery ain't anybody's fool an' he ain't
gonna miss any of it. 'Twon't be long 'fore he starts back-trackin'
on Jensen, an' then he'll run spang up agin the fack that we already told him that this here Jensen was killed in my office. That
there Susie, she reco'nized you. She recommembered this here
Detweiler. Mebbe there's others she'll reco'nize includin' Deedie.
An' then, o' course, mebbe there's somebody we ain't figgered on
a-tall, somebody mebbe that used the elevator, an' Susie'd miss
seein' 'em. Reckon effen she ever realizes that, she'll git 'em to
put the phone exchange right spang in the middle o' the lobby,
'stead o' stuck in that cubby hole by the stairs. I don't see how
come she ever let 'em put the house phone 'round the corner
where she cain't see whose usin' it. Susie's plumb curious, she is."
Judge Massie shook his head. "Don't reckon nothin' serious is
gonna happen, Amy, 'cept mebbe you'll be in fer a bad spell, an'
effen you got a clear conscience . . ."

She spoke quickly. "Oh, I shan't mind the bad spell, now that
I have Frankie with me again." She stopped just on the right side
of being coy. "I've been lost from him so long."

"After this is cleared up, my dear, do you suppose we could
take that . . . er . . . honeymoon the Judge suggested—possibly
Miami and . . ."

Amy almost wrecked the car in the lunge she made for the
little doc. "You sweet . . ."

Amy's volatile enthusiasm died quickly in the close, malodor-
ous morgue.

"That there smell ain't what you think it is," explained the
Judge. "It's mostly dead air an' dead gas an' mebbe the dead
hopes that folks has brought here . . . an' left."

But none of the gloom had penetrated to Charlie Burton, keeper of the morgue. He calls his stiffs "customers" and potters around among the cold vaults with an air of cheerful pride. He ushered them into his gloomy little office with a grin.

"After my latest customer, eh? Well, he's in fine shape, scarcely damaged at all." At Amy's shudder he nodded toward her. "Relative? Want to see him, miss? Oh, just a friend." At the Judge's brief explanation he nodded. "Sure. Emery'll be along in a minute. He's just up the hall checking the bullets." His very temporary and professional solicitude for Amy's feelings vanished under his pride. "Yes sir. We got a couple of neat ones. You'd be surprised the state some of 'em come here in. Had one that was chawed up by a ship's propeller. He was a mean one to get together right. Never did find his left hand."

Willie whistled softly. "Bet he was a beaut."

Amy shivered against the little doc, and Burton apologized hastily. "Sorry, miss. Didn't aim to startle you none." He turned to a less squeamish audience, the Judge, who had unerringly picked Burton's own chair and was tilted back in it, his palm-leaf fan working rhythmically. "We had a sight o' visitors after we run that actor fellow's picture in the paper, but ain't a soul identified him."

"So you figger he was an actor feller, huh? Perty shrewd figgerin', I reckon. Hear tell there was a pellet o' nose putty in his mouth."

"That's right. That's part of how we figgered he was an actor. Had grease paint mixed up in it, and he had grease paint in his hair and around his nose. And he was doping," added Burton mysteriously, "and a lot of them actor fellers takes dope. We found the punctures in his arm."

Judge Massie allowed his spectacles to slip along his nose so that he could peer quizzically over them. "Reckon it occurred to you folks that mebbe that would sorta indicate the grease paint was took off after he was dead."

Burton shook his head slowly. "Nup, can't see as it does."

Judge Massie fondled the uppermost of his chins. "Effen you had a lump or mebbe jess a little pellet o' greasy nose putty in yore mouth, what'd you reckon you'd do?"

Charlie eyed the Judge suspiciously. "Jedge, you ain't kidding me? I'd spit it out."

"This feller didn't. Figger he was sorta normal an' reg'lar, don't you? Figger effen he could spit it out he woulda, don'tcha?"

"Guess maybe you're right."

"So, effen he didn't spit it out, musta been a reason. Figger the reason he didn't spit it out was 'cause he was dead."

Burton was still skeptical. "He could have been gagged just after he'd got it in," but there was no real vitality to his argument.

Judge Massie checked his points with his palm fan against his fingers. "Fust, it was a pellet or lump. Therefore he didn't smash it up strugglin' against a gag. Two, he didn't struggle or mash this here pellet because he warn't able to, an' three, he warn't able to because he was dead."

"Danged if you ain't right, Judge," Burton commented admiringly. "I guess you got something there," he scratched his head, "but danged if I know what."

Emery stalked into the room and looked around. "Where's Miss Storme?"

"Well, dog my cats!" The Judge started out of his reverie. "I plumb forgot them two. Reckon they'll be comin' 'long presently. It's sech a beautiful night." The Judge was covering his own anxiety with a faint, ingratiating smile.

"Yeah? Well, I'm wonderin' the same thing you are—did she do it? Or maybe you know, and maybe you're helping her escape." He pointed at the Judge. "I wouldn't put it past *you*."

Willie thrust himself belligerently at Emery. "She didn't do it. She's a swell kid. She's . . ."

Emery glared down at Willie, whose earnest face was crimsoning under the steady glare. "And who are you to be calling anybody a kid?" And Emery struggled against a grin—and lost. "Okay, kid, she's swell, but she was in the Judge's office this afternoon and Jensen was probably killed there." He regained his frown and aimed it at the Judge. "Yeah, I'm beginning to believe you were right about this afternoon. Maybe he was killed there. And I ain't forgetting it was in your car, Judge. I could do with a little explaining of that. Yeah, we just got a report from the wrecking company that hauled it up. If Wolfe hadn't been on your trail from the time I left until after the accident, I think I'd clap you in jail as accessory after the fact."

Willie faced the big detective, pulling him around with a tug on his sleeve. "See here, me an' the Jedge . . ."

Emery appealed to the Judge. "Call off your dogs, Judge."

The little doc protested, "But my dear sir, the Judge could not possibly have . . ."

Emery glared at him. "And you, too. You ain't got such a clean nose that you can go poking it around."

Dr. Carlyle felt gingerly of his nose and then smiled uneasily. "You're jesting, of course. Besides, I very fortunately have an alibi for the time of the murder."

"An alibi for the time of the murder, eh? And what would you want with an alibi?"

The little doc coughed. "I didn't precisely want it, you see. It was given me, so to speak. I was . . . er . . . apprehended by the police. He gave me a parking ticket."

"Let's see it." Emery held out his hand and the little doc began another of his patting searches, locating it only after Emery had snorted irritably two or three times.

"Hmmm . . . Cassidy. Three-forty-five. Looks okay, but we'll check it anyhow. Not that we have anything on you, Doc, but you never can tell." He flipped the paper. "Even this is a pretty close squeak from what we've been able to figure on the time things happened in that office—if they happened there." He frowned down at the little doc. "Remember, we're keeping an eye on you. Guys that are handy with alibis generally have a reason." He beckoned to Burton. "I want to see you a minute about the position of the bullets. The coroner thinks something is funny."

"He usually does," stated Burton pessimistically.

The two men left the room, and Amy jumped from her chair and ran to the little doc. "Frank, they said if they got something on you. Oh, if they ever find out about me and what I've done to you! Oh, my darling, what have I done?"

The Judge waved her back to her chair with his palm fan. "You ain't done anything . . . yet. But effen you keep gittin'

dramatic on us they'll be lookin' 'round fer somethin'. The doc's
alibi is good enough fer us—but fer them? Well, they ain't as sure
of the times as we be, an' even if they was, it's like Joe Emery
said, a perty close squeak. So you jess sit tight an' keep lookin'
at the little doc like you have been. It'll be mighty nigh enough
to corn-vince a blind man you love him. Corn-vince *anybody*,
even me."

"But I do love him. I never stopped loving him, only . . . ."

The little doc patted her hand. "Don't, my dear. I neglected
you, I know," he smiled sadly, "and I'm not very romantic."

Amy clung to his hand. "You *are*, Frankie. Oh, you're kind
and thoughtful and generous—and that's romantic. Maybe not
the moonlight and roses and sweet music, but who cares for that
kind of romance, anyway?"

"We do!"

Deedie and Pete stood in the doorway, posturing elaborately
like a gay nineties' photograph, Deedie staring wide-eyed over a
little bouquet, Pete holding his hat stiffly, arm crooked. "Don't
we look like a happily married couple?"

They weren't even fooling themselves, and certainly not the
wise, discerning eyes of Judge Massie. They didn't look happy,
and they didn't look married. Judge Massie coughed. "They ain't
gonna feed you to the lions tonight . . . come in." Their gaiety
was all in the posturing. They were a couple of scared kids.

Amy gazed at them, stunned, sensing the pose and not quite
understanding. Then she did the one sensible thing. She rushed
to Deedie and caught her in her arms. "You poor, sweet dar-
lings." She held out a hand across Deedie and grasped Pete's
hand. "Congratulations, Peter, but why scare her to death?" She
patted Deedie's shoulder. "Don't shiver and shake so, darling.
People have lived through getting married and even, in time,
learned to like it."

Willie flushed deeply and stalked toward Pete, hand outthrust. "Congratulations. The best man won."

That eased the tension. The Judge, watching from under
drooping lids, hoped that Pete would have sense enough not to

laugh. He didn't, although the restraint must have been difficult. He shook Willie's hand firmly, the tightness around his mouth fading into a shy grin. "Thanks, old man. We can't all win."

Deedie released herself from Amy's hug and flung her arms around Willie, who squirmed ecstatically. "You're sweet, Willie, and you're one grand fellow. Aren't you going to kiss the bride?"

Willie drew back for an instant and then darted a peck at her cheek, getting red in the face and scuffing the floor with his shoe. "I hope you're happy," he mumbled gulpily and stalked back to his chair.

The little doc fumbled at his glasses and coughed politely a couple of times. "Congratulations . . . er . . . er . . . congratulations."

Judge Massie heaved himself grumblingly out of the chair. "Jess about time I get settled fer a mite o' reee-laxin' somethin' comes along. Never knew it to fail. Howsomever, reckon I cain't pass up a chance to kiss a bride, pertikerly as perty a one as this. Come here, Deedie." The Judge cocked his massive head on one side for his kiss on the cheek.

Deedie kissed him lightly and then clung to his arm, talking a little breathlessly. "We got to talking about getting married—on the way here—and, well, it didn't seem disrespectful, not after the way Dr. Jensen has behaved so."

Pete took up the explanation hastily, not quite looking at the Judge. "Deedie's going to need someone to stand by and, well, who could stand by better than her husband? I hope Sylvia will forgive us."

Amy almost cooed with delight, however specious it might be. "Deedie, you look radiant . . . and a little scared, but you'll get over that." She was talking to fill in the blank that Pete had left. "Frankie, isn't it exciting? A wedding . . ." She chattered gayly on, making a grand pretense of being oblivious to the guarded misery and false bravura of the two youngsters and to the Judge's spurious enthusiasm.

The Judge was content to let her rattle on. He eased himself back onto the keeper's worn swivel chair and made a great effort to appear to be reee-laxin'. But from under the shaggy brows he studied Pete's taut cheek planes and his clenching hands. He surveyed him from rumpled hair to still muddy boots, and shook his head. His babyish lips moved softly as if he were telling himself a not particularly pleasant bedtime story.

Amy's polite, brisk chatter died away as Emery entered with Dr. Cranshaw. The irascible coroner nodded curtly once around. "Hello, Amy. Nice party. Sorry I had to leave. All right, Joe, I've made my report. Now may I go eat?"

"Oh, sure, go ahead." Emery said it with a casualness that indicated he had other things on his mind. When the doctor had gone the big detective sergeant still stood there, evidently trying to reorganize his case. Finally he spoke abruptly. "Dr. Jensen was shot after he was dead—a long time after he was dead!"

"What?" Pete started. "How can you tell?"

Emery waved a hand at the door. "That's the coroner's business—coagulation of blood, bruised tissues, things like that. And he's generally right."

Pete stared at the detective. "I didn't know you could tell things like that." He hesitated. "I mean, it would never occur to me that anybody would be able to tell whether a man was dead when . . . I mean, if a man's dead and he's got bullet holes in him, I'd think the bullets killed him. How did he die?"

Emery shook his head. "I don't understand it myself. According to Doc Cranshaw one shot killed him and the others were fired an hour or so later."

Amy closed her eyes and shuddered. "What a wanton, brutal thing to do!"

Deedie stood rigid, her young mouth trembling. "It seems horrible, doesn't it? But I don't suppose he felt anything."

"Kinda queer," the Judge mumbled, "but mebbe I agree with Alice in Wonderland—there's been so many queer things that only the unqueer things would seem queer. Now this here sorta fits into the rest o' the things an' begins to make a pattern. Yessiree bob! Makes a pattern fer murder."

Emery looked at him. "What does?"

"Eh?" The Judge glanced up. "Must be gittin' old, talkin' to m'self. Said this here sorta fits in with them queer doin's last night, when there's a murder and the corpse gits up an' walks away. Then this aft'noon in my office, there's a murder and the corpse gits up and walks away. And now this here same corpse is shot after he's dead—after he's been killed in an accident. Effen that there ain't a general picture o' queerness I hopes never to see one; an' yit, this here pattern o' contradictions must fit, effen we knew some one little thing. Moughtn't be much . . . jess a mite of a thing."

Emery didn't have the energy to snarl at the Judge. "Yeah, a pattern of contradictions is right, but Wallaby Jo will straighten 'em out. Trust a hop-head to tangle things up." He recollected his mission suddenly. "Oh, will you folks just step this way? We have a routine for identification. First, the description and clothing . . ."

They trooped down the hall and into an office lined with lockers. On a table in the center lay two groups of clothing, neatly stacked and ticketed. Deedie saw them and crept into Pete's arms. "I can't look."

Pete nodded toward one pile. "Those are his, all right . . . and could you make the rest of it easy? Deedie can't stand much more." He patted her shoulder comfortingly.

Emery nodded toward the other pile. "They're our actor fellow's. So many people been here to try to identify him we just keep 'em out."

Judge Massie inspected the actor fellow's clothing carefully, turned over a garment with the edge of his palm fan, and then studied the doctor's clothing. He looked around for a comfortable chair, but there was none at all. He beckoned Emery over and whispered to him. Emery frowned and nodded and then went off on an errand. The others looked after him for guidance.

Judge Massie used his palm fan like a traffic semaphore. "Jess a minute; Joe Emery'll be comin' right back. Jess gone to fix somethin'."

In a moment Emery returned, less worried but eyeing the Judge dubiously. He led them down into the vault where Pete and the little doc made formal identification of the body. The two women stood a little apart, but Judge Massie peered down at the dead face. Then he glanced up. "You know, I feel a heap better fer knowin' fer certain-sure that he's really dead. Ain't sayin' I really doubted it, but, after a feller's been murdered twice an' got up an' walked away, I feel a mite easier in m'mind effen I *see* him dead."

Pete asked for a release of the body for burial, but Emery told him that would have to wait until after the inquest. Emery then led them back to the office and became very efficient about making out papers, getting signatures and then blotting them too thoroughly, until it became obvious even to the little doc that he was waiting for something. Only the Judge seemed placidly unaware of any stalling. He had lowered himself firmly and apparently permanently in the keeper's chair. He errumphed only once when it seemed that Emery couldn't fumble the papers gracefully any longer.

Then Benny, the police photographer, came running in, waving some damp prints. "Damned if you aren't right, Emery. Those bullets check in every particular. Look."

Emery stared at the prints and then shifted his gaze to the Judge's placid face. "Damnation, Judge, you were right. That actor fellow and Dr. Jensen *were* shot with the same gun. How in hell did you figure that one out?"

Judge Massie waved his palm fan casually. "Had to be. Part o' the pattern—the general queerness o' things."

14

FLOWERS FOR A CORPSE

Pete and Deedie were so deep in their own general fear at what they had done, and so thoroughly miserable with happiness that they didn't hear. And Amy was so busy being inconsequential and cheerful that she wasn't listening. But the little doc got it.

"Dear me." He stared at the Judge and then at Emery. "So that's your corpse without a murder? Shot with the same gun that killed Jensen. But . . . why, bless me?" His frown of concentration cleared. "But of course. This actor fellow and the queer one of which the chauffeurs spoke would be the same man, and the shots in the arm would be those glandular injections I deduced—the glandular injections that changed him from a shambling man to one whose face gradually seemed to fit him."

Emery nodded confirmation. "Haven't had time for a complete check, but the organs don't show traces of dope, so he may have had gland injections."

Judge Massie, firmly entrenched behind the morgue keeper's desk, moved the handle of his palm fan between his fingers tented across his paunch so that he could gently fan himself without too much motion. The Judge disliked unnecessary motion. "Me, I sorta figgered somethin' like that. 'Course, I had to git them bullets checked to figger it complete, an' even yit we cain't be sure. Ain't nobody yit identified this here actor feller as the queer one—reckon one o' them chauffeurs kin do that. Anyhow, it sorta ties them two murders up together."

Emery sat back, nodding approval as if the Judge were something he had invented and taken a patent on. "I'll tell you, the

Judge has something on the ball. Right out of a clear sky he says to me, 'Joe, check them bullets.' Didn't you, Judge?"

Judge Massie wriggled uncomfortably in the swivel chair until it creaked ominously. "Well, now, I got a sort o' confession to make. It warn't 'xactly out of a clear sky, so to speak. It was a plumb muddy sky. But I knowed somethin' nobody else knowed, an' I seen somethin' nobody else 'pears to have seen. Y'see, I recommembered the doctor's underdrawers."

Emery gazed at the Judge with a slight lessening of his enthusiasm, as if he wasn't quite sure he was right in the head. "And what has his underdrawers got to do with it?"

Judge Massie peered over his spectacles at the little doc accusingly. "All on account o' him. Don't 'spect he recommembers, but onct he got me into a game o' golf, 'long early this summer. Played at the Country Club—effen you kin call what I done playin'."

"Dear me, so we did. A foursome with . . . er . . . Dr. Jensen and . . . oh yes, James Harvey. You offered to play a round."

Judge Massie frowned. "I was coerced. That there Jim Harvey is the coercin'est man. Howsomever, three of 'em played, an' I worked at this here game. An' we came up to the showers an' I pertickler noticed Dr. Jensen's underdrawers, bein' as I wear ol' fashion jaegers as more becomin' to a man o' my figger."

"Why, bless me, I recall them now. I remember commenting on his . . . er . . . ah . . ."

"Underdrawers," Emery helped out bewilderedly.

"Thank you. His underdrawers. I rather admired them, you know. Quite lively. It had never occurred to me that a man could indulge a natural love of color so intimately and yet so . . . er . . . inconspicuously."

"An' speakin' o' color, did you notice them socks o' this here actor feller? Reg'lar rainbow an' brand new, but one of 'em was tore at the ankle."

Emery tried to brush that aside to get at the underdrawers. "Sure, and he had abrasions on his left ankle to account for it, but what the hell have these purple pants got to do with a murder?"

Judge Massie glanced up in mild surprise. "Them underpants is the key. Both me'n the little doc noticed 'em. Dr. Jensen told us he had 'em made to order, an' when I seen 'em among these here clothes from the actor feller, why it jess natchelly come to me. Folks don't lend their underpants 'round indiscriminate-like. An' there was another pair jess like 'em 'mongst Doc Jensen's things. Them things sorta ties men together. An' then when they both been shot, I figger mebbe if they were 'sociated in life, mebbe they were 'sociated in death. Sorta simple an' fundamental, when you come right down t'it."

Emery chuckled. "Ain't he the berries? Well, who'd have thought a pair of purple pants would maybe hang a guy?" And then, as if he recalled his duty to his department, he added, "Of course, we'd have checked the bullets sooner or later. We just hadn't gotten around to it. But I still think it's right smart of the Judge to figure it out just from a pair of purple pants." He banged the desk and stood up. "Well, that settles one thing. We start back at the house, checking everything in it. The house is the place, and we'll pick up Mrs. Jensen. She done it."

Deedie, who had been only half listening, sprang to her feet. "No! No! She didn't do it. I won't let you . . . you can't . . . I'll . . ."

Pete caught her shoulders. "Hold everything, dear. They can't arrest Sylvia and the sergeant knows it. For one thing, the little hop-head had the gun. For another, Sylvia wasn't anywhere near the wreck where Jensen was killed."

Emery thrust his fingers against Pete's vest and emphasized his points with light punches. "No? She was at the wreck, bright boy. The trooper got her license number, and besides, she said so herself. But," he underscored with a heavy punch, "Jensen wasn't killed at the wreck. Somebody bumped him off in the Judge's office, and Mrs. Jensen was there too. And so were you, and so was Miss Storme, and so was the little doc, and so was his missus, and so was another guy we ain't identified yet, and so were maybe some others that the telephone girl didn't see. Oh yeah, we've been checking, even telephone calls." He turned to the Judge. "I must say you're a cautious devil, Judge. From where'd Willie phone me, a public phone? We traced all your calls and we only found that one to Judge Ames goin' out, and one guy who kept calling you all afternoon while you were up at Jensen's place. That telephone operator didn't get his name, which is a wonder. She's got plenty of curiosity."

"That's how come I sent Willie outside the buildin'."

The little doc was impressed. "Dear me, I had no idea you were so thorough. And you can check anyone's telephone calls?"

Emery hesitated between drama and truth, and caught the Judge's eye. He decided on truth. "Well, not exactly. Only where there's an exchange. The girls keep a record of outgoing calls so they can charge 'em to the right party. On incoming calls the girls can't check where they're from, of course—just the hour and who gets 'em. They're pretty careful on a new exchange so the company can have a check on how many trunk lines are needed. The girls don't bother with interoffice calls—those inside the building." He grinned at the Judge. "That girl up at your place has got one keen eye, Judge, and she ain't so bad looking."

"Got two children, ain't you, Joe?" muttered the Judge.

Emery bridled. "That ain't affected my eyesight any. Anyhow, this girl gave us plenty of dope on all of you—what we didn't already know, and we knew plenty. Doc Jensen had demanded a sanity commission to declare his wife insane, and she had applied for a divorce. Someone killed her dog and she had an autopsy performed. Pete Coleman is broke. That'll give you an idea of how much we know."

Deedie's chin went up. "I knew he was broke before I married him."

Emery roared, "You what? Married him? Thunderation, lady, he's, why, he's a suspect."

"And so am I. You just said so." Deedie shrugged off Pete's protecting hand on her arm. "And I also had a very good motive. Dr. Jensen tried to rob me of two hundred thousand dollars."

Pete thrust himself between the detective and the girl. "She doesn't know what she's talking about. She's just saying that to show you that you can't dash up to the house and arrest Sylvia. Deedie couldn't possibly have done it. She was with the Judge all afternoon, and besides, there's that hop-head."

Emery drew out his handkerchief and mopped his forehead. "Maybe I was hasty, but look here. This Mrs. Jensen admitted shooting someone last night. Called us up and told a daffy story about finding a body when there wasn't any body, and then said she dreamed it, and then said she really did it. Only she *didn't dream* it, and she *did do* it, see? Because we found the body, old Purple Pants. She could have bumped him off, carted him away, and then phoned us."

Judge Massie, from his reee-laxin' in the swivel chair, coughed a warning. "Don't git carried away with yore enthusiasm, Joe; mought be a long walk back. Jess figger it out. Miz Jensen couldn't possibly have got rid o' sech a cumbersome thing as a body, effen she had killed the man. Dead bodies is right onhandy to git rid of, 'specially fer a woman. She took a taxi straight to my office—I s'pose you checked that, too."

"Yeah, we did," Emery admitted. "We checked that last night at the cab stand. Her story sounded phony even then, and we couldn't take a chance. Maybe it was hysterics, maybe it wasn't. We even checked the time the servants left. All right, Judge, I guess you're right—she couldn't have had much time." Emery was arguing more with himself than with the Judge.

"Ain't figgerin' mebbe she jess sorta walked out, casual-like, an' says to a cab driver, 'Gimme a hand. I got a dead body hangin' round that's gonna be awful embarrassin' in a little while.' Or mebbe you asked 'em that?"

"All right, all right. She didn't take it away in the cab." Emery flapped his hands helplessly. "So what?"

Judge Massie aimed his palm fan at the detective. "An' then she didn't take it away in the cab, an effen she didn't have time to take it some other way, then she didn't take it; an' effen she didn't take it, she didn't commit this here murder—or, leastwise, you cain't arrest her fer it, yit."

"She shot somebody!" protested Emery.

"An' agin you're wrong, Joseph Abernathy Emery. She *said* she shot somebody, but you'n me both know that that there shot she fired is still stuck in the jamb of her own bedroom door, an' couldn't nowise be the bullet that kilt either o' them two men."

Emery was only balked temporarily. "Okay, so I can't arrest her yet—but I can search that house from top to bottom, and I'm gonna check every damn thing in it, from soot to soup-bones."

Amy protested. "Oh, you mustn't! You can't!" She hesitated. "I mean, it would be so cruel to Sylvia, right at this time. She shouldn't be disturbed."

"Lady, in case you forgot, this here is a murder—two murders, in fact. We can't be considering anybody's feelings right now. Somebody didn't think much of those guys' feelings when they bumped 'em off."

"But surely," Deedie interrupted, "you can't intend to harass my sister when the Judge has proved to you that she couldn't have done it."

Emery shook his bull head. "Not what you'd call *proved*, but I can see just what sort o' case the Judge would make out of what I've got now. But after I've gone through that house and the Judge's office . . . but I think I've got most of the dope on that." He swung around on Amy. "And if you hadn't burned up those films I mighta had more. I'm just beginning to realize how important they are. Just the same, we'll turn up plenty—letters, maybe even some threats, though mostly folks who write threats don't carry 'em out. And furthermore, I'll want to talk to every one of you and the servants too. Let's see." He glanced at his watch. "It's pretty near eight now. I'd like to talk to them all about ten. Maybe we can get enough lined up for the inquest." He glared around the room. "If none of you have anything on your consciences, you'll be there. I'm just asking now. I could haul all of you down here, but I'm asking you to meet me at the Jensen's house at ten, and maybe we can do this on a friendly basis."

Judge Massie nodded, heaving himself ponderously to his feet. "Don't know as you could be fairer, Joe. Reckon effen I'd jess had a swell case knocked out from under me I wouldn't be feelin' so generous. 'Course, you still got this here Wallaby Jo, though there don't seem to be much p'int in him killin' this here actor feller, an unknown man. 'Course, he moughtn't be unknown to Wallaby Jo."

Emery waved them out of the room. "I've sent for your chauffeur, Miss Storme—excuse me, Mrs. Coleman—to see if he can identify this actor fellow as the queer one he was talking about. That ought to clear some things up. I'll know by the time I get out to your place."

It was a glum crowd that huddled on the steps of the morgue. The little doc spoke first. "Judge, if you and Willie would partake of dinner with us we should be happy to have you. Then we can join the others at Storme's Grote at ten and hear what Emery has to say. That should be most interesting."

"I think it's horrible," Amy shivered, although the August night was warm, "going through all of Dr. Jensen's personal things."

"One way to prevent it would be to clear up this here case 'fore he gits a chance at 'em," suggested the Judge mildly.

"What could we do?" Amy's voice was scornful.

"Well, ma'am, we know's much as the p'lice, an' mebbe a mite more. Effen we kin jess take them things and shuffle 'em 'round a bit 'til they fit into this here general pattern o' queerness, mebbe we could git at the answer. 'Course, there's a piece missin', or we'd know. Jess find that there piece an' we got it. Might be a tiny thing, jess a little bit of a thing, but it'd fit . . . an' make the rest fit."

Deedie held out her hand to the Judge. "You've been very kind to stick by us in this, Judge Massie. Wouldn't you like to come to Storme's Grote for dinner and talk to Sylvia? I think probably it would help her. And of course you, too, Willie." Her young face twisted in a grimace of pain. "It will be our wedding supper . . ."

"I don't think I could eat anything," croaked the lovelorn Willie.

"Mought not be a bad idea, but I 'spect a man o' my corporosity would sorta crowd that there roadster o' yourn, so mebbe we'll git the little doc to drop us by. He lives close by, don't he? Said he did."

"Just over the hill. It's about a mile by road, but only a short walk across the lawns. We'll see you then, at dinner."

The two newlyweds walked stiffly out to the car, their efforts at nonchalance pitiably transparent.

"It ain't gonna be easy for 'em to break the news to Sylvia," commented the Judge as he forced his bulk through the door of the Carlyle's sedan.

Dr. Carlyle started the car with a jerk that flung the Judge into the back seat. "I still cannot see why Dr. Jensen killed Sylvia's little dog. In spite of what we have learned recently, Dr. Jensen was not, psychologically, the sort of man to kill Chu Chin needlessly. He must have had a reason."

Amy sniffled into her handkerchief. "He wanted to hurt Sylvia . . . and possibly me."

"Don't figger it thataway," stated the Judge jerkily in his efforts to adjust his bulk comfortably to the little doc's erratic driving. "Don't figger you come into it. That there dog was kilt 'fore the doctor knew you'd come over an' talked to us. Like the little doc says, it ain't like him. What do we know he was doin'? Trying to make Sylvia doubt her sanity. Killin' the dog wouldn'ta added to that. Ruther, it'd be th' other way 'round. Nosirree bob! He was heap cleverer'n that. Look at the way he done it. He made her b'lieve she'd said stupid or embarrassin' things. With that there motion picture corn-traption he'd made her think she'd seen him, an' then made her think yesterday was Thursday. Or mebbe she really did fergit. Mebbe he'd put her through so danged much she jess couldn't think straight by then. Mebbe we'll never know. Then, o'course, there's that queer one an' the tricks the doctor got him to play."

The little doc turned half around in the seat. "You really think this queer one was part of his trickery?"

"Sorta fits into the general queerness o' things, don't it? Recommember what the chauffeur said about this queer one bein' in the house—an' nobody knowed it, or didn't let on they did? An' recommember how the chauffeur said the queer one was imitatin' the doctor's walk an' gestures an' even expressions? That there Leonard laid it to gratitude an' hero worship—said it was the only decent thing the doctor done. Well, mebbe it warn't so decent. Mebbe it was trainin' from the doctor so's Sylvia would see two of her husband, one downstairs an' one up, an' wearin' different clothes. Mebbe recommember the doctor an' the queer one was jess about of a size, an' with a tech o' make-up . . ."

"The grease paint!" shrieked Amy, horrified, "and that makes the actor fellow and the queer one the same."

"Don't *make* 'em the same, but sorta fits, don't it?"

"Horribly."

"An' you gotta recommember that Sylvia was already jess about as wrought up as she could get when she seen him . . . an', Great Land a' Goshen, she musta been perty nigh plumb daft when she saw him lyin' on the floor there, after she'd shot . . ."

"But," Amy was puzzled, "how did Dr. Jensen get him to play dead so convincingly—and why?"

"Why? Jess figger it out. The p'lice figgered Miz Jensen was a mite teched in the head after they heared the story. Reckon a sanity commission woulda believed jess about the same thing. Only he warn't playin' dead. He *was* dead."

"Oh, no! No!" Amy protested. "Sylvia didn't shoot him. You said yourself that the bullet was still in the door."

Judge Massie nodded. "An' I didn't say she shot him. I jess said he was dead. She shot that there movin' picture."

"But . . . but . . . why, Judge, how do you figure that?"

"Recommember that Sylvia said he was 'cold, quite cold.' Well, a man that's jess been shot don't git cold. Takes 'bout an hour fer the human body to git cold enough fer a person that jess teches it to say it's 'cold, quite cold.' I don't reckon she imagined that, 'cause we kin prove she didn't imagine the rest o' it. We found the movin' picture machine an' the bullet. Looks to me like he musta really been there—an' dead."

"Judge," Amy's voice sank to a hoarse whisper, "do you realize what you're saying?"

"Been tryin' to git you to realize fer ten minutes. Yes'um. I figger Dr. Jensen killed this here queer one whilst he was dressed up like the doctor, an' put him in Sylvia's room whilst she was lyin' down restin' . . . though I also figger mebbe he give her a light sleepin' medicine. He woke her up somehow an' started his movin' picture of himself, an' he was danged clever. Bein' a psychiatrist he knew jess what to expect, an he'd put the gun near her hand . . . an' it happened."

"Why . . . why didn't you find the body when you went up there with her?" Amy was getting over her horror and was frankly curious.

"He didn't want her accused o' murder; he jess wanted us to think she was crazy, so's he could handle the estate . . . which he couldn't effen she was hanged fer murder. When she died, his income stopped."

"But, who moved the body?"

"Well, Dr. Jensen had about two hours from the time she left 'til we got back, an' the body was found not more'n five-six miles away."

"But you still haven't given any reason why Dr. Jensen should have killed Chu Chin."

"Great Jumpin' Jehosaphat! He didn't do that. This here queer one done it. I figger Dr. Jensen admitted killin' it jess so's we wouldn't start lookin' fer the real feller an' find out the doctor had killed a man. That woulda plumb upsot his plans." Judge Massie tapped the little doc on the shoulder. "You kin turn in here, an' mind that there rhododendron bush. Sylvia sorta prizes it."

Amy was silent for the short drive to the big house, now brightly lighted. She smiled wanly at the Judge as he thrust and wriggled his way out. "That was a horrible story, Judge, but it absolves Sylvia, doesn't it?"

"Figger it should. Aim to absolve m'clients. Awful good fer the trade, absolvin' clients."

And as the car pulled away the last thing the Judge saw was Amy's white face staring out the window.

The dinner had not been a social success, although Willie, despite his broken heart, had covered himself with glory and gravy by making away with one complete duckling and four helpings of potatoes. Sylvia had excused herself to the Judge and had taken Deedie and Pete upstairs, as she said, to settle the details of this absurdly sweet marriage. The Judge had found himself a deep chair and was profoundly reee-laxin'. Even the palm-leaf fan only rose and fell to the regularity of his breathing. Willie lay stretched on the lounge, suffering a pleasant torpor.

A shot crashed the pleasant quiet!

Judge Massie was on his feet before Willie could untangle himself from an afghan, and was pounding down the hall toward the library. Benson, his face a little green, met him at the library door and pointed in. The Judge switched on the lights.

Near the window, an inert heap in the midst of her beloved flowers, lay Amy Carlyle, dead!

15
IN TWENTY-FOUR HOURS

The lustrous gold of Amy's hair fell across the bronze of the gladioli. One white arm lay against the shattered fragments of the tall green vase, a startling contrast to the wine red of her gown. And she was dead, quite dead. The petulant lines of selfishness were erased from the handsome face until it looked delicate and childlike, except for the sightless staring of her blue eyes, incredulous that death should come so swiftly.

Judge Massie moved heavily across the room and knelt beside her. Benson, the butler, stood shivering in the doorway.

Slowly the door between the library and Dr. Jensen's private apartment opened. Benson watched it in fascinated horror and then, with a scream that was more of a squeak, turned and fled. Judge Massie swiveled his great head around and saw the figure in the doorway. He stood up, futilely trying to hide the body from Dr. Carlyle.

The little doc stepped into the room and peered around the Judge. His face went sickly white, and the Judge put out an arm to steady him.

"My God, I killed her!"

He pushed the Judge aside then, and knelt beside her, staring down at the dead face, groping for her hand. "Amy . . . Amy . . ." He appealed helplessly to the Judge, "Is she dead? Is she?" And then, at the Judge's sorrowful nod, he hauled himself erect, leaning on the table. "I killed her. If I had only hurried . . ."

Judge Massie laid a gentle arm across the little doc's shoulder. "Hold on a minute, Doc. Get a grip on yourself." He drew the little doc gently away from the supine figure. "Take it easy, Doc. You jess don't know what you're sayin'." His arm tightened around the doctor's quivering shoulders and braced him firmly. "It ain't fitten you should break now. It's too important. You didn't kill her."

Without his pince-nez the little doc looked lost and blind. He turned a twisted, suffering face up to the Judge. "If I had hurried I could have saved her. If I hadn't waited so long! I saw her slip away and I should have known. She came over here to get the letters she had written . . . to him." The little doc blinked. "She felt she had to . . . to protect me. I sometimes think she was afraid I had killed him and the letters would prove I had a motive. She stole back the key she threw away this afternoon. You remember when she saw Mr. Wallaby Jo here, from this library window—that's what she was doing, getting back the key. I should have known it then. It was all so clear, so terribly clear. Upstairs, Emery said he'd search for evidence of motive, and she burned the film and then crept down to get that key. It's so terribly clear—and I didn't see it. She slipped away, right after dinner, while I was changing my shoes. I should have hurried, but as soon as I knew she was gone I came across the lawns." His near-sighted eyes were seeing it all again—his futile, fumbling efforts with his shoes, his scurrying to catch up with his long-limbed wife, and then . . . this. He shivered. "She's so beautiful."

Judge Massie turned him away, walking him slowly toward the door. "She died among the flowers she loved. That's somethin', Doc."

The little doc nodded. "Among the flowers she loved." He turned back for a last, long look, and then allowed himself to be led away. "Among the flowers she loved. That ought to mean something, Judge."

Judge Massie stopped in his tracks and looked at the little doc. He repeated slowly. "That ought to mean somethin' . . . Great Jumpin' Jehosaphat, it does! It means . . . Doc, I reckon we know who did this here thing."

The little doc whimpered softly. "But why did Amy have to die?" Slowly the truth dawned on the little man. He looked up and met the Judge's eye. "Judge, could you let me handle this? It . . . well . . . it belongs to me now. Let me . . ."

Judge Massie squeezed the little doc's shoulders. "Doc, it ain't gonna be pleasant, an' it's gonna be a risk."

The little doc caught the Judge's hand in both of his. "Thank you . . . and nothing is a risk for me, now. I've got nothing to lose. Everything I had is . . . back there."

The door at the end of the baronial hall burst open and a swirl of figures crowded in, twisting around some central struggle that resolved itself into Benny, Legge, and Emery wrestling with an infuriated Detweiler. In a moment Legge had the dapper lawyer's arms pinioned behind him, and Emery stepped away, straightening his tie and coat. He nodded briefly at Detweiler. "We heard a shot and we caught this bird doing a sneak around the house. Anything wrong in here?"

Judge Massie glanced down at the little doc, who tried to smile. "I'm all right now. Just let me go somewhere and think this out." And he walked stiffly into the drawing room.

Judge Massie waddled over and stood before the now-chastened Detweiler. "Didn't figger you had that much fight in you. It's right interestin', corn-siderin' . . . yes, sir, right interestin'."

"You're crazy, Judge Massie. I didn't do anything. These ruffians . . ."

Judge Massie silenced him with a scowl and a wave of his hand, and turned to Emery, telling him of what had happened in the library.

Pete thundered down the stairs as he finished. "I heard a shot, and went to look for the girls. Is anything wrong?"

Deedie came running along one gallery and Sylvia walked more slowly down the other.

Judge Massie glanced up. "Land o' Goshen! Thought you three was stayin' together . . ." He broke off. "So long as none o' you been hurt, reckon I shouldn't say nothin'."

Emery told them of the gruesome find in the library. "And we got the guy that done it."

Sylvia and Deedie, clinging together, cast frightened glances at the library and then Sylvia stared at Detweiler.

"Charles Detweiler? Oh no! Why, he's our lawyer!"

Detweiler tried to hold himself sprucely. "I've told them this is absurd, Mrs. Jensen. I was just here on perfectly legitimate business connected with the estate. I heard a shot and, as I was investigating, these ruffians seized me."

Emery sneered. "Perfectly legitimate business don't generally call for a man to sneak around a client's house peeking in windows and shooting women."

"I didn't shoot anybody." Detweiler jerked convulsively, his voice hysterically high. "I didn't . . ."

"He had a gun," Emery hefted a small automatic in his hand, "and that looks legitimate, too . . . or maybe it's your calling card." He nodded toward the door. "Take him to headquarters, boys, and book him on suspicion of murder."

Judge Massie looked at the struggling lawyer protesting his innocence. "Reckon it was me you was aimin' to kill, warn't it?"

"Yes, damn you! Yes, it was you, damn you!"

The little doc stood in the doorway to the drawing room. He spoke quietly. "There is no need to swear. If you will all just step into this room, I have something to say." His voice caught and he waved a hand vaguely at the room. He had control of himself, a control so rigid that it hurt to look at him. There was something magnificent about the little doc at that moment. He turned to Emery. "Will you have someone look after my wife?"

Emery detailed Benny and Garrison, who had stood in the doorway like a bulwark, to guard the library.

The little doc ushered them into the drawing room with a firm finality that even Emery obeyed. Detweiler came, persuaded by Legge's pressure on his arm. The rest of them followed. Mrs. Hardecker, Leonard and Edward and the other chauffeur, and Wilks, the gardener, entered from the dining room, ranging sullenly along the wall. The little doc pointed out seats for the others and then stood with his back to the doorway, his thin mouth tight, his eyes behind the pince-nez hard and dry. He squared his shoulders.

"I shall take only a moment of your time. With the kind permission of Judge Massie, and with his invaluable aid . . ."

"Judge Massie's permission?" Emery straightened belligerently. "Now see here, who . . ."

The Judge's glance was mild. "Who has arrested at least three wrong suspects?"

Emery subsided and waved the little doc on. But the wave of the hand was only a gesture of officialdom.

The little doc went on, "I shall attempt to reconstruct what happened during the last twenty-four hours, culminating in the . . . the death of my wife." One hand pressed against his mouth to still the trembling of his lips.

"Twenty-four hours?" Sylvia raised startled eyes to the mantel clock. "And so much has happened."

The little doc nodded bleakly and went on, "Judge Massie has permitted me to take over the work he has done because of the very bitter, personal interest I have in this affair. It has robbed me of the one person I loved, and my only desire is to be the instrument through which justice is done." He paused, glancing around the room. "Had I been less dull-witted I could have saved my wife. I had all the facts but I could not see them in a clear and logical order. It remained for Judge Massie to point them out."

The little doc glanced uncertainly around and encountered the Judge's encouraging smile. He stood a little straighter. "It's difficult to know where to begin, but suppose we start with Dr. Jensen's efforts to drive his wife insane."

"But why didn't he kill me?" Sylvia leaned forward earnestly. "It would have been more . . . more merciful."

"I doubt if Dr. Jensen knew the meaning of mercy, Sylvia . . . but his real reason was the fortune. If, you died, his interest in it ceased. The fortune was to be divided then—your share to some institution and Miss Cordelia's share to her. But with you committed to an asylum, he controlled the fortune."

Sylvia shuddered in Deedie's arms. "He did that to me . . . just for money!"

"We know some of the efforts he made to show you were insane, Sylvia. You've told us about the things he pretended you'd said, things that worried you almost to the point of believing yourself, well, not coherent. We know about the motion pictures he projected on your wall. We know, or suspect, that he had another man secretly in this house to confuse you further. I think the servants will confirm that." The little doctor glanced along the line. Leonard and Edward nodded in unison.

"We know," the doctor checked off a point on his fingers, "that this morning, having laid his groundwork and pushed by circumstances, Dr. Jensen applied for a lunacy commission to adjudge Sylvia insane; and that at about three-twenty he went to Judge Massie's office, for what purpose we'll never know. And there, sometime between three-twenty-seven, the time Willie left, and three-thirty-seven, when Judge Massie returned, Frederic Jensen was murdered in the Judge's inner office."

Pete Coleman shook his head. "You don't know that. Jensen was found in Edgewater Quarry, in the Judge's car."

Judge Massie, sunk deep in an overstuffed chair, craned his several chins around and peered at Pete. "The little doc's statin' facts, son, things we been told. Jess like you told us you took Doc Jensen's body out'n my office and took it out to the Quarry in my car. There you put three more bullets in it . . . and pushed him and the car over the edge."

Pete's face went white. He shook off Deedie's restraining hand. "I . . . I told you that?"

"Yup, son, 'pears like you did. Ain't but three people knowed that was my car down there—'sides the p'lice. The little doc, me, an' the feller that done it." Judge Massie twinkled gravely. "An' Miss Deedie will be plumb glad to know he was dead when you found him in my office."

Deedie turned slowly from studying Pete's face, a rekindled light in her eyes. "You mean that, Judge? You're positive . . . Pete didn't . . ."

Judge Massie shook his head. "Nup. He didn't murder Doc Jensen, even if you did see him hidin' that gun under a rock. You did see him, didn't you?"

Deedie sighed happily. "From the back window. It had me worried."

Judge Massie nodded. "You see, like you, I seen the black mud on his shoes—same sorta mud this here Wallaby Jo had on his shoes. So I knowed Pete had been in the back lot where Sylvia keeps the mulct for her garden." He glanced at Wilks, the gardener. "She does, doesn't she?"

Wilks nodded grumpily. "When she thinks about gardening. Goin' to rack and ruin."

Judge Massie accepted that gravely. "An' Pete was the man that hid the Spanish automatic under a rock." He turned to Emery. "An' Wallaby Jo wasn't lyin'."

Pete sighed heavily and stood up. "Okay. You worked it out very cleverly." His eyes shifted momentarily from Judge Massie for one last, long look at Deedie. "I killed him. And I'd do it again.

Judge Massie held up a restraining hand. "Pull in yore heroics, son, an' sit on 'em. Miss Deedie didn't kill him neither. You're a couple o' idjits, both o' you, marryin' each other so's you wouldn't have to testify agin th' other. Nice sort of idjits, though, thinkin' a husband can't be made to testify agin a wife—nor wife agin husband—which ain't strickly true."

"I did kill him." Pete thrust himself forward, glaring at the Judge.

"Nup," stated the Judge with finality. "You knowed Miss Deedie follered Jensen to my office. You come along as soon as you could git away from the bank to perteck Deedie from him— an' found him dead. You drug his body to th' elevator, put it in my car, an' you took it to th' quarry. You shot him three times there . . . jess to corn-fuse th' issue . . . which you done, all right."

"I shot him in your office and then I . . ."

"He didn't." Deedie swung around Pete's guarding shoulder and scowled at the Judge. "He didn't shoot Jensen in your office because I did. He laughed at me and I . . . I sat there like an idiot, tearing my handkerchief . . ."

"We found a piece . . ."

"See!" Her voice was triumphant. "That's proof I was there. I . . . I picked up the gun and I . . . I shot him for what I'd learned he'd done to Sylvia."

Judge Massie turned to a bewildered Emery. "Two confessions. Take yore pick. Only, o' course, didn't neither of 'em do it. But they're nice idjits, jess the same."

Deedie's momentary daring was deserting her. "How can you be so sure I didn't kill him?"

Sylvia had been watching the two of them and now she leaned forward. "Are they confessing because they think I did it? Are they trying to protect me?"

Judge Massie shook his head. "They think each other did it. Pete couldn'ta done it 'cause I seen him still in the bank when I went up to meet Jensen who was already dead."

"I did . . ." Pete began stubbornly.

"An' Deedie didn't kill him 'cause o' that there telephone call."

"What?" Color flooded back into Pete Coleman's face. "You mean that?"

"'Course I do, Deedie was with me from ten minutes to four till long after the doctor's body was found. She couldn'ta phoned out to this here house at four o'clock an' pertended to be Dr. Jensen, even if she coulda done the pertendin' . . . an' the murderer is countin' on that telephone call as an alibi."

"You mean it?" Pete stared down at the Judge and suddenly grinned. "Thank God!"

"And he didn't do it?" Deedie's finger stabbed Pete's chest, and then, somehow, climbed along his lapel to his shoulder. "Oh, Pete, I've been such a fool."

"Both complete idjits. Deedie, I hope Pete beats you, reg'lar." With a final smile at the two youngsters he turned back to the little doc. "'Scuse me. Jess settin' one little point straight."

"It seems you settled several."

"But you may've noticed there ain't any confession comin' from Mister Detweiler. He's bein' very silent."

"I didn't!" Detweiler started up and then cringed before the ring of eyes. "I didn't kill him. I knew he was dead, yes. I saw him there but I didn't kill him. I didn't."

The Judge's voice was quiet but stern. "You had motive . . . motive an' opportunity."

"Motive?" Sylvia looked up from between Deedie and Pete whose hands she held.

"Yes ma'am. You see, this here slick lawyer was takin' money out'n the estate, and Jensen threatened to expose him."

Detweiler moaned and sank back in his chair, wailing softly, "I didn't kill him."

"What Detweiler didn't know was that Jensen never meant to expose him. He jess wanted to scare him, so's when Jensen made an application to administer the Storme fortune, Detweiler wouldn't raise any objections. He couldn'ta, or Jensen really woulda had an investigation. But Detweiler was too valuable to Jensen. He wasn't puttin' a petty crook in jail if the petty crook would help him rob the estate."

"I didn't do it. He was dead when I got there. He was."

"I figger you're tellin' the truth . . . fer once. Not 'cause you're tellin' it, but 'cause o' evidence. Now we know Jensen was shot with the gun that was already on the desk—the one I took off'n Sylvia. So it had to be somebody that Jensen would trust, to let 'em git that there gun. It had to be somebody that talked to him first and, Detweiler, if you hadda talked to him two minutes you'da knowed you didn't have to kill him—jess work with him. An' you'da done it. You're that sort o' cheap crook. But you ain't a murderer."

"Thank . . ." Detweiler began.

"Don't thank me, thank the truth—effen you'd know it when you met it." The Judge turned to the little doc with a nod that was almost a bow. "'Scuse me agin. Jess clearin' up some o' this corn-fusion."

Dr. Carlyle coughed dryly. "Thank you, Judge. Frankly, I hadn't grasped all those points myself. But let us consider another suspect, Mrs. Jensen. She had the strongest motive and an equal, if not better, opportunity than these others. She was at the office and she was even at the scene of the so-called accident at the quarry. The crime was committed with her gun, ordered for her in her name by her husband as part of his plan to confuse her into believing she was doing things of which she was not aware. She even had time to put through that call which the murderer was counting on to make us think Jensen was alive at four o'clock.

She admitted wrecking the doctor's laboratory, but not as thoroughly as it was later wrecked by the murderer, who wanted to destroy something. However, that person didn't think as quickly as my wife . . . or didn't have the opportunity. Amy burned the films. She didn't want you to see her in them, being made love to. Doubtless she was right. And there were times when I found myself wondering if she might not have killed him."

"Oh, how awful . . . to make us suspect those we love." Sylvia shivered and leaned against Deedie's arm, smiling vaguely. "You see, I haven't suspected anybody because I just didn't care what had happened to him., I was just glad he was . . . gone."

The little doc nodded. "But I knew it couldn't have been Amy because, well, this goes back further than Amy. It starts, well, way back." Dr. Carlyle turned with quiet dignity toward the servants grouped near the dining room door. "Judge Massie established fairly accurately that this unknown actor was, in reality, the queer one you men reported seeing around here."

Leonard nodded solemnly. "The cops had us down there to identify him. He's the same feller."

The little doctor turned to Mrs. Hardecker. "You said, some time back, that the cook was complaining of missing food."

"She always is." Mrs. Hardecker's dark face glowered.

"It could have been taken to feed this extra person, this man kept secretly in this house?"

"I guess so. I hadn't thought of it that way. Cook's always complaining."

"So you said, and the men have stated that such a person was here. How is it you, as housekeeper, weren't aware of it?"

"I, well, I *was* aware of it. I didn't know why he was here. I just knew he was here, and that Mrs. Jensen wasn't to know. The doctor said it would upset her. I believed him."

"How did he explain this man's . . . his absence?"

"He . . . he said he had sent him back . . . back to the . . . the asylum where he got him. That his case was hopeless."

"Instead, Dr. Jensen killed him, staged the ghastly scene in his wife's room to make her think she had committed a murder, and then went downtown the next morning to set in motion his plan to take over the Storme estate . . . and he was killed! More than that, my wife came here tonight to get letters she felt were . . . er . . . indiscreet, and we found her—among the flowers she loved." For an instant the little doc achieved a magnificent dignity. "Gentlemen, ladies . . . those flowers killed my wife."

Emery sat forward eagerly and then, at the little doc's last words, started to relax, an expression of annoyance on his face. Suddenly he leapt to his feet.

"She's got a gun!"

The little doc peered around at the detective in mild surprise. "I knew that. I'm going to take it away from her."

And with slow, impressive dignity he started walking toward Mrs. Hardecker, his eyes on the gun clutched against her hip. "You killed Amy because of the flowers, didn't you? They were . . . too beautiful."

"Don't come any closer! Don't! I'll shoot!"

"Do you think it will make any difference to me? You've killed all I had to live for, so killing me won't matter. They'll hang you . . ."

"I had to kill her. She knew . . ."

The little doc's mouth trembled and he shook his head. "That's the terrible part of it. She just stopped because the flowers were beautiful. She never guessed. Amy wasn't very smart." The little doc continued his slow, steady advance. "Give me the gun." He held out his hand and Mrs. Hardecker stepped back, thrusting the gun out at him, her finger whitening on the trigger. The little doc drew a deep breath. "If you hadn't killed Amy there might have been some excuse. He was your son, wasn't he, and Jensen killed him?"

The woman crumpled then, seeming to fold inward, and the gun clattered to the floor. The little doc stooped and picked it up, looking down at the woman's shuddering back. "I'm . . . I'm sorry."

Emery darted forward and took the gun, staring over the little doc's shoulder. "She did it?"

Deedie pulled herself out of Pete's arm. "Oh, Dr. Carlyle, she might have killed you!"

"It wouldn't have mattered, and it would have caught Amy's murderer. I was just afraid she might hurt someone else." The little doc smiled gravely. "But I believe the Judge was taking care of that."

They turned to see the Judge thrusting a revolver into his belt band. It was the one Emery had taken from Detweiler.

Emery examined the gun he had taken from Mrs. Hardecker, held it to his nose and sniffed. "It's been fired recently."

"She killed Amy with it . . . because of the flowers."

"Flowers? Now, look," Emery appealed to the room, "people don't get killed over flowers."

"When they're an alibi, they do, Joe," Judge Massie nodded to the crumpled figure, "and them flowers was her alibi. Mebbe Miss Deedie will recommember. When we druv up here this afternoon, Mrs. Hardecker was carryin' 'em, recommember?" Deedie nodded and the Judge went on, "Said she'd jess been gatherin' 'em, like she'd been out in the garden all along. An' we jess natchelly figgered she had been. On'y them flowers ain't on the market yit as bulbs. Jess special fer florists." The Judge appealed to Wilks. "Do you have Evans Bronze Beauties?"

"Not in that garden. You can't get Bronze Beauty bulbs. Oh, I see . . . she bought them flowers."

Judge Massie nodded. "Amy saw 'em, too, and wanted 'em. So she asked at the florist down by my office, an' he tole her the bulbs weren't fer sale yit." He looked down at Mrs. Hardecker, who was struggling to sit up. "Bought 'em jess after you shot th' doctor, didn't you?"

The housekeeper, dry-eyed now, and staring bleakly straight ahead, nodded. "Just after I killed a murderer."

"You thought fast, didn't you? Flowers to account fer yore bein' out o' the house, an' a telephone call t'make us think you was there."

Emery shook his head. "Somebody phoned her that Dr. Jensen . . ."

Judge Massie pursed babyish lips and frowned. "She *said* somebody phoned . . . an' that's where we slipped up. Now, Joseph Alexander Emery, you already proved nobody phoned *from* the office, recommember? An' nobody phoned *in* from th' outside. Checked with Susie yoreself. So Mrs. Hardecker musta been phonin' from *inside* th' buildin', interoffice calls not bein' recorded. An' effen she was inside th' buildin' she couldn'ta been out here, gatherin' flowers that ain't even on the market yit." The Judge signaled Emery to help Mrs. Hardecker to her feet. "It musta been a terrible jolt when you called m'office, Mrs. Hardecker, an' nobody was excited 'bout findin' the doctor's body."

"I nearly went crazy then." The housekeeper ran a hand through her severely drawn hair. "I knew I'd shot him, but nobody said anything about him. Just surprised that he'd called the house. That's when I got panicky. I bought the flowers and came out here . . . to the house . . . and waited, expecting *him* to turn up." She shook her head slowly. "And all the time he was really dead. I don't know which was worse—waiting for him to come back, knowing I'd tried to kill him, or having him turn up . . . dead. I hated him!" The bitter anguish in her voice cut through the room. "Hated him!"

"He killed yore son, didn't he?"

The housekeeper's head snapped up and she glared at the Judge, and then her face softened. "Yes, he killed Jimmy . . . my poor, helpless Jimmy."

"He'd promised to cure him, hadn't he?"

Mrs. Hardecker nodded. "And for a while Jimmy seemed to be doing so well I thought he was cured. It was cretinism, you know . . . something wrong with his glands. And Fred said he could cure it with injections . . . but nobody must know. It was to be a secret until his cure was complete . . . but he never meant to cure him. He was just using him—using him to terrorize Mrs. Jensen—and then he killed him."

Judge Massie nodded slowly, his several chins quivering. "An' last night when you fainted you didn't faint on account o' the blood, but from relief."

"I thought Jimmy had . . . had killed Fred." Her eyes pleaded with the Judge. "Jimmy was a good boy but he had a temper . . . a horrible temper, and he didn't know what he was doing when he . . . he . . . sort of went wild."

"But Jimmy had killed the Pomeranian."

The housekeeper nodded dully. "It bit him, and he kicked at it and then beat it. Fred told me about it when I saw him in your office. Fred tried to explain why he killed Jimmy. You see, when Jimmy went wild he just struck out at anyone . . . even me. Fred told me Jimmy went crazy when the dog bit him and he killed the dog and then tried to kill Fred. He said they had a fight and he killed Jimmy accidentally . . . but I don't know what to believe any more. You said there weren't any marks on Jimmy except the dog bites." She looked up at the Judge, hatred suddenly welling back of her eyes. "But I think Fred meant to kill him all along. I think that was part of his plan. You see, he *did* get Jimmy almost well, and put nice clothes on him and taught him to walk and act like a sane person. But it was just so Jimmy could confuse Mrs. Jensen. It wasn't really a cure."

"But how'd you know Doc Jensen hadn't sent Jimmy back to th' asylum?"

"The picture in the paper this morning . . . that was my Jimmy. The paper said he was left in the woods . . . in the dark." Suddenly she started to cry, great, racking sobs that shook her gaunt, bony frame. "Jimmy! My Jimmy! He was always afraid of the dark . . . and the woods."

"Could you jess tell us how y'did it? When an' how?"

She looked up and dragged a knobby hand across her eyes. "I don't know the time. This afternoon—it must have been after three—I slipped away from the house and followed him to your office. I tried to talk to him, but he was raging. Mrs. Jensen was trying to get a divorce, and that had upset his plans. And he wouldn't listen to me when I tried to talk about Jimmy. Just said he was a stupid . . ." She stopped the ugly word with her hand and stared at the Judge. Slowly she drew down her hand. "And he ought to know."

"Jimmy was Jensen's child, huh . . . an illegitimate child?"

The woman nodded. "I was studying to be a nurse, but I couldn't make it. The sight of blood made me ill, that was the truth, and Fred was an interne, not making enough to marry . . . and we . . . we had Jimmy. I took care of him for years, working at anything I could get until Fred married money. He got me this job as his housekeeper so he could help Jimmy, he said, but all along he planned to use him."

"An' in th' office?" the Judge prompted.

"There was a gun on the table. Fred showed it to me, and laughed. He said that gun would break Mrs. Jensen's divorce and send her to the asylum. He played with it and even loaded it a couple of times . . . and kept putting the shells in and taking them out. Finally, he tossed it aside, loaded . . . and I grabbed it. I threatened him with it . . ." One knotted hand massaged her cheek and she shook her head. "I don't know what I expected him to do . . . except that when he laughed at me I . . . I shot him. Then I was scared. I ran out. There was an empty office and I hid there, expecting a commotion, but there wasn't any. I waited . . . and then I phoned . . ."

"From inside th' buildin'," the Judge nodded to Emery.

"And no one seemed to know he was dead. I was terrified. I made up that story about papers, and then I started home. I saw the flowers and bought them. I don't think I meant them as an alibi . . . not really. They were . . . sort of for . . . for Jimmy."

"Did you wreck the laboratory?" Emery put in.

The gaunt woman nodded. "When I got home. I hated him so, I wanted to . . . to destroy. Somebody had been there and pulled down a movie projector and I . . . I just went crazy for a minute . . . tore at things . . ."

Judge Massie steered her back to her story. "But when Miz Carlyle saw th' flowers . . ."

Mrs. Hardecker pulled herself back with an effort. "Flowers? No, it didn't frighten me at first. And then I heard her call them Evans Bronze Beauties, and I knew I'd bought the wrong kind . . . and I . . . My boy was dead . . . I'd killed the one man I loved . . . and there she was, the woman who had everything—a fine home, a husband, and she'd even taken Fred—staring at those flowers . . . I knew she knew, so I killed her. I guess that's . . . that's all." She hardly glanced at the others, but her eyes went to the little doc. "I couldn't shoot you. Maybe you'd be happier if I had. I know I'm going to be when they get through with me."

She held out crossed wrists to Emery. "Shall we go?" and there was the dignity of grief about her that held the others quiet until Emery had taken her away.

As they left the little doc turned to go but the Judge laid a hand on his arm. "Doc, I was wonderin', would you mind helpin' me out? I got a heap o' thinkin' to do an' would you drive me home?"

It seemed cruel to ask a favor of the bereaved man, and even Willie seemed hurt. Dr. Carlyle looked up, hurt and startled, and met the Judge's eyes. "Drive you?" Then he smiled shyly. "Certainly, Judge, you're very kind. It would have been difficult to go home alone."

Willie's brief scowl lightened and he took the little doc's other arm. "We can have a man-to-man talk . . ." and Willie's eyes switched briefly to the perfidious Deedie, "a real man-to-man talk."

At the door the Judge turned back and grinned amiably at Pete. "Seems a married man oughta be gittin' a job. Come 'round an' see me in a day or so."

Pete colored. "I'm sorry, sir. I shouldn't have tricked Deedie into this marriage. I should never have doubted her, and then I wouldn't have made such a sorry spectacle of myself . . . and hurt her." He turned stiffly to Deedie. "I'll go away . . . right now. And you can have the marriage annulled. It wouldn't be legal anyway . . . if I left on the day of the wedding."

The Judge paused and turned back. "Young man, That's a moughty lib'ral interpretation o' th' law."

Deedie winked solemnly at the Judge. "It certainly is, Judge." She pointed to the mantel clock. "And anyway, this *isn't* the day of our wedding . . . It's after midnight."

ADDENDUM

1953

ABOUT THE AUTHORS

Douglas Stapleton was born Samuel Granville Staples (1907-1972), growing up in Virginia. (In the 1950s, his mother is referred to as Mrs. H. C. Link of Virginia Beach, so the 'Harry Link' in this book's dedication might be Douglas' stepfather). Douglas Stapleton may have started out as a pen-name, but appears to have been taken on for most professional use. According to one newspaper article, Stapleton "started out as a song-and-dance man with Eleanor Powell in her first success, 'The Wedding of the Painted Doll,' became historical correlator for the *Encyclopedia Britannica*, advertising man with General Foods, program manager for a radio station and radio commentator and (in Washington) administrator for the W.P.A. and later Radio Expert for the executive office of the president." After service in the naval reserve and teaching at the Ft. Monmouth signal corps O.C.S., he worked as an advertising executive in New York for a wide variety of TV and radio programs. As an author, Stapleton wrote a multitude of books, articles, short stories, radio plays, and television comedies.

It was while working in New York that he met and married his (third?) wife, Dorothy, in 1941. Dorothy Tucker Aden (1917-1970) was from Bastrop, Louisiana, where she had worked as a political speechwriter, theatrical company press agent, licensed engineer, radio station operator, film director and producer, and creator and writer for the army radio serial, 'This is Your Judge Advocate.' She moved to New York to become director of radio, TV and films for Grey Advertising, where she met Douglas.

While on their honeymoon, they co-produced a Broadway play, 'Questionable Ladies,' and wrote their first novel together, *The Corpse is Indignant*. For this, and only this mystery, Dorothy used the pen-name Helen A. Carey. In future collaborations, the pair went by Douglas and Dorothy Stapleton. They continued to work together on radio shows, monthly magazine columns, and other projects. *American Magazine* called them "the people who work 48 hours a day." (For relaxation, they both obtained their pilot's licenses.) They 'retired' to Virginia Beach in 1951, becoming involved in community work and some further mystery writing for Arcadia House (*Late for the Funeral, Corpse and Robbers*, and *The Crime, the Place, and the Girl*). This retirement didn't last long, as they had moved to Monroe, Louisiana, in 1953 to help operate a new radio station, though it shut down the next year. Their mystery novel writing ended after the mid-1950s (though short stories for mystery and science fiction magazines were published into the 1960s), and both Douglas and Dorothy appear to have lived their final years in Los Angeles, California.

When *The Corpse is Indignant* was published in 1946, it was advertised as 'A New Judge Massie Mystery.' No previous stand-alone novel featured this character, but the book's original description notes that Judge Massie was one of Douglas Stapleton's short story (or even short novel) magazine detectives, likely published in such pulps as Street & Smith's *Detective Story Magazine*, *Crack Detective Stories*, or *All Fiction Detective Stories*.

References:
'Novel contract signed by former Bastrop girl.'
Monroe (LA) *News Star*, Feb. 11, 1953.

COACHWHIP PUBLICATIONS
CoachwhipBooks.com

NIGHT IN GLENGYLE

JOHN FERGUSON

COACHWHIP PUBLICATIONS
CoachwhipBooks.com

DEATH COMES TO PERIGORD

JOHN FERGUSON

COACHWHIP PUBLICATIONS
CoachwhipBooks.com

COACHWHIP PUBLICATIONS
CoachwhipBooks.com

COACHWHIP PUBLICATIONS
CoachwhipBooks.com

THE
BEACON HILL
MURDERS

THE
BACK BAY
MURDERS

THE ROGER SCARLETT MYSTERIES
VOL. I

COACHWHIP PUBLICATIONS

CoachwhipBooks.com

THE STRAWSTACK
MURDER CASE
K I R K E
M E C H E M

COACHWHIP PUBLICATIONS
CoachwhipBooks.com

The Serpentine Club Investigates
Murder in Washington, D.C.

THE CAPITAL
MURDER

James Z. Alner

COACHWHIP PUBLICATIONS
CoachwhipBooks.com

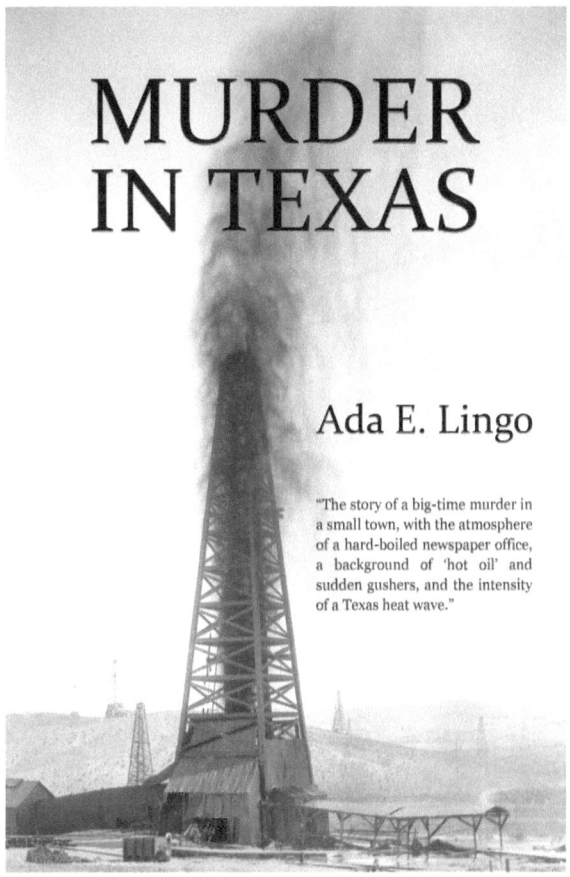

MURDER
IN TEXAS

Ada E. Lingo

"The story of a big-time murder in
a small town, with the atmosphere
of a hard-boiled newspaper office,
a background of 'hot oil' and
sudden gushers, and the intensity
of a Texas heat wave."